Tempest

GRACE JOHNSON

Tempest at Stonehaven

scottish shores

Tyndale House Publishers, Inc.
WHEATON, ILLINOIS

Visit Tyndale's exciting Web site at www.tyndale.com

Scripture quotations are taken from the *Holy Bible*, King James Version.

Designed by Melinda Schumacher
Edited by Rick Blanchette

Library of Congress Cataloging-In-Publication Data

Johnson, Grace, [date]
  Tempest at Stonehaven / Grace Johnson.
    p. cm. — (Scottish shores : 1)
   ISBN 0-8423-6250-9 (sc)
   1. Scotland—History—19th century—Fiction. 2. Wreckers (Plunderers of
ships)—History—Fiction. I. Title. II. Series.
PS3560.03774T46 1997
813'.54—dc21

97-12400

Printed in the United States of America

03 02 01 00 99 98 97
7   6   5   4   3   2   1

ACKNOWLEDGMENTS

My gratitude for special help from Rick Blanchette, Faye Larson, Ken Petersen, and Joan Stadel. And special thanks to Dottie Campbell, my wonderful typist and encourager!

DEDICATION

To Jonathan, Heather, and Jeremy—with whom I have spent golden hours!
Always remember that you are a wee bit Scottish, for your great-great-grandfather
Everson Rider MacKinney was a tall, handsome Scotsman.

Characters

Annie Mackinnon . . . . A widow, schoolteacher

Captain Mackinnon . . . . Annie's husband, lost at sea

Donal Mackinnon . . . . Annie and the Captain's son, has gone off to sea

Duncan Carmichael . . . . Fisherman, devout Christian

Margaret Carmichael . . . . Duncan's wife

Griselda Carmichael . . . . Sixteen-year-old daughter of Duncan and Margaret

Meg Carmichael . . . . Twelve-year-old daughter of Duncan and Margaret

Eppie Carmichael . . . . Seven-year-old daughter of Duncan and Margaret

Davey Morrison . . . . Sailor, adventurer

Malcolm Donnovan . . . . Sailor, Davey's partner

Jonathan Stoat . . . . Lighthouse keeper

Rob Rafferty . . . . Drifter

Letty Rafferty . . . . Rob's wife

Liza Rafferty . . . . Seven-year-old daughter of Rob and Letty

Elvira Elphinstone . . . . Wealthy, powerful matron of Stonehaven

Fiona Elphinstone . . . . Elvira's pretty niece

Ian Fraser . . . . Sheepherder, Fiona's suitor

Hector . . . . Sheepherder

Thomas Blacklock . . . . Carpenter, coffinmaker

James Turner . . . . Visiting evangelist

CHAPTER 1

A Strange Company

The storm had died to only a whimper of sighing wind, and a quiet had settled over Scotland's great North Sea in the spring of 1882. The waves moved, ever restless, yet exhausted from their tempestuous fury earlier in the night. They lapped now with a gentle rhythm against the great granite rock that rose above them in sheer, unbridled majesty.

The rock held the rambling remains of a great stronghold, Dunnottar Castle. Immense with a forbidding grandeur, dramatic with wild and hoary towers and battlements, it brooded as a melancholy giant over the water.

Inside the walls, men, perhaps a dozen of them, moved with as little sound as possible. There was heavy breathing and some scraping of feet—as well as an occasional curse—as bulky and oddly shaped bundles were carried up the ancient timbered staircase.

At the bottom of this unusual procession, an open door to the sea let in tentative light from a moon that played with scudding clouds. A torch held by someone in the forefront lit the way in wild patterns over stone walls and down a portion of the staircase. Those at the midsection of the staircase bumped into each other and swore under their breath in nearly utter darkness.

Reaching the top, this mysterious company followed the torch along a narrow passageway to a large door that swung inward on rusty hinges. Inside, the torch splayed in curious flickerings over a windowless room of modest proportions, although not small. Several crumbling casks were piled in one corner. Over the rest of the room tumbled an array of trunks, boxes, and bundles. Strewn here and there, as if having escaped from their prisons, lay all manner of offal—or at least so it appeared in the murky light. Bottles and chains and tapestry and clothing. A ship's log. An old bed board. A small ebony elephant with ivory tusks.

Without any word, the men deposited their baggage as far from the door as possible and then left.

Their leader lingered. He leaned against a clammy wall, tugged at a full beard, and sighed with weariness. His clothing was rumpled. One leg of his heavy but loose-fitting pants was torn to the knee. His pants and rough shirt were covered with dark stains. He closed his eyes, and one might have thought him about to collapse in exhaustion.

But shaking his head and rousing himself purposefully, he stood straight—a tall, muscular figure. He held his torch aloft and gazed about him. His eyes seemed to linger on each parcel, caressing each shape, fondling every visual oddity until he smiled in immense satisfaction.

After some minutes, he turned toward the door, extinguished his torch, and felt his way along the dark corridors with a practiced hand.

When at last he came out into the night, stars framed the walls of the great five-storied keep that loomed over the courtyard.

He paused, eyeing its gables and turrets. "Ye'll not be tellin' no secrets now, will ye?" he murmured softly. "Same as me precious

cream-colored, black-nosed sheep." A grin spread across his face.
"It's no bad to have sech gentle creatures to give a man somethin'
respectable to do by day."

And so he went back to his other life.

CHAPTER 2

Dunnottar

Annie gripped the post of the big wooden gate that led to her home. She clutched it ferociously until her knuckles were white, angry that life had dealt her yet another blow.

She stared down the path that led past a row of thatch-roofed cottages and disappeared in a stand of larch and mountain ash just before the long, lonely moors on the way northward to Aberdeen.

But there was no faint dot of a familiar figure in the distance. When Donal had walked away, he had turned back only once and waved. He was gone. Her only son—just seventeen years old—gone to join the merchant marine.

She grimaced. Hadn't she been only seventeen when she'd faced life alone? But Donal seemed so young. *So young!*

"I have to go, Mama. I'm like my father," he had said.

Like his father—like his father. It drummed in her mind. "Please, God! *Please*—No!"

She was tempted to sink down upon the dirt and grasses by the gate in a tragic heap. But it was not a fitting thing for a village matron—let alone Stonehaven's only schoolmarm.

Instead, she pulled herself up, graceful and slim in the early morning's foggy shadows, and turned resolutely toward the large, gray stone house. It had been built proudly by the Captain, Donal's father, from granite blocks taken from a quarry near Inverness and brought down the great Caledonian Canal and then overland to Stonehaven. The Captain was like that, doing everything with ever more flourish, if possible. Thus, the house stood elegantly on the hillside looking down upon the humble rows of huts, barns, and sheds that tumbled downward toward Stonehaven's bay.

The front door had been left slightly ajar. As she entered, the growing light of dawn gently touched the simple pine furniture and a few elegant mahogany pieces that were softened by pillows and an afghan in muted shades of rust and blue. The rising sun cast its rays through the east window and across a large sandstone plaque the Captain had mounted above the fireplace. "Man Proposes, God Disposes," it proclaimed. It had been made during the Captain's brief fling with religion, before his avid attendance at the kirk had as quickly ceased as it had begun, before his confidence in God's power had given way to an abiding fatalistic philosophy. "What shall be, will be," he used to say, "and we can no more change it than a sailor can tamper with the tides."

Annie eyed the plaque now, thinking that whatever the words meant, her life had not been as she would have wished.

Unbidden, a dark and horrible memory pushed its way into her consciousness, even as she silently screamed, *No!*

She had stood in this same room in the early morning—three and a half years ago—clutching a gold locket and a note in her hand. She had crumpled the note in an agonized frenzy and had twisted the locket chain until it tore the skin on her fingers.

And the Captain had stood calmly, a few paces away, hands on his hips. He had looked at her directly and had spoken in even tones. "Ye really found it necessary to search through my private possessions, did ye, Annie?"

"Who is she?" Annie had hissed, her heart thudding so violently she had been sure he had heard it.

The Captain had walked past her while she waited in a trance—waited for the rest of her world to fall down. He had reappeared with his large duffel bag, the one in which she had found the locket and the note.

He had held out his hand. "Give them to me." And she had done so. She was used to obeying the Captain. She had slammed them into his hand with as much force as she dared—which wasn't much.

He had moved toward the door and turned, a slow, condescending smile spreading across his handsome face. "There is nothing to be concerned about, Annie. These things—a mere note and locket—mean nothing. Absolutely nothing."

And he had gone.

She never saw him again.

No one knew this awful episode, the *manner* of his leave-taking. Not Donal. Not anyone in Stonehaven. As far as anyone knew, he had simply gone off to Edinburgh, gone off to do a captain's duty.

She turned from the parlor, hoping to block out the dark images, the memories that stung and tore at her heart.

But what flooded in to take their place were thoughts of Donal. Donal, who had been her focal point—her son, of whom she was so proud. Donal, who was kind and honest and with whom she had shared the dailiness of life. Donal, who too suddenly had thought himself a man and had marched off to Aberdeen, seeing only adventure, not the grief he left behind.

She wandered aimlessly from the parlor, along a small hall, and up a flight of stairs to her room. She had a thought of throwing herself on the canopied bed and crying. Instead, catching sight of herself in a large oval mirror above the walnut dressing table, she hesitated, then sat down on a stool and, propping her head on her hands, stared at her reflection.

She knew she was at least pretty, if not beautiful. The Captain would not have romanced anyone who was plain, she thought half bitterly. The eyes that looked back at her were dark and framed by thick brown hair pulled demurely to the back of her head and tucked into a great comb that had been handed down by her grandmother. Her skin was still soft and smooth, for she had not worked out-of-doors as had most village matrons. Her mother had always told her she would have been a great beauty had it not been for a mouth a bit too wide. "But just stand straight, and ye'll have all the elegance ye need," Mama would say. "If tragedy catches up to you, no one will know it." Mama felt good posture and strong faith could take care of everything.

Annie had tried good posture. She had tried that day when Mama and Papa, who had died of typhoid fever within hours of one another, had been laid to rest in the little graveyard by the kirk. She had turned away to face life alone, back straight and head high, though privately wondering if her first seventeen years had fitted her for the task.

And when the Captain left on that dreadful day, she had waited until Donal had gone off to the bay, where he braided rope for the nets and baited fishhooks, before she had sobbed, almost uncontrollably. After that she had gone out and about her business—as Mama had taught her—keeping her secret safe and hanging on to what she had. She hung on to Donal and her position as Stonehaven's schoolmarm.

But what about faith? What had happened to the faith she had once held? All that was left was an aching, lonely emptiness.

Abruptly Annie stood up. The house seemed to close in upon her. She had to get away—away from the house, away from Stonehaven. And there was only one place to which she could flee: Dunnottar Castle.

She moved quickly out of the room, down the stairs, through the parlor, the great door, the walkway, and out of the gate. Then she turned and sped down the path.

Early morning mists from the sea drifted over the ragged rows of huts that clustered about the bay and rose ever upward on the bracken-covered hills. Two women, who carried great baskets of cod and obviously were ready to stop and pass the time of day with the village schoolteacher, trudged toward her. But with only a nod, Annie hurried past.

She passed fishermen's wives and children searching for shellfish—winkles, mussels, oysters, and scallops left by the receding tide in the southern part of the bay. Two small girls waved as Annie sped by. On this day even they could not tempt her to stop.

She veered southward along a footpath up and over the Bervie Braes, where peat smoke from chimneys hung over thatch-roofed cottages and crofters tended their fields.

Reaching an open field, she picked up her skirts and ran. Her eyes blurred with tears, but she knew the path. She had no idea how many times in her thirty-seven years she had come this way. But she felt her footsteps would be sure, even in the dead of night.

At last she reached the bluff. Annie stopped to catch her breath, shielding her eyes against the morning brightness of sky and water.

The bluff dropped off precipitously to a narrow valley or den a hundred feet and more below. But beyond this chasm rose an enormous spur of rock jutting out into the North Sea, silhouetted against the rising sun. It was a magnificent and mysterious sentinel against sky and water, one which drew her on.

She brushed at tears with her sleeve and plunged down the precarious path, at times clutching at rocks or long grasses to steady her descent. Reaching the valley known as Ninian's Den, she paused in its shadowed coolness only momentarily before starting up the steep incline toward Dunnottar. She relished its difficulty as she panted from the exertion, for there was no energy left (at least for the moment) for other emotions.

About halfway up, a short flight of stairs appeared, leading to a tunnel. She passed into darkness that was only faintly etched in gray light. Musty dampness chilled the wind caught in the passageway, and she shivered.

With some relief she came out into the warmth of daylight and then up a broader flight of stone steps to what was once a heavy gate.

Beyond it, Dunnottar Castle rose before her. The sprawling complex of the ancient and partially decayed baronial establishment dwarfed Annie. Thick walls, dull in pinks and grays of sandstone and granite and hoary with lichen and moss, caught the early morning shadows. Their darker shades seemed to whisper of a stormy and dramatic past of plunder and burnings, of medieval intrigue within the galleries and stairways and narrow passages, and of legend.

Annie had "found" the castle long ago—intrigued by its remoteness two miles from the village, challenged by the difficult descent and arduous climb and a ten-year-old's love of adventure. Being of a solitary nature, she told her mother only that she had gone "walking and climbing about." It became her place to be—to ponder and sometimes to escape. Of course, as time went on, those closest to her had come to know that she found some odd kind of solace or pleasure from these occasional forays. None had asked to join her, discouraged no doubt by the difficult climb and most uninterested in a castle that had not been inhabited in the last century and a half.

Still, the village folk were fond of repeating the legends of Dunnottar Castle. Some said a Marischal wandered the halls, searching for his wife who had been carted off to the mainland three hundred years ago and burned at the stake. Others said ghosts with candles moved over the bluff on stormy nights. And still others claimed that if one listened carefully, the low moaning of the famous Covenanter prisoners could be heard borne upon the wind.

Annie had listened to these tales, her eyes large, wondering which, if any, of the stories were true. She had explored some of the castle's structures and passageways—but never very far, for they were dark and musty and forbidding.

A small gust of wind blew at Annie's skirts, and she stopped still, listening. What was it? An odd, scraping sound from within the ancient walls? Her heart began to thud. The noise stopped, and there was only the sighing of wind about the corner of the weathered rock. She was about to move on when she heard it again. A grating or scratching? She froze, every sense alert, but heard no more.

She cleared her head with a shake. Surely it was only the wind; she would not let her imagination run away with her.

She moved quickly, past the gatehouse buildings, the five-storied keep with its crowstepped gables, the smithy, stables, and finally a chapel with two walls in ruins.

She stood in the kirk yard, irresolute, glancing about her. She sat down on a stone that had been hewn into a rough bench and stared at the plundered and crumbling walls of the old kirk. A vaulted alcove was barely discernible.

She found herself wondering who had worshiped there long ago. Had they only gone through the motions, or had there been true faith? Had they once been taught about *the Presence?* And when the storms of life had come, had *they* remembered?

Had *she?*

When Annie was a child, Mama always had taken her to the village kirk, and Papa, too, when he was not fishing. Papa never had much to say to Annie—probably because she had not been a boy to help at sea—but each night he was home he read the Bible by candlelight and admonished Annie to say her prayers before bed, his way of dismissing her for the night.

But when it was Mama and she alone, Mama would place the big Bible lovingly on her knees, pat it, and say, "Now, lassie, ye listen to yer ma, and I be tellin' you what the Good Book says."

Annie had come to feel that the *telling* of the stories and truths was directly because Mama's ability to read was limited. But no matter. Her father's reading had more to do with habit, but Mama's words danced and sang and thundered.

"Do ye not see him, Annie? Over yonder by the sea?" Then her voice would get softer but take on a grand quality as if she were announcing royalty. "The Lord Jesus—that's him—his robe tucked up to his knees so's he could stand where the waves was coming in ('cause folks was crowdin' around so!) and his legs brown in the sun. An' then he's a-kneelin' down to touch a man with the most awful pus-stinking sores. Seems like he never could do enough to show he'd come to take up with folks what was about as low as a body could get!"

Most often Mama told her stories about Jesus by the *sea*, until Annie saw him in her mind's eye along the shore of Scotland's great North Sea. How much Mama embellished events with her vivid imagination didn't seem to matter, for after all, it was clear Mama *knew* Jesus.

And Mama said that Jesus was God. "Not just a nice man or some highfalutin teacher. But God come down to us! God sayin' in Jesus, 'I'm wantin' to be with you and stay by you fer always iffen ye'll jest be askin.'"

So Annie had asked. One time when she was eight years old and had torn her best dress, which Mama had already patched at least five times, and Papa had scolded her for getting tangled in his fishing seine that was all laid out for him to untangle. She had crept away and knelt beside her little straw mattress with a heavy heart and had asked Jesus to come and not ever leave.

She had not forgotten the feeling of peace that had come—a kind of lightheartedness tempered with the solemn feeling that she had entered a new dimension of life, that the Presence of Jesus with her also meant a new accountability, that she must measure the events of her days against what Jesus would want her to do.

Annie now stood up and turned away from the kirk. Something had happened in the meantime, and her heart was empty, her faith seemingly as devastated as this kirk.

She moved restlessly to the furthermost edge of the bluff, around which ran a stone wall—high in places, crumbling to a low ledge in others. On every side a sheer drop to the sea below, where the waves beat, foaming in rhythmic cadence against the rocks.

A mournful cadence, like funeral drums, she thought. She peered at the sea's horizon. Somewhere out there the Captain's ship had gone down. She wondered again what kind of storm had torn it apart, and she shook her head to clear such thoughts. In the three years that she had been a widow she had come often to Dunnottar to mourn for her husband, the Captain. This seemed the best place, for there was no marker to grieve beside. How much she mourned the cold fact of his death and that now he could never change—never come back to her—and how much she mourned the death of life as it had once been she could not tell. But mourning seemed the appropriate thing to do, whatever the motivation.

Annie watched a sea mew circle above her and sweep out to sea. And now Donal would follow. Pain tore at her heart. *Please, God—not Donal, too! I can't lose him, too!*

Strange—the churning, ever changing North Sea before her was indeed her enemy. And yet she was drawn to it, mesmerized by its rhythm, soothed by its magnificent expanse sweeping away to the horizon.

Perhaps it was because Mama had loved the sea so much. Even its storms, unless Papa was out to sea in one. "Annie," she would say, "life is like Scottish weather. Ye can't depend on things stayin' the same for more'n ten minutes. So what's a body to do when the storms come unless she's got somethin' to hang on to?"

Then Mama's eyes would light up with a special something that Annie knew came from inside. "But iffen ye have the Presence of Jesus, and yer hangin' on tight, it's downright exhilaratin' to see what he'll do—how he'll bear you up!"

"But sometimes I feel awful upset, and I can't feel anybody close by!" the little Annie had once objected.

Mama had folded her hands in her lap and looked out to sea. "That's just how Jesus' friends thought. They was out to sea, and the wind was powerful fierce, and the waves was washin' over the boat, and they was about certain they'd drown."

"Because Jesus wasn't there?"

"Oh, he was there all right," Mama had answered. "He was just asleep, so I guess they'd clean forgot about him. Well, they woke him up and asked him if he cared that they were about to be done in. Then, Annie, just as calm as could be, he took care of that storm—when the time was right."

"Because they'd woken him up?" Annie had asked.

Mama had been silent a bit, then had shaken her head. "Nay, lassie. He knew what he was doin'. But then again, mebbe he was lookin' for them to *talk* to him. A pity they waited till they'd done *everything else* before they turned to him."

Then Mama had fixed the little girl with her eyes. "Lassie, ye done asked Jesus to come into yer life."

Annie had nodded.

"The storms of life'll catch up to you, sure as sure! But remember

14

these words of yer ma—the Presence of Jesus is with you in yer boat, sometimes asleep. *That's* the times yer going to wonder if he's there at all. But he is! Jesus' friends were sure they were gonna perish. But the boat didn't sink, Annie! *It didn't sink.* Remember it: Jesus will *never* leave you! *Even when ye can't hold on to him, he'll be holdin' on to you!"*

Annie stirred restlessly. After the death of her parents, she had spent lonely days trying to remember Jesus' presence was with her and sometimes doubting everything. And two years later, when the dashing, debonair Captain entered her life, it seemed increasingly not to matter just what one believed philosophically. Then, there was only the present. Bright, golden days of romance and dreaming. How much life could change!

She stared at the sea, noticing that the darkening clouds had turned the water a deep green. A rift in the clouds sent a shaft of sunlight across the great rock and the sea beyond.

Annie stood up to leave as a few raindrops spattered about her; she was not in the mood for a drenching just now.

As she passed the chapel ruins, something on the ground caught her eye, something that glittered. Her eyes went wide. Stooping down, she picked up an object and stared in fascination.

It was a bracelet. Delicate silver filigree held small enameled panels on which were etched tiny flowers and leaves. She turned it over in her hands and glanced about. She shook her head. No one ever came up to Dunnottar. *Where had it come from?*

The wind picked up, and more raindrops fell. She dropped the bracelet into her apron pocket and hurried toward the keep and down the side of Dunnottar to Ninian's Den. Not slowing, she half ran, half crawled up the other side to the bluff.

Rain had not fallen on the other side, and the sun looked to be trying to break through. She dropped to the grass and held her head in her hands. Suddenly she was very weary.

Abruptly clouds replaced the sun, and Annie shivered.

"Miz Annie! As I live and breathe!" said a voice surprisingly close.

Annie jumped to her feet, whirling about. Before her stood a man in loose-fitting trousers and a ragged jacket. "Rob Rafferty! I didn't hear you coming."

Bushy eyebrows went up and then down from under a mop of reddish brown hair that waved and curled in all directions. Strong hands clutched a shepherd's crook—a sturdy piece over which he had half hung his large frame. "I wadna thought to see you so far from home all by yerself."

"And you, Rob Rafferty. I wouldn't have thought to see you with a shepherd's crook in your hand."

"Ah, 'tis a sheepherder I am just now. It's no bad to be working fer Ian Fraser." He jerked his head in the direction of the black-nosed, cream-colored sheep in the distance.

Annie smoothed her skirts. "And if you can be keepin' yourself out of the whisky bottle, the job may last," she observed pointedly.

Rob Rafferty smiled, showing a row of yellow-stained teeth. "Ah, Miz Annie, as Robbie Burns hath said, 'Freedom and whisky gang the gither.'"

"Which leaves you *free* most of the time, doesn't it?"

Rob Rafferty stared at her for a few moments and, seeming to find no suitable retort, shook his shepherd's crook in the direction of darkening clouds. "Storm's brewin' yonder, Miz Annie. Ye best be gettin' yerself home."

Annie nodded politely. "Tell the missus and your little Liza I asked after them." She turned to go.

"Mem—"

Annie stopped, inwardly sighing. "Aye?" she asked without turning.

"I wadna mention it, but ye bein' me young un's schoolmarm and all—"

Annie swung around. "And *what*, Rob Rafferty?"

"And a well-thought-of lady in the village," he added hastily. "I'm thinkin' in such poor weather with the mists and all, me imagination must have run clean away—"

Annie arched her brows. "Aye?"

"And no doubt I dinna really see you up at the castle."

"And if I was, what of it?" she challenged.

Rob Rafferty's eyes turned dark with dire portent. "Ye'd no want to be going to such a place! It's full of sea demons, it is!"

"That's simply a village tale," said Annie, trying to be patient and at least fairly polite and not wishing to discuss her own journeys. The last thing she wanted was to have Rob Rafferty joining her.

He was undeterred. "Full of sea demons! When the dark comes down, there's shadows and demon lights! I *seen* 'em, Miz Annie! Movin' along the castle bluff yonder!"

"I must go." Annie swung away from him and began to walk at a steady clip back toward the village. "Good day to you, Rob Rafferty," she called firmly.

Rob Rafferty's voice echoed across the field. "It's no place to be fooling around with! Nobody goes up to the castle!"

Annie's hand instinctively went to her apron pocket. She fingered the filigreed bracelet.

"*Nobody*," he shouted after her.

CHAPTER 3

A New Day?

Annie awoke as she had every morning since Donal had gone away—with a feeling of anxiousness and a knot in her stomach. The curtain at the open window stirred slightly as dawn sent a faint hint of daylight into the room.

She felt so alone. Abandoned—by both her husband and her son, each in a different way. She had been dreaming of Donal. They were at sea during a storm. Donal was high up the mizzen-mast while she had clung to the deck rail and screamed for him to come down. Then came a terrible crash as the ship broke apart, and she had found herself kneeling on shore cradling an old rag doll and crying softly, "It's all I have left—just the doll!"

She turned restlessly on her side. The old rag doll lay somewhere in the attic. She had not seen it for a long time—not since childhood. Mama had made it painstakingly out of leftover mattress ticking and stuffed it with straw. Annie had taken it to bed with her whenever she was lonely or sad and cried onto its faded gingham dress. Until she turned twelve and decided firmly that she must put away childish things.

Mama had looked just a bit downcast about it. "Remember,

lass," she said as she tucked the doll into an old box, "don't ye get caught gettin' rid of what you'd best keep. Oh, *possessions* ain't of much matter." Mama had let a meaningful pause fall. "It's things of the *spirit* I'm thinkin' of."

Annie blinked. Had she dreamed of her old doll because of her prayer last night? The first prayer she'd prayed in a long time, at least one which went beyond a sort of exclamation cry for help.

She had knelt beside her bed—even that had seemed a bit strange—and asked God to show himself to her somehow. She found herself wanting to know if Jesus was still within calling distance. The prayer had been brief.

In the weeks since Donal had gone, she thought long and hard. She fought to go about her life and to stay on an even keel. But, grateful as she was for her school pupils, school wasn't enough. There was still that dreadful return to an empty house each night—to an aching, lonely sadness. She longed for something or someone else. And so she had prayed.

Now as the soft light of dawn grew more sure, it seemed that into her heart crept a small sensation of something different. Expectancy perhaps? The thought that God had indeed *not* forgotten her although she had largely forgotten about him? Perhaps there was something new or adventurous or even wonderful just over the horizon?

She sat up, climbed out of bed, and moved to the window. The sun had come up, and its light came sweeping over the sill. A butterfly dropped gracefully before her, its delicate wings of orange and brown fanning the air gently.

Mama always said all sorts of things could be a sign that the Presence of Jesus was with one. Even a butterfly?

Annie had gone down to her breakfast with a more lively step than usual. Perhaps, even, Donal was *not* sick and *not* lonely. The one letter she had received had sounded cheerful. Perhaps his superiors would be kind to a lad of only seventeen. Though, doubting the latter, she let one small sigh escape.

She was grateful to be relieved of the possibility of sinking back into too many doleful thoughts when at the end of breakfast Meg arrived.

Of all her pupils, twelve-year-old Meg Carmichael was the one with whom Annie felt the most kinship. There was something special about Meg's charm, her earnestness, her dreamy-eyed flights of fancy. Annie thought of her as the daughter she had never birthed.

"Sit down here, Meg," she said, pointing, "and have a wee bite of toast while I straighten up."

Seated, Meg leaned on one elbow and, cupping her chin in her hand, chewed her toast thoughtfully. "Don't ye ever wish ye could *leave* Scotland, Miss Annie?"

"I don't think I've ever thought just like that," Annie said slowly. "I'm not sure life would be easier or better someplace else."

Meg clasped her hands. "Oh no! I don't mean to find something *better*. Just different and adventuresome and far away—to perk up a body's mind with new sights and things that we never thought of before."

Annie put the last dish away and smiled at her young charge. "So tell me, Meg, where would you like to go?"

Meg's eyes danced. "I'd go to India, and I'd live in a palace of white marble and have servants to do all the work, and I'd ride around in one of those little carts with the two big wheels and see snakes being charmed clean outta their baskets and see all those people taking a bath in the river at once and—"

"Oh, Meg—Meg!" Annie threw her arms around her. "But I really couldn't let you go! You know I couldn't get along without you."

Meg returned the hug. "I dinna suppose I'd ever *really* get a chance to go, but iffen I do it in my mind, it's a bit like having it happen, don't ye think?"

They heard a knock at the door, and Annie answered it to find Griselda, Meg's sixteen-year-old sister. She was a pretty, diminutive lass with great dark eyes and soft brown hair. On this particular day she appeared to have been running, for her cheeks were flushed, and she was breathing hard.

"Good mornin', Annie. And have ye heard from yer Donal lately?" she asked politely.

"Not since three weeks ago. I guess I can't expect it to be as often as I'd like."

Meg stirred. "I suppose Mama sent for me?"

Griselda shook her head. "I came because—oh, Annie! There's a square-rigger's going to anchor out in the bay this very morning! Word of it came in on the telegraph from Aberdeen to the marine station. And the ship's putting off some cargo and some folks that are going to stay—not go back with the ship!"

Meg smirked knowingly. "I ken what yer thinking, Griselda. 'Twon't be any ladies on the ship. So that leaves just menfolk. And maybe they'll be charming and handsome and sweep you clean off yer feet." She threw an arm out dramatically. "And ye'll ride off with one of them to live in a castle somewheres!"

Griselda blushed. "Oh, Meg, now yer blethering! But I *am* going down to the dock. Things have been so quiet around here lately—we could use a bit of excitement. Annie, come with me. Please?"

Something inside Annie gave a start. Could this be an answer to her prayer? Immediately she told herself how utterly ridiculous the thought was. "I don't think so. I've plenty to do here," she answered sensibly.

Meg started toward the door. "Well, ye'd better hurry down, Griselda, before Fiona gets to 'em." She stopped. "Miss Annie, have ye ever watched that Fiona Elphinstone? She is really something! Just put a handsome man anywhere within sight of Fiona, and she flirts up a storm in no time!"

"Fiona's keeping steady company with Ian Fraser, isn't she?" offered Annie.

"That doesn't stop her. She flirts with anyone that's good-looking. Annie, please come." Griselda's eyes pleaded. "Anyway, it's not good for you to keep to yerself so much."

Meg stopped by the door. "Miss Annie, ye said yerself yer needing more school supplies. We could walk down to the market. And then ye and I can watch and see who flirts best—Griselda or Fiona."

Annie hesitated. "Oh, all right." She gathered up her purse, stuffed a supply list into it, and threw a light shawl about her shoulders. "I'll walk with you, but *only* for supplies. I'll leave the romance strictly to Griselda and Fiona," she said, determined not to get carried away by any flights of fancy. On the other hand, she said to herself as she closed the door behind her, perhaps one *should* keep an open mind to the future. . . .

Margaret Carmichael, a sturdy woman, arms akimbo, observed her fisherman husband ensconced in the midst of an array of creels, fish lines, and bait.

"The ship should be in soon, so I'll be going, Duncan," she stated in definite tones.

"And I'll not be stopping you, Margaret," replied the mild-mannered Duncan.

"As the ladies' representative from the kirk, it's only fitting that I should."

"Aye."

"Newcomers'd be a sight grateful to have a wee bit of friendly advice. Not to mention finding out where this thing and that is."

Duncan pulled at his line. "Not to mention checking to see if there was one braw enough to come calling on our Griselda?"

Margaret smoothed her apron, carefully tucked a recalcitrant strand of hair into the bun on the back of her head, and picked up a large basket. "I also have supplies to pick up," she said firmly, indicating the conversation was at an end. She turned to glare at a small girl of seven years who was up to her elbows in a pail of fish bait. "Eppie! Get yerself out of that mess, and come along and help carry."

Duncan watched them go. He smiled and shook his head. "If there's one that's both charming and single, may the Good Lord help him!"

CHAPTER 4

The Arrival

Davey Morrison—sailor, adventurer, and a few other things—leaned on the rail of the *Saucy Nancy* as it rode gently in light winds in Stonehaven Bay. He was a tall man with a full beard, neatly trimmed, broad-shouldered with an air of jaunty confidence and at least a hint of debonair worldliness. It was his eyes that gave a suggestion of something else—deep set, intelligent, but now and again reflecting a shadowed melancholy.

Before his view, shops, sheds, and thatch-roofed homes clustered about the harbor and perched on slopes that rose gently toward heather-streaked hills beyond. Some cottages were constructed of pitch and straw; others were whitewashed sandstone with small doors set into the gables, for easier hauling in and out of fishing gear, he supposed. To his right on a narrow spit of land stood the lighthouse. Reef Point, he knew it to be. But his eyes were drawn to the south, where the ruins of Dunnottar Castle could be made out atop the mighty rock projecting into the North Sea. It was here his attention lingered.

"Davey." His companion, a slim man with long, curling hair, leaned close. Both men were dressed in dark dungarees and heavy, loose-fitting jackets. He tapped Davey on the shoulder. "Davey Morrison! If ye can come outta the trance yer in, the dinghy's ready to take us. We're at our destination, ye know."

Davey Morrison hoisted his gear and followed the other man thoughtfully. "Aye, Malcolm, we're at our destination!"

The two men stepped off the dock into what appeared to be the usual Saturday morning village bustle but with the addition of curious eyes of the overt who, Davey guessed, had come down to peruse the newcomers, and the equally curious but shy who stayed at a distance and pretended they had other things to do.

Davey put his duffel bag down and had reached into his pocket for a slip of paper when a shriek rent the air and a small missile came hurtling out of nowhere, hitting him in the thighs with such force that he nearly lost his balance. He recovered himself to find a small girl at his feet.

She leaped up, not a little aided by the quick movement and strong arms of a woman who dusted the child off and gave her a little shake. "Eppie! If I've told you once it's a hundred times to act like a lady and not to be running around like that not looking where yer going and slamming inta a body! And a stranger at that!"

"I was just running to catch the ball, Mama."

"Well, ye'd best apologize to the man—to Mr.—?"

"Davey Morrison." Davey smiled down at the child with her dark eyes and pigtails and smudged pinafore. "And who are you?"

"I'm Eppie, and I'm seven years old, and I'm sorry I bumped you; and yer awful tall, ain't you?"

"Well, I suppose so, Eppie. That's just the way I grew."

"Oh, ye must excuse her." The woman held out a rough hand. "I'm Margaret Carmichael."

"How do you do, Mrs. Carmichael."

"No—no—just call me Margaret. Nobody in Stonehaven goes on formalities."

"Margaret, then," Davey said. He gestured toward his companion, who was kneeling on the ground in the process of tightening a strap on his duffel bag. "And that's Malcolm— Malcolm Donnovan. Best sailor to ever sail the sea!"

Margaret beamed at them both. "Are ye to stay a spell now?"

Davey nodded. "I reckon we may do just that."

There was a sudden swish, and Davey found standing before him the most beautiful creature he had ever seen. If he had not been as sophisticated as he was, he would have drawn in his breath in awe.

She had positioned herself between him and Margaret, forcing the older woman to move back a step. Davey blinked. This girl had the largest blue eyes and thickest eyelashes and most flawless skin he could ever imagine.

The girl nodded and dipped in a half curtsy. "I couldn't help but hear your names." She pushed a stray blonde curl behind her ear and smiled charmingly, including Malcolm in her look. "And that you're to be in Stonehaven for a bit. I just wanted to welcome you. My name is Fiona Elphinstone." She smiled again.

Davey felt himself melting. "Aye—Miss Elphinstone. How nice to meet you." Davey felt himself close to stammering.

She reached into a pocket. "I have something here." She handed him a small card with the name *Elvira Elphinstone* and an address printed in dainty letters. "I live with my aunt—that's her name—and if either of you would want to learn anything of the history of Stonehaven or the surrounding area, Auntie and I—" again the smile—"we would be happy to have you call. Auntie knows *everything* there is to know!"

Davey thought he might be in a dream. Not only was this entrancing creature standing before him, but she had given him an invitation to come calling. He mumbled something warm and polite, he hoped.

A man strode up to them. "Ah, Fiona! Here y'are." He took her arm possessively. He was as tall as Davey with thick, sand-colored hair and beard. He was dressed in the rough clothing of a crofter and was, Davey decided, handsome in a rugged way. "Perhaps ye'd introduce me to the gentlemen?"

Fiona moved just enough to remove her arm from his grasp and busied herself with straightening her collar (which was already straight) and smoothing her skirts (which were already smooth). "Ian, this is Davey Morrison, and over there, Malcolm Donnovan." She nodded toward Ian. "Ian Fraser."

Ian looked Davey up and down. "I've not seen you in these parts before."

"Because I've not been here before."

"What's yer business, Davey Morrison?"

Malcolm ambled toward them. "Davey here's an artist," he offered.

Davey was not sure who was most surprised—himself or Ian Fraser, who spit out, *"Artist?"*

Davey, however, found himself picking up the gauntlet. "Mr. Fraser, you were expecting us to be ignorant and smelling of seaweed?"

Ian Fraser's brow wrinkled in puzzlement. "Why would ye come here? Stonehaven's not what ye'd call a thriving metropolis."

"Ah, but what's more picturesque—" Malcolm gestured toward the sea—"what with the stretch of sand down there rolling along to them high bluffs with the castle." He stopped. "By the way, what do you call the castle?"

"Dunnottar," said Ian after a pause.

"Actually," interjected Davey, feeling himself bound to explain Malcolm's sudden invention, "I only sketch for my own amusement. Malcolm here and I signed on to a whaling ship a year and a half ago and—"

"Before that we was on a Venetian galley to Palestine," interrupted Malcolm. "Rotten food, but the shantymen sure knew how to sing up a storm to pass the time of day."

"Anyway," continued Davey, "we figure it's time for a new adventure. Thought we might sign on to a fishing boat. Figure Stonehaven's as good as any other."

"Well, I can't help you. It's not my line," Ian concluded brusquely.

"What do you do?" asked Davey.

"I herd sheep." He reached again for Fiona's arm. "Best go, Fiona." He nodded toward Davey and Malcolm. "Good day. And I hope ye find what yer lookin' for—as long as it's something possible."

Was it a challenge? Davey wondered. As they walked away, Fiona turned back toward them with a smile full of warmth and charm. *And was that an invitation?*

Margaret Carmichael again moved in. "Folks are expecting Fiona Elphinstone to be pledged for marriage to Ian Fraser any day now," she observed pointedly.

Davey nodded politely as he tucked the small card into his pocket.

Margaret clasped her hands, beaming again. "Let's see now, Master Davey, ye done met my Eppie. And this here's Griselda, my oldest." She motioned to a pretty girl who stood shyly a few feet away. "Griselda's a good hard worker. Does mighty fine needlework, too."

Griselda curtsied, smiling and blushing.

"And over yonder by the shop, that's my Meg, my twelve-year-old. The other one's the schoolmarm, Annie Mackinnon."

Davey felt something inside him stiffen. "You have only one

schoolteacher?" he managed to ask, realizing it a rather inane question for such a small town.

"Aye. Annie keeps to herself quite a bit. Kinda quiet. But then her husband, a sea captain, was lost in a storm, and now on top of it her son, Donal, has gone to sea, too. Don't make Annie too happy."

Eppie scampered between them and plumped down at Malcolm's feet. "Wisht I was a boy, so's I could go to sea."

"Aye! All that adventure!—Shootin' up pirates, rescuin' sinkin' ships—"

Eppie's eyes grew wide. "Ye do?"

"Aye! There's nothin' like deep-sea adventures!" Malcolm glanced at Griselda and grinned disarmingly. "Say! How about if ye two lovely ladies show me around the village?"

Griselda glowed. "That would be fun."

"Oh, Mama, please?" Eppie leaped up exuberantly, knocking Margaret's basket and spilling its varied contents.

"Eppie! Eppie! Aye, ye both may go. But first help me get this stuff up and back in the basket."

Davey was still watching Meg and Annie, who were leaving the village square. Malcolm picked up his duffel bag and leaned close to Davey. "Get to know the schoolteacher," he said softly.

"Why?" Davey shot back in a whisper.

"Schoolteachers have sharp eyes and are liable to know more 'n anybody else."

"I just may do that."

"Ye could charm the stars outta the sky. Now use it to some good purpose." He turned to Griselda and Eppie. "Come, come, ladies, we're off to see Stonehaven!"

"Malcolm!" Margaret called after them, "ye and Davey come for supper soon. We'll have fresh herring, and I'll bake scones to go with 'em." She turned her attention back to Davey, who was still staring at the retreating figures of Meg and Annie.

"Seems like a nice young man, Malcolm Donnovan."

Davey pulled his attention back to Margaret. "Aye, he is that."

"Now yer going to need a place to stay. Doory Wilson has some extra rooms and an idea to making a bit of money. Nice beds—not too lumpy. And she'll cook for you, too." She pointed. "Third house on the left. Tell Doory I sent you."

"I'm much obliged. Thank you, Margaret." He hoisted his duffel bag, thinking the voluble woman before him an extraordinary source of information. "By the way, is there anything special around Stonehaven I should be seein' before we're off to sea again?"

"Well, now—of course, we got the kirk up yonder. Wait! I reckon you'd like to be going out to the lighthouse at Reef Point, ye being inta ships and the sea. Must get lonely for Jonathan, the lighthouse keeper, out there, though the children and Griselda go out and chat up a storm with him. Bet he'd like a visit."

"Sounds like a good idea."

"Jonathan's a fine man—though a mite strange sometimes. Leastways, 'twould seem so to hear some folks tell it. Oh, mercy, just look at that sun, high in the sky and I ain't yet started on the fish and a dozen other things. I'd best go, but I'll be having you soon for a good supper."

Davey nodded affably and turned to go. Then he stopped. He may as well ask her now as later, he reflected. "What about Dunnottar Castle? It makes a fine sight from the sea."

Margaret stood very still, fixing her eyes on Davey. "Davey Morrison, ye can't go against the spirits!" Her eyes glittered in earnestness and fear. "Just *fergit* Dunnottar Castle, and I guarantee ye'll be saving yerself a peck of trouble!"

"What did I tell you, Miss Annie," chattered Meg as they left the village square. "Ain't that Fiona Elphinstone somethin' else? Did ye see how she moved right in on the tall sailor, battin' her eyes and makin' so sweet and soupy?"

"Aye, she was busy—that I'll be grantin' you," Annie answered distractedly.

"Griselda says sometimes Fiona's just downright sickening, that's what!" Meg eyed Annie thoughtfully. "What did *ye* think, Miss Annie?—of the tall one. I thought he was downright handsome!"

"I suppose," Annie answered slowly, thinking the tall sailor *did* have a certain dashing air about him. But what was it that bothered her? Was there something that reminded her of the Captain? "Well, handsome isn't all there is to be thinking about. Not by a long ways!" she said firmly.

CHAPTER 5

Davey and Annie

Davey's demeanor was casual and relaxed as he lounged against the outside of the shop, hands in his pockets, but his eyes scanned the crowd restlessly.

It seemed that all of Stonehaven filled the village square. A festive din of voices rose and fell on the night air. Children chased one another and played hide-and-seek behind the skirts of their elders. Bagpipes wailed, and in an open area a half-dozen men danced with wild abandon, twirling and panting. A dozen others joined them, and the beat of the dancing accelerated, aided by rhythmic clapping and bottles of whisky that passed from person to person among the watchers.

Torches secured in buckets of sand at either end of the dancing area illumined the faces of those who stood closest. Davey thought he might have seen Eppie darting in and out. To his far right he found Fiona Elphinstone with Ian Fraser close by. She seemed to sense his stare, for she turned slightly, smiled, and gave a small, unobtrusive wave of her hand, which Davey acknowledged with a nod and a heightened pulse. He fingered the little card, still in his pocket. Yes—he would "go calling."

Across the square he saw Malcolm with Griselda. In the three days since their arrival, Malcolm had found more than one occasion to be in Griselda's company. He could scarcely blame Malcolm for being taken with such a pretty lass. Could Malcolm, at age twenty-eight, have any serious thoughts about someone twelve years younger? But then, Malcolm was quite unable to resist a pretty lady of whatever age.

Still Davey's eyes searched.

Abruptly the dancing ceased, and the crowd fell back and regrouped, leaving an open area at one end.

Down the main avenue and snaking rapidly toward them came a line of flashing fire that entered the clearing in the crowd. Fireballs attached to long wires and handles were swung by young men who ran in a circle, goaded by much cheering and clapping.

The nearness of one fireball caused people immediately in front of Davey to pull back suddenly, and a woman fell against him. He caught and steadied her.

It was Annie Mackinnon.

"I'm sorry. Thank you," Annie murmured, smoothing her skirts and only half glancing at her benefactor.

"Pleased to be of service, Annie Mackinnon."

Startled by his resonant and unfamiliar voice, Annie swung fully around to gaze into the face of the tall stranger. Her heart gave an odd lurch as she recognized the sailor she and Meg had glimpsed and discussed a few days ago. "Beg pardon, but how do you know me?" she asked primly.

"Margaret Carmichael pointed you out." He smiled, but not with his eyes. "And I never forget a name—or a face. Now it's only fair to introduce myself: I'm Davey Morrison."

Annie nodded politely, determined not to get carried away by a simple chance meeting. "Aye, Mr. Morrison. Eppie and Meg Carmichael have spoken of you and Mr. Donnovan since your arrival." She nodded again to close off the conversation and turned back to the fire spectacle, feeling vaguely uncomfortable about the man behind her but not sure why. Did his charm remind her of the Captain? His looks were different enough.

Now the participants formed two long lines and ran in a crisscross formation, swinging the fireballs with ever more vigor.

Davey Morrison leaned close. "Do you mind telling me what all this means?"

Annie moved just enough away to indicate she was not ready for a cozy conversational exchange. "It's supposed to chase away evil spirits."

Davey shrugged. "Every village seems to have its own customs. How many do you suppose believe in it?"

Annie considered. "Probably about three-quarters of them do." She paused. "It's a noisy thing—makes my head pound. I really shouldn't have come. Good evening." She turned away and struck off at a steady clip.

Davey Morrison immediately fell into step with her. "Then may I not see you to your door?"

Annie stopped. "Why?"

Davey thrust his hands into his pockets. "I've been hoping to bump into you somewhere." He grinned. "Of course, not quite so literally."

Annie surveyed this unorthodox stranger, tall, bearded, with the rugged outdoor look of a seaman. His clothes looked clean, if somewhat rumpled. But his eyes—they were inscrutable. She wondered, briefly, how old he was. Probably younger than she. She frowned. "I really don't understand."

Davey rocked briefly on his heels. "Well, Mrs. Carmichael tells me you're the only schoolteacher in town. And I have a great interest in the history of Scotland, especially its villages and other smaller places. So I thought you could give me some information." He smiled, and this time the smile reached his eyes. "I promise to try and not ask too much."

Annie regarded him gravely. "Come along then." She began to walk southward along the harbor, Davey keeping step. The voices of the festival faded behind them.

"Is Stonehaven village very old?" he began.

"Aye. Six hundred years and more, I should say. At one time it was known as a thanage and later on became a barony. Now it's what they call a royal burgh." They passed a stand of silver birch, and just beyond a great oak tree she indicated a small but sturdy shed. "That's the marine station. They research any unusual catch the fishermen bring in and send reports to the university in Aberdeen.

"Most are fisherfolk or crofters," said Annie as they turned inland. She motioned toward a picturesque stone edifice partly in ruins and a tumbledown deserted farm beyond. "The church of St. Caran's," she explained, "was partly destroyed by a raid in 1560—which produced a tale. The townspeople unroofed it to prevent further sacrilege or black magic. It's said that the owner of Redcloak Farm just beyond stole some of the church beams and for his wickedness, blood rained down on him. Hence the name Redcloak."

They continued on past the school, a deserted and overgrown well, and the present kirk. Keeping pace beside her, Davey was attentive, asking the right polite questions. But whenever Annie glanced up at him, she found him regarding her with an intensity that struck her as odd and made her slightly uneasy. The moment their eyes met, a curtain came down, and her companion shifted to a look that was only casual and polite.

She was relieved to reach the stone hedge, beyond which stood her house, guarded by tall oaks, with a full moon riding above it.

Annie turned to her companion. "I'll be going in now, Mr. Morrison. I hope I've been of some help."

Davey nodded but made no move to go. "It's a fine house you have there."

"My husband built it."

"Mrs. Carmichael told me he was lost at sea. My sympathy."

Wondering why he was prolonging the encounter, she unlatched the gate.

"We haven't yet spoken of Dunnottar Castle. It makes a grand sight from the sea," he said.

"I'll grant you it's imposing."

"Do you know its history?"

"Aye. The castle's more than five hundred years old. Partly in ruins now. Who knows what part of it's liable to fall down next?"

Davey shifted on his feet. "I was hoping—just perhaps—that someday you might be willing to accompany me up to the castle and tell me a bit more about it." He smiled charmingly. "As sure as I'm a deepwater sailor, I'd not let any of it fall down on you."

Annie hesitated only momentarily. "I'm thinking not."

"Can you give a reason why?"

She regarded him soberly. "I don't need to be a schoolteacher to know it's a mite peculiar that you'd be paying me attention instead of asking some bonnie young lassie in the village to give you a tour."

Davey leaned on the gate. "Ah, but you're a bonnie lady yourself, Miss Annie."

Annie felt her cheeks grow warm and was thankful for the shadows of night. Davey Morrison did have a charm about him, but she was not about to let it affect her good sense. "Good evening, Davey Morrison," she said firmly.

When she had entered her house and closed the door, she leaned against it. Her brow wrinkled in puzzlement. "What *is* it that you're after, Davey Morrison?"

CHAPTER 6
Thomas Blacklock

Thomas Blacklock detested Davey Morrison. Not that anyone knew it; Thomas was too timid for that.

Thomas had seen Davey from afar on the day of his arrival—along with Malcolm Donnovan. Thomas had listened to comments from the edge of the gathering by the dock, and since that day the same remarks were repeated over and over wherever Thomas went about on his few errands. How handsome, how rugged, how sure of himself Davey Morrison was! This fawning of the villagers over him made Thomas ill, for Davey Morrison was everything that Thomas Blacklock was not.

They did speak of Malcolm, too. How charming and humorous Malcolm Donnovan was! Therefore, Thomas did reserve some measure of disdain for Malcolm as well.

Thomas was tall and thin with a particularly long, skinny neck and narrow, hunched shoulders. He had a subservient air and the look of one who wondered where the next blow would come from and when it would fall. Beneath a receding hairline his black eyes held a hunted expression, and he was apt to frequently moisten his lips and nervously tap one foot.

Thomas Blacklock looked like a loser, and indeed, the circumstances of his life seemed to bear that out.

He had gone off to Edinburgh nine years before to learn veterinary medicine, a hard road intellectually and one that took all he had to keep abreast of his studies.

He had lived in a small third-floor apartment fronting a long, narrow alley. His loneliness drove him, from time to time, to a small chapel of worship about a half mile away. The hymns and truths he learned there had begun in some way to sink into his soul, although to what extent he could not have said. But as the struggle to master his studies had become more difficult, words of certain hymns had taken on a personal meaning, aided by the fact that the one talent Thomas Blacklock had was a melodious singing voice. The only other thing that he might have thought a redeeming characteristic in what was otherwise his personal wasteland was a love of poetry.

Perhaps it was these two things, the melodious voice and the poetry, that caused Jenny Haggart to allow Thomas to come calling. Jenny Haggart was a very pretty girl he had met at the chapel, and Thomas was almost immediately hopelessly in love. But alas, it was not many weeks until Miss Haggart had dropped him for another.

This failed romance and the increasing difficulties with his studies led to a nervous disorder that put an end to any career he might have hoped for in Edinburgh and in veterinary medicine. He returned, beaten and apologetic, to Stonehaven. A total failure in his own eyes and, he supposed, in the eyes of others as well.

Necessity drove Thomas to search for a means of sustenance, and he found he had some ability in the line of carpentry. He sought small jobs on homes and barns and sheds and thus became a joiner. This led to his building of coffins when needed, and eventually to being considered Stonehaven's undertaker. "He has the look of one what has to do with death," the townspeople whispered to one another.

Occasionally he was asked to care for a sick cow or sheep or dog, as the villagers knew he had managed at least part of his veterinary training and therefore, due to lack of competition, was their only recourse.

And so Thomas had found his niche in the life of the village. But as he went unobtrusively about his tasks, there was no one to wonder whether he was content or lonely or sorrowful.

The kitten mewed piteously.

Seven-year-old Liza came flying over a hillock, skirts and hair streaming behind her. She had heard a thud followed by an animal's shriek. A wooden prop of a rotting lean-to had given way, pinning the creature to the ground. Liza tugged frantically to dislodge the post as the animal squirmed and cried. With her mightiest pull she wrested it enough to free its victim.

Liza dropped to the ground beside the kitty. "Oh, Dusty, Dusty!" she cried. "Poor, poor kitty!" Ever so gently the child stroked its gray fur with her fingers and gazed with consternation at the mangled hind legs.

The kitten tried to purr and mew at the same time, but it couldn't move.

"I'll help you," Liza murmured. "Ye kinna just lie here." With utmost care she knelt, spread her apron before her, and laid the kitten on it. She gathered it up in her arms and started back toward the thatch-roofed hut she called home, but she stopped and stood still, thinking.

Her papa had come home late last night. He had been drunk, and there had been so much yelling that Liza had squished as far down in her little bed as she could and pulled the old quilt over her head, trying not to hear. Now it was almost midday, and still her father lay in a stupor in the cottage. The daughter of Rob Rafferty knew when it was best *not* to be around.

But someone had to help her with the poor little thing. *Who?* Suddenly she knew what to do and set off with determined step, all the time crooning softly to her tiny burden.

Thomas Blacklock was busy planing a piece of wood to make shelves for a village home. He was so intent on his task that he jumped when a small voice behind him said, "Master Thomas?"

He looked down in puzzlement at the child with great dark eyes, long reddish blonde hair, and clothing ragged but painstakingly mended. She was carrying some sort of small lump in her apron. "I dinna hear you come in."

"I'm Liza Rafferty."

"I know who ye are."

"My kitten's dreadful hurt. Could ye fix him?" The child's eyes pleaded.

Thomas frowned. "Don't know too much of cats. Let me see it."

Liza held her apron toward him, and Thomas carefully lifted the hurt animal and laid it on his worktable. When he did, the kitten let forth a series of agonized wails. Thomas patted the creature and spoke gently until it subsided into soft, frightened mewing.

Liza watched anxiously. "A terrible big post fell on him out by the back shed."

Thomas carefully poked and prodded.

"Is he going to die?"

"It's just the two back legs. But they're mangled bad."

"Can ye fix 'em?"

Thomas looked at her. "Are ye sure it's worth saving? Lots of cats around."

Liza's eyes grew large, and her lip trembled. "He's my Dusty! He's my own kitty! And I love him!"

42

Thomas surveyed the cat. At last he said, "I'll round up some stuff and see what I can do."

While Thomas sat on a stool making two tiny splints, Liza stood beside him watching every move. Finally satisfied that all would be well, she glanced curiously about the room. "It's a big shed you have." Noting a cot and some cooking utensils at the far end, she asked, "Do ye live in here, Master Thomas?"

"Aye."

"Just by yerself?"

"Aye."

"But have ye no pets?"

"No pets."

"I saw a horse outside," she ventured. "He could be yer pet. Does he have a name?"

Thomas shook his head.

"I'd name him Blacky because he's black. My kitty's name is Dusty on accounta she's gray like dust but mostly because Dusty has a nice sound to it."

"Aye," agreed Thomas. "It's a good sound, Dusty is." Carefully he placed a splint and began to wind a small cloth about it. There was a silence, and he could feel the child's puzzled eyes upon him.

At last she said, "Master Thomas, are ye lonesome sometimes?"

Thomas stopped what he was doing. He turned to look at her. No one—not *anyone*—had ever asked him that before. And never having been asked nor ever expecting to be asked, he had never considered whether or not he *was* lonely. The great hollow feeling inside him seemed his lot in life—something meted out by Providence and not to be disputed or challenged. Since he didn't know what to say, he returned to his work without saying anything.

"'Cause sometimes I get lonely," Liza continued, seemingly undisturbed by Thomas's silence. "And the man what talks to us at the curing shed says folks can be powerful lonely even iffen they got all kinds of people around 'em."

"A curing shed sounds an unlikely place for that kind of talk."

"He's a man what comes down from Peterhead. He says we should just call him Brother Turner on account he ain't no church minister. Anyhow, Mama and I go, and folks sing and pray, and when I git tired, I lean up against Mama and go to sleep until Brother Turner says something real loud."

Thomas, finishing up the second splint, smiled.

"Anyone kin come. Ye could come, Master Thomas."

Thomas opened his mouth to say something but thought better of it.

Liza leaned one arm on the table, thoughtfully cupping her chin in her hand. "Brother Turner says Jesus kin fill up the empty spaces what's inside of us."

Thomas found a phrase of a forgotten hymn trying to penetrate his consciousness. What was it? Something about Jesus being a friend of sinners? Giving up on the verse, he stood up. "Splints are all done."

"Kin I take him home now?"

Thomas's brow wrinkled. "Think ye best leave the little thing here. It's going to be a mighty sick kitty for a few days. I'd best see to it."

Liza's eyes seemed to search Thomas's face. At last she nodded. "I'll come by ever' day." When she reached the door she turned. "Could I name yer horse for you?"

"I reckon," said Thomas.

Liza smiled happily. "Then he's Blacky!" And she was gone.

CHAPTER 7

The Curing Shed

James Turner clutched his Bible and blinked against smoke from a peat fire set in the middle of the room. Oil lamps smelling of salt fish and smoke illuminated the faces of the villagers who sat on stools and a long bench or on the dirt floor. Some simply leaned against walls infested with fungi and cobwebs. Nets, ropes, buoys, and rows of dried fish hung from smoke-blackened rafters.

"The Resurrection *proved* Jesus was the *Son of God!*" The evangelist's booming voice filled the shed. "And *where* did the Son of God *go* with his resurrected body? At that point he could have convinced *anybody*, would ye not think? He could have gone to the temple—or to the Sanhedrin—or to Governor Pontius Pilate—or to the fancy palace to see King Herod! He could have sat down with 'em and said, 'Look at me and believe.' *He'd conquered death!*"

His voice dropped to softer but measured tones. "Here's whar he went! Jesus went to make breakfast by the sea for a bunch of smelly, dirty, discouraged *fishermen* who'd deserted and denied him and who never had seemed to get it through their thick skulls what he'd been talking to them about for three years! *That's who he went to!*"

James Turner's eyes moved over his audience. About two dozen, he judged, had crowded into the shed. There were two or three crofters from the edge of Stonehaven, along with their wives and children. There was Duncan Carmichael with his daughters Griselda and Meg. Duncan had taken to having long talks with James Turner, talks that spiritually warmed both men.

And there was Letty, Rob Rafferty's wife, and their sweet child, Liza. Some in the group had prayed that Rob Rafferty would come to the meetings, and a couple of folk had prayed he'd *not* come.

All eyes remained upon James Turner. "First he helped 'em with their fishing, and then he made breakfast for 'em! And then *he served them!* Would ye not think 'twould be the other way around? *Why? Why?*

"Not so's to say to them, 'Never mind what ye done or what ye are.' Nay! But to say, 'Ye need to come up *higher*. Ye need to follow *me!* I got work for ye to do!'

"What work was it? To feed his sheep! To be *lights in the darkness!* To be—"

Abruptly James Turner fell silent, and all eyes followed his to the door of the curing shed. The large form of Rob Rafferty loomed in the opening, silhouetted against the darkness of the night. Letty drew in her breath and pulled Liza closer.

"Come in, Rob Rafferty." James Turner motioned toward the far end of the bench. "We got a seat for you there."

Rob Rafferty placed a hand against the doorpost. "Nay, I'll not be attendin' yer meeting. But I might just ask a question or two."

The evangelist nodded affably. "Aye."

Still clutching the doorpost, Rob Rafferty leaned forward. "We got the minister up ta the kirk. What do we need with a bigmouth like yerself coming around to stir things up?" He snarled drunkenly. "Light? Light, ye say? Ain't we got light fer the soul up ta the kirk?"

James Turner was not flustered. "Aye, ye have. But how brightly it burns and whether yer own soul draws light and warmth from it, *that* is for a body each to decide for himself."

Rob Rafferty seemed to think that one over, at least as much as he was able in his present condition. "Where are ye from, and what makes ye come here?" he growled, but in a subdued tone.

"I'm a cooper and a herring curer from Peterhead. And I'm here because I got a fire in my soul that won't let me rest. I got to pass on what Jesus has given to me—light in my soul and a filling up of the empty space I had inside before I joined up to be his follower."

Rob Rafferty stared drunkenly at the evangelist. Finally he said, "'Tain't no divine light! It's demons! That's what it is!" Slowly he turned away and faded into the night.

There was an awkward silence, during which Letty looked distressed and Liza blinked at tears.

"It appears to me we got something to pray about here," said James Turner.

And pray they did.

When Rob Rafferty had appeared at the curing shed, a tall, gaunt figure had fled. Now as Rob Rafferty moved away into the night, that same figure crept back, keeping close to trees, hedges—whatever shadows were available.

The figure slunk close to the curing shed and lowered himself again to the ground beneath the one small window that was open. He clasped his arms around his knees and pulled them up close to his chest.

And Thomas Blacklock listened. Intently.

Inside, people spoke in simple words to Jesus, who had left heaven—and even the high and mighty of earth—to involve himself with weak, foolish, undependable folk.

Now and again someone began to sing, and others joined until the praises or the petitions fairly shook the little shed.

The music took Thomas back in time. Again he was in the small chapel in Edinburgh wondering if what he heard could be meant to have anything to do with him personally.

A silence had fallen within the curing shed. Not an awkward kind of silence but something deep and profound that reached out to the lonely man outside. He thought about Liza's words. And he became acutely aware of an empty—nay, even a *yawning* space inside himself.

Another hymn began.

> "I hear the Savior say,
> 'Thy strength indeed is small,
> Child of weakness, watch and pray,
> Find in me thine all in all.'"

Thomas found himself on his knees beside the shed. With his face almost to the ground he prayed to be forgiven for paying scant attention to the Almighty all these years, for never having believed that his Son could want the likes of Thomas Blacklock in his kingdom.

And he prayed to be forgiven for hating Davey Morrison.

CHAPTER 8
The Lighthouse Keeper

Jonathan Stoat paced the lower room of the lighthouse. With pent-up energy he rubbed big hands through thick, dark hair.

Shadows from a kerosene lamp played across the massive stones that formed the tapering walls and the triangular angle irons that held the ceiling in place.

The usual dampness was only partially obliterated by the warmth of a peat fire that burned low in a fireplace set into the south wall. And, as always, there was the never-ending watery thud of waves against great rocks just outside the sturdy ramparts.

The lighthouse keeper moved resolutely to a rough oak table and contemplated his ledger. Numbers, dates, lists, and comments were arranged in very small and terribly neat handwriting that belied the obvious strength and verve of the man who was its author.

He sat down, rearranged a few papers, and selected a pen. In his usual orderly fashion he inscribed *May the thirtieth—*

The pen blotted, leaving an ugly smear. He swore and hurled it across the room. He glared for a long moment, then slowly got up, the square shoulders suddenly drooping. He crossed the room, picked up the pen, firmly broke it in two, and discarded it in a waste bin.

Feeble light filtered into the room from a small rectangular window. He moved to it and stood looking out at gray sky and sea. "Why?" he said softly.

He was hard at work at his ledger when he heard a soft rustling on the other side of the room. "Good day to you, Master Jonathan," piped a small voice.

Jonathan turned to see Rob Rafferty's daughter, Liza. She clutched a basket with a cloth over it. The tediousness and responsibility of his work, along with the unwelcome thoughts he couldn't shake, made a visit by almost anybody a welcome occurrence, but the child who stood before him was one of Jonathan's favorites. "Liza! Upon my word, I didn't hear you. If ye'll just be waiting a moment, I'll be finishing my journal."

Liza moved to the side of the table. "Do ye like to write?"

Jonathan continued his task. "It ain't a question of like. A lighthouse keeper's got to keep his journal every day."

"I think I'd get tired of it." She peered over his shoulder. "What do ye note down?"

"Oh, the weather mostly, and supplies I'll be needing." He closed the ledger and carried it to a cabinet on the other side of the room. "Sometimes a special bird I seen." He squatted down beside the child. "Do ye know I saw a fulmar this morning?"

Liza's brown eyes grew large. "Ye did? I saw a stormy petrel on the way over."

"They're the most cunning little things, dancing along across the water."

Liza held out her basket. "Mama sent bannocks and a crock of cream for yer supper."

Jonathan lifted the cloth. "Oh, my—jest looking at them

things makes me mouth water. But there's way too much for me. Speck ye could help me out a bit?"

Liza nodded, and Jonathan set to taking cups and plates from the cabinet. "It's quiet out," she commented, "but I like when the wind blows the waves up."

"Do ye now?"

Liza nodded firmly. "God makes the wind."

"I speck so," Jonathan murmured after a pause.

Liza hopped up on a stool. "Do ye like storms, Master Jonathan?"

There was a long silence. Then finally he spat, "I hate storms!" He sat down and distractedly took a bannock, then poured cream into Liza's bowl.

Liza's brow wrinkled in puzzlement. "But why are ye a lighthouse keeper then, Master Jonathan? Ye be right out in the middle of the wind and the waves. Papa hates storms, and he says he'll stay as far away from the sea as he can. Papa says he'll never go out in a fishing boat again ever in his *whole life!*"

The lighthouse keeper stared at Liza for so long she finally fidgeted uncomfortably. At last he said, "I have to do it, Liza. I just have to—that's all."

Liza contemplated her friend, and her eyes grew sad. "Sometimes ye feel bad about somethin'?"

Jonathan put his spoon down. "I don't know why life has to seem so hard on a body. Some things just never go away."

"I'll stay by you, Master Jonathan. And Mama says Jesus pays special attention to us in hard times. Probably 'cause we're paying special attention to him."

"Liza," said Jonathan thoughtfully, "I think ye understand a heap of things even big folks don't."

Liza dug into her biscuit, chewing contentedly as a silence settled over the room. Finishing, she stared pensively into her empty bowl. "Papa's always talking about ghosts and demons, and it makes Mama cross, and she tells him to stop, but he doesn't."

Jonathan inclined his head sympathetically, reflecting that Liza's only possible resemblance to her father—a drifter for whom Jonathan had no use—was that her blonde hair had a reddish tint. Fortunately it seemed that in all other respects the child took after her mother.

Liza looked up. "Do ye speck there's demons, Master Jonathan?"

He rose to get the teapot that hung over the fireplace. "Well, now," he said slowly, "I speck there is. But to be honest, I'm thinkin' they ain't wandering about doing what yer Pa thinks they is. Ye want a spot of tea, Liza?"

She shook her head. "Papa thinks they're 'specially up at Dunnottar Castle. I went to the castle once, down by the beach, but I heard strange noises, so I ran back, and Mama told me never to go again."

Jonathan poured himself some tea and sat down. "Sounds like good advice. Ye'll mind yer mama now, won't ye?"

Liza nodded solemnly.

"Yer ma knows best." Jonathan sipped his tea thoughtfully.

"Mama 'specially got religion," Liza said suddenly. "There's a man what come down from Peterhead, and he has meetings in one of the fish-curing sheds. And they sing real loud sometimes and clap their hands and pray for a powerful long time. But Papa says it's just demons making them do it." Liza leaned toward her friend earnestly. "Master Jonathan, do ye think demons could make anyone do what they hadn't a mind to do already?"

Jonathan set his cup down with a clatter. He stared at her, his eyes darkening. His mouth worked convulsively as he twisted his hands. Then he turned his gaze away and became as still and frozen as stone.

Liza picked up her basket and backed away from him, her eyes wide with puzzlement and concern. "I best be going. God be with you, Master Jonathan," she said softly.

There was no answer.

CHAPTER 9

Davey Asks Questions

Davey swung out on the narrow tongue of land that led to Reef Point Lighthouse. A late morning sun was pulling up a breeze to ruffle the waters of the North Sea and refresh its inlets.

Seagulls winged their way eastward while a sea mew circled above Davey. So intent was he on watching them that he almost didn't notice a small girl off to the side of the path. Crouched on a flat rock, she was a wee bit of a thing and still as could be, a basket beside her, and her eyes fixed on the horizon.

Davey crouched beside her. "See anything special out there?"

The child looked at him quickly, appraisingly, then turned back as she had been. "Stormy petrels are a bit hard to see sometimes, 'specially iffen they're gray. See there." She pointed. "That one's gray, and it's a bitty one. See it skimmin' along on top the water? Don't it look like he's walkin'?"

"It sure does. Out on the sea we used to call 'em Mother Carey's Chickens."

"That's a funny name."

Davey cocked his head. "Sailors say funny things sometimes."

The child stood up with her basket. "I know who ye are, Master

53

Davey! Eppie talks and talks about you and Master Malcolm. An' I know which one ye are on accounta yer so tall."

"I see. Well, since you know who I am, shouldn't I know who you are?"

She nodded. "I'm Liza, and I got some biscuits for Master Jonathan. Ye want to walk with me?"

"I'd like that because I'm on my way out to see him, too," he replied as they set off together.

"I go and see Master Jonathan lots of times, whenever Mama lets me. Do ye want to know what my most favorite bird is? A fulmar, because it's big like a duck and it's a white color and has a long yellow bill. And ye know where it builds its nest? Way, way up yonder on them high-up bluffs."

A few minutes later at the lighthouse, introductions had been made, and Davey found himself seated at a table with Liza and the lighthouse keeper. They exchanged pleasantries about the weather, Liza's birds, and how long Davey had been in Stonehaven.

As Jonathan busied himself to brew a pot of tea, Davey noticed that the lighthouse keeper moved methodically, but he also sensed a certain pent-up power in the man. He was not tall but brawny, his face and hands were rough and ruddy from the weather, and his eyes darted quickly, seeming to miss nothing. Davey guessed him to be about forty years old.

Davey glanced about the room. Ledgers and supplies were stacked on the floor and on a long counter in a precise neatness—which, as Davey looked at them, seemed suddenly odd. Book stacks faced the same way, no end or corner sticking out further than the next. Papers had obviously been laid with utter care. Cans and jars of supplies had been categorized and stacked one upon the other in fastidious orderliness. Absolutely nothing was out of place.

"Looks like you're keeping a good light, Jonathan."

"Thankee." He poured the steaming liquid into Davey's and

Liza's cups. "Don't get too many visitors out here at Reef Point. Gits lonely, too much time to think sometimes." He stared off into space but pulled himself back almost immediately. "But I got a job to do, and I'm thankful the Good Lord's given me enough strength to do it."

"Has Reef Point Light been here long?"

Jonathan put the pot on the table and sat down. "Oh, sixty-five years, maybe. I been here the last eighteen or so."

Liza broke a biscuit in half. "Reef Point's a *very* big light!" She punctuated it with a firm nod of the head.

"Yep," said Jonathan. "She can be seen fifteen and a half miles out to sea."

"I can see the light. Even in a *storm* I saw it," said Liza proudly.

"She takes on a boiling sea real good, I'll say that for her."

Davey's eyes traveled around the tower room. "How do you fuel the light?"

"Kerosene. In the closet over there." Jonathan jerked his head in the direction of a small door near the tower's entrance. "Kept in a big drum."

Davey eyed the closet carefully. "I suppose you'd be needing to keep it locked up," he said slowly, "for safety's sake. So the wrong person couldn't get into it."

"Ye betcha, Davey." Jonathan patted his belt. "Wear the key to it right here on my belt." He rose and moved toward the fireplace with the pot.

"Sounds wise to me." Davey took another biscuit. "These are right tasty, Liza. Did you help your mama bake them?"

"Aye. They're my favorite." The little girl smiled.

Davey finished the biscuit, picked up his cup of tea, and sauntered thoughtfully across the room. He watched Jonathan pick up a cup and move toward the table. "Must be a great satisfaction to know you're part of saving lives at sea."

Jonathan's hands tightened on the cup, and he stared straight ahead.

Davey surveyed him carefully and then turned to gaze out the window. "Jonathan," he said with studied casualness, "do you know anything of . . . *wreckers* hereabouts?" At the last phrase he turned quickly to study the lighthouse keeper's reaction.

The cup dropped from Jonathan's hands, shattering on the floor. "No! No!" He was staring wildly. "They—no!" He began to breathe in short gasps.

Surprised by so violent a reaction, Davey moved toward the man swiftly. "Jonathan! Here—let me help you. Sit down, please."

Now seated, Jonathan continued to stare ahead, unaware, as far as Davey could tell, of his surroundings.

Liza was on her knees picking up cup fragments. "He gets this way sometimes. I think he's looking at somethin' in the back of his mind and it don't make him happy."

Jonathan's eyes glazed. "Dark! Dark! The wind—and the—the fog—"

Liza ran to him and leaned close, trying to make Jonathan see her face. "Please, Master Jonathan—don't! Look! It's me. Liza. I'll help you."

The lighthouse keeper stood up. He looked around wildly, strode to the wall beside the fireplace, and leaned his face against it. His voice, at first muffled against the stones, grew to a shriek. "The cries! I can't bear the cries!"

Liza ran to Davey and clung to him in terror. "Master Davey, I never seen him so bad," she sobbed.

Davey patted her but kept his eyes on Jonathan. "It's all right, Liza. Don't fret so."

Liza still clung to him. "Master Davey, what's wreckers?"

CHAPTER 10

This and That

Late afternoon clouds blotted out the sun and sent faint light through two small windows into the schoolhouse and over the rows of empty oaken desks.

Annie, at her desk alone, tapped her pen absentmindedly and stared at an old globe that stood on a shelf, beneath which ranged rows of worn volumes in varying sizes. Realizing that the afternoon's light was fast fading, she arose and lit a kerosene lamp.

A sense of isolation seized her. The schoolroom, silent and deserted by the children who loved Annie and who drew her into their world, seemed now to cast only a somber, cheerless air.

She sat down at the desk and drew the letter from a small satchel. She spread it before her and read it again. This was only the second one she had received from Donal in the six weeks he had been gone. He sounded busy and reasonably content—and only slightly homesick. But surely he would tire of this life and come home eventually. . . . She folded the sheet and tucked it away again.

She sighed, eyeing the stack of papers to her right that waited to be marked and graded. It was totally uninspiring, but she resolutely moved them to the center of the desk. Selecting a pen and dipping it in the inkwell, she set herself firmly to the task at hand.

She had gone halfway through the pile when the door opened and Davey Morrison entered.

Her heart skipped a beat. *How ridiculous,* she thought. *Why on earth should I have any reaction at all to this almost total stranger? Even if he and his friend are the talk of the village!* The fact that he had walked her home one evening certainly meant nothing.

"Miss Annie, I'm sure you weren't expecting—I mean—the reason I'm here is—" He stopped and grinned. "I think I should start from the beginning."

"That sounds appropriate," said Annie in a reasonably friendly tone. She decided she ought to at least be polite. Besides, just now *any* interruption seemed welcome. "Would you care to sit down?"

"Thank you. I would."

She motioned toward the desks. "I doubt you'd fit into any of these. Why don't you try that bench." She couldn't resist adding, "It's for naughty children."

Davey lowered himself onto the sturdy seat. "I believe I could be properly placed in that category!" He fumbled with a small bag. "Anyway, after visiting the lighthouse yesterday, I bumped into—so to speak—one of your pupils, Meg Carmichael, and we became acquainted."

"Meg is very easy to know."

"Quite a talker—most delightful. At any rate I found out how greatly she loves you."

Annie smiled. "The feeling is mutual."

"And she told me that just now you're studying the countries of the East."

"Aye."

Again he fumbled with the bag. "I have some things here from my travels. I thought you might like to see them—to show the children. You may keep them as long as you like." He laid before her a string of marbleized brown beads, a brass bell, and a small engraved cylinder.

Annie glanced up at Davey. Looking into his eyes from so close, she had an odd feeling that she had known him before, which, of course, absolutely could *not* have been. Yet despite what she told herself, she felt drawn to him. She was curious about him and found that she wished their conversation to continue.

She busied herself with the objects on the desk and then picked up the bell.

Davey pulled the bench closer. "The bell's from India. It's reputed to ward off evil spirits." Pointing to the beads, he said, "Those are prayer beads from Arabia."

"And this?" Annie held up the ivory-colored cylinder.

"That," proclaimed Davey grandly, "is the Amulet of Kandehar!"

Annie arched her eyebrows. "Indeed?"

"It's from the tomb of Antiochus I, a tomb carved into rock on the east terrace of a mist-filled valley along the Euphrates. A fitting place of drama and grandeur!"

"An impressive beginning," said Annie. "And how did it come to be there?"

Davey leaned forward, hands together, resting his elbows on his knees. Annie wondered if he were making up his story on the spot.

"The amulet belonged to a king who had inherited it from his father, Seleucus, a general under Alexander the Great. Seleucus led an expedition against the Nabataeans in Petra." Davey's eyes gleamed. "In a small vault of a rich sheik—whose head he cut off—he found the amulet! It protected him from evil and treachery for the rest of his life. And he willed it to Antiochus as his greatest treasure."

Annie smiled. "I applaud your presentation."

Davey grinned. "Well, it must be true because that's what the little man in the shop in Dubai told me. Cost me two shekels."

Annie fingered the amulet thoughtfully. "It would seem that people are superstitious the world over. But none more than in Scotland."

Davey wrinkled his brow. "Aye, I've found sailors a superstitious lot."

"As are fishermen." Annie stacked the papers neatly one upon another and put them in a drawer. She glanced sideways at Davey. He sat quietly, giving her his full attention. Suddenly it seemed he might become a friend, someone she could confide in. "Meg tells me it's a great point of dissension between her parents."

"How's that?"

"Well, Duncan has 'got too much religion' as Margaret puts it, and now on board ship the men kneel down and pray together before they let down the nets."

"Seems rather harmless."

"That's not what she objects to. It's his disdain for certain rules—such as, if on the way to the boat a fisherman meets an old woman or a woman with red hair, he must turn back or go through some ritual of cleansing before starting out again. Certain words aren't to be spoken. And his wife mustn't comb her hair at night while her husband's at sea, or they might be drowned with their feet tangled in seaweed. Duncan doesn't hold to this kind of thing any longer."

"I can imagine Margaret to be a strong voice, shall we say." Davey studied his hands. "It appears to me most folk mix a bit of piousness with more than a little superstition."

Annie got up to walk about the room, picking up and straightening. "Aye, a rather strange mixture of druidism and

Christianity." She carried several books to a shelf under a window. "I suppose they feel that if God should fail them, the ancient taboos and rites will come to their rescue. Or is it the other way around?"

"And you, Miss Annie?"

Annie turned to look at Davey and found him studying her intensely. There was that something in his eyes again that she could not name. She carefully laid the books on the shelf. "I wasn't raised to be superstitious. Papa held to a few of the ancient taboos, though." Annie wrinkled her brow. "I wonder where the line is crossed, where these ancient customs become evil."

"It all seems harmless to me. Some downright funny."

Annie shook her head slowly. "I don't know just *where* the line is crossed. But I do know many of the customs come from a fright of evil spirits or the devil himself, a desire to placate him. I know it can quickly become devil worship." Annie stared out the darkening window. "Strangely, folks who hold to superstitions most fiercely are liable to mix certain parts of the Bible with it."

Davey pondered his hands. "Maybe because in both cases— superstition and religion—it's something to hang on to, something *outside* ourselves." One corner of his mouth tipped in an ironic smile. "*If* one needs it."

Annie arched her eyebrows. "I suppose a sailor such as yourself, Mr. Morrison, who's been everywhere and done everything, needs nothing?"

Davey smiled. "Aye, Miss Mackinnon, you have it right!"

Annie studied him, not sure if he was serious. She sat down, her eyes thoughtful. "When I was a child, Mama taught me that Christianity wasn't religion—elsewise a body could go off in all sorts of directions. It is a *person*—the Presence of Jesus." She stopped, not sure how to continue.

"And do you have this—Presence?"

"I did once. Now . . . ?"

A silence fell, and Davey stood up. "I suppose I should be getting on." His smile held as much charm as anyone could wish for. "I've enjoyed this."

Annie, watching him go, thought it had been a more pleasant time than she wanted to admit. Even to herself.

Thomas Blacklock had spent the day repairing rotting boards in the Wilson barn. Walking back across the fields and down toward his shed, he eyed the sky. Murky gray clouds seemed to hang oppressively low.

All day it seemed to him the air had hung heavy, a portent of something . . . something that made Thomas uneasy.

The moment he pushed the door of his shed open, he saw it: a torn piece of brown paper, anchored by a rock on the dirt floor. He picked up the note and read it with dread. Then slowly again. Shaking inside, he slumped to a stool and spread the brown paper on his knees.

Tonight, the note said, *come to the forest just beyond Jenny's Bog. Come as soon as it be dark, and be bringing no one with you.*

Thomas stared about his shed with unseeing eyes while within himself the feeling of oppression grew.

Later, darkness had come with no stars to guide him. Thomas made his way following vague shadows and his knowledge of the countryside uphill along a row of pine, through an open field, and past the old ruined croft house known as Jenny's Bog.

Confronted by the forest, he paused and drew in his breath. The note had said "just beyond."

He entered the woods and stood uncertainly, trying in vain to see beyond mountain ash, oak, and fir. An owl hooted in the distance, and a twig crackled close by. Thomas's heart beat faster. Whom or what was he waiting for?

A tall figure suddenly loomed before him. It seemed to have a loose-fitting coat and trousers and perhaps some sort of mask. "Thomas Blacklock?" said its raspy, muffled voice.

"Aye," Thomas managed to get out feebly.

"Sit down."

Thomas, used to following orders, felt behind him for a fallen log or stump. Finding none, he sat on the ground against the trunk of a tree and waited.

The figure paced before him perhaps five or six feet away. Finally the man said, "Do ye know Davey Morrison and Malcolm Donnovan?"

"Aye." Thomas's heart slowed. Perhaps it was not such an ominous meeting after all. "They come to Stonehaven a fortnight ago, mebbe."

"Do ye have a shine to 'em?"

"Nay," said Thomas quickly, "I dinna."

The man stood very still. At last he said, "Then, Thomas Blacklock, ye can earn for yerself pounds iffen ye do what we tell you. Ye could use a bit more of the riches of this world, could ye not?"

Thomas considered. His income had always been meager, and just now, except for the Wilson barn, there seemed to be fewer jobs than ever. "Aye," he answered softly.

"Then this is what ye shall do," the raspy voice went on. "Ye shall go about yer work, and ye shall listen—in the shops and at the harbor and on the pathways—and especially at the Wilsons' where ye are working. And ye shall tell us *everything* ye know of the comings and goings of Davey Morrison and Malcolm Donnovan."

Thomas felt suddenly uncharacteristically bold. "Why is it ye want to know?"

The figure was silent for so long that Thomas found himself nervously licking his lips while one eye twitched. At last the man moved toward him a step. "Let's just say we have a business to take care of. And it helps us in that business to hear of these two. So we shall be meeting here in a week with yer observations. But before ye go, tell me all ye can, and this little bag'll be fer ye to take home." He pulled a small bag from his pocket and held it toward Thomas.

Thomas took it.

Twenty minutes later he was on his way back to his shed. He clutched the little bag and hoped his situation was not akin to that of Judas Iscariot. But a man had to get by, didn't he? And in spite of his prayer at the curing shed, he still had no love for Davey Morrison.

Griselda picked up a fresh apron, shook it out, and tied it around her waist.

She had done the usual chores with more than her usual energy. The haddock had been smoked and hung on a rack in the back of the kitchen. She and her mother had taken the mattress she shared with Eppie and Meg (which had become flat) and stuffed it with new chaff carried down from Wilson's barn—followed by sewing the end with linen thread. Later Duncan would hoist it into place. Meanwhile, Eppie had made great sport of bouncing on it until Margaret hauled her off to help brown the oatcakes.

Chores in the Carmichael house seemed endless to Griselda. She had grown up accepting her lot in life. But now at age sixteen, other horizons loomed. Griselda had begun to feel closed in, sometimes even put upon. She longed for just a bit of the excitement and adventure of other places, other ways of doing things. Like she had read of in some of Annie Mackinnon's books.

However, all was definitely not gloomy. She smoothed her skirts and gave a little twirl. Malcolm Donnovan was going to come calling this afternoon.

She took out a large mirror and propped it on the table and sat down on a stool before it. She had to make sure her hair was just right.

Suddenly she sighed and leaned her elbows on the table. Brother Turner had said at least half a dozen times that one who was a follower of Jesus ought to take great care whom he or she got mixed up with, on account of Jesus' caring about everything to do with a person's life. Going to meetings at the curing shed had awakened and furthered in Griselda a faith that had been given to her by her father when she was a wee girl and had been tended ever so slightly at the kirk. Now she wanted, heart and soul, to be a follower of Jesus.

Or did she? Malcolm Donnovan was a whole new world of fun and charm. Well—she shook her head firmly at the image in the mirror—she was not "getting mixed up with" Malcolm Donnovan! He was merely a nice friend dropping by on a visit.

She heard her mother's step in the hall and leaned forward, fussing with her hair again.

Margaret appeared in the doorway. "So Malcolm's going to come calling, is he?"

Griselda peered into the mirror. She blushed slightly. "Oh, he just said he'd stop by for a bit."

"Well, ye kin ask him and Davey to come by for a supper soon as they can. Yer father finally brought home a good catch of herring." She wiped her hands on her apron.

"I'll ask," replied Griselda, still intent on her hair.

Margaret nodded in satisfaction. "That Malcolm's took a real shine to you, Griselda."

Griselda stopped. She eyed her mother thoughtfully as she sighed inwardly. *Fiona.* Why was there always something about to spoil one's joy! "He may be just as taken with Fiona, whether she's about to be pledged to Ian or not! Maybe both Davey and Malcolm are."

"Oh, Fiona kin wave her little lily-white hands at them and flutter her eyelashes like she does, but you're the better and sweeter! Don't ye worry none about her." Margaret gave her apron a vigorous shake to emphasize her feelings.

There was a knock at the door. With a last quick glance in the mirror, Griselda went to open it. She could practically feel Margaret beaming as she followed.

"Greetings, ladies," said Malcolm with a jaunty air and bowing over a bouquet of red roses and white daisies. "And these are for the lovely Griselda!" He thrust the flowers into Griselda's hands.

Margaret's face went white. She put her hands up as if to ward off an attack. Griselda's eyes went from Malcolm to her mother. "Mama—" she remonstrated, distressed, for she knew what was coming.

Margaret's eyes glazed with fear. "Nay, laddie! Ye kinna bring the likes of them inta the house!"

"Excuse me?" said Malcolm.

"Flowers. Red and white flowers tagither means *death!* That there's to be an early *death!*"

Griselda clutched the flowers. Whatever should she do?

"Red and white together?" inquired Malcolm, incredulous.

"Laddie! Laddie!" wailed Margaret. "Ye kinna go against the spirits!"

CHAPTER 11

Thomas and Liza

Thomas sat on a fallen log in front of his shed, mending a horse harness. Liza had spent time nuzzling the horse she had named Blacky and now was inside with the kitten that Thomas said should not be out on such a cool afternoon.

Liza had come every day to see her pet and to visit with Thomas. Thomas had begun to look forward to these visits, though he found it hard to admit such a thing.

Liza burst through the door. "Dusty *purred*, Master Thomas! Even real loud, he did."

"He's getting a mite stronger, that one is."

"Kin I be taking him home soon?"

Thomas shook his head. "Best wait a bit. It's been real nip and tuck with him. But don't worry none," he added, seeing her crestfallen face. "He's gonna make it, he is."

Liza plumped down on the log beside him. "Did ye work up to the Wilsons' barn today?"

"Aye."

"Master Davey and Master Malcolm board there."

"Aye."

"Do ye see 'em?"

"Not over much." Thomas glanced at Liza sideways. "Ye see 'em?"

Liza nodded. "Griselda's sweet on Malcolm. Leastways, that's what Meg says. And Eppie told me Malcolm brought Griselda red and white flowers and Eppie's ma got upset and Griselda had to throw the flowers out!"

Thomas chewed that one over. "Ye see Davey Morrison?"

"Aye. He's lots of places in the village, and he likes to ask questions. I heard him asking the clerk at the market about Dunnottar Castle, but she dinna ken anything."

Thomas tugged at a strap. "Ye remember anything else he asked?"

"He went to see Master Jonathan out to the lighthouse, and Master Davey asked him *lots* of questions!"

"Such as?"

"'Bout the light and what makes it go and about—wreckers—" A strange look came over Liza's face, as if perhaps she'd come to a topic best not discussed. Abruptly she rushed on. "Master Davey's traveled *all over!* And he brought things from other countries to Miss Annie so's she could show us. Meg thinks Master Davey's getting sweet on Miss Annie on accounta she saw him walking her home one time. But Meg thinks practically ever'body's gettin' sweet on someone!" Liza cocked her head, studying Thomas. "Are ye sweet on anybody?"

Thomas shook his head. "Know anything else about them two fellers?"

"Just that Griselda told Eppie they're both handsome but Malcolm's the most fun." A pause. "Do ye like poetry, Master Thomas?"

"Aye."

"I saw a wee book inside, next to the kitty box, is what made me think of it." Liza popped up. "Could I bring it out and see iffen I could read it?"

Thomas saw no problem in that, and Liza shortly returned, book in hand.

She turned the pages. "There's so many big words."

"I'll find you a piece." Thomas thumbed through the well-worn little volume. "Here's one by Robert Louis Stevenson for you to try."

Liza studied it. "I don't think I ken all the words. Would ye read it to me, Master Thomas?"

Thomas took the book. He read as Liza stood before him, hands behind her back, mesmerized by a voice singularly melodic as it rose and fell with the cadence of the poem.

"In the Highlands, in the country places,
Where the old plain men have rosy faces,
And the young fair maidens
Quiet eyes;
Where essential silence chills and blesses,
And for ever in the hill-recesses
Her more lovely music
Broods and dies.

O to mount again where erst I haunted;
Where the old red hills are bird-enchanted,
And the low green meadows
Bright with sward;
And when even dies, the million-tinted,
And the night has come, and planets glinted,
Lo, the valley hollow
Lamp-bestarr'd!

O to dream, O to awake and wander
There, and with delight to take and render,

Through the trance of silence,
Quiet breath!
Lo! for there, among the flowers and grasses,
Only the mightier movement sounds and passes;
Only winds and rivers,
Life and death."

When he had finished, Liza stared at him for some moments. "It was just like ye was in another world! I dinna ken the words, but ye make it sound like music!"

Thomas looked embarrassed. "Poetry be muckel like music."

"Miss Annie read us a poem about a wee mouse. Do ye know it?"

"'Wee, sleekit, cow'rin, tim'rous beastie, O, what a panic's in thy breastie!'" quoted Thomas.

Lisa clapped her hands. "That's the one! Miss Annie said Robbie Burns wrote it, and he's Scotland's very *best* poem writer! But do ye know what, Master Thomas? Miss Annie said he lived a dreadful wild life and drank himself clean to death!"

"Aye."

"Master Thomas, what makes folks say good things and all the while they're doing something dreadful that nobody knows about?"

Thomas stared off across the fields. "Mebbe sometimes a body gets caught in a trap, and he don't want to do it, but he don't want to stop neither."

CHAPTER 12

Elvira Elphinstone

Elvira Elphinstone, at the window in the back parlor, surveyed the yard. She nodded in satisfaction; her new gardener was doing well. Tenstemona, with their pinkish red bell-like clusters, grew next to rosebushes and azaleas. In a far corner, heather crept in and out beneath queen of the meadow bushes and arching ferns. Beyond these, larch, silver birch, and great oak trees shadowed the lawn.

She turned from the window. Elvira was a tall, slim woman, somewhere between middle and old age. Thick gray hair swept back from a still handsome face and was anchored in an imposing bun by a large ivory comb.

She walked with a quick step to the corner and picked up a gold-tipped mahogany cane. She glanced above the fireplace at a great picture of a heavily bearded gentleman. Elvira smirked and shook her cane at him. "You should smile, Colin, to know how well your granddaughter keeps your estate, and see the respect Stonehaven pays to the name of Elphinstone!"

She stood proudly for a moment in the middle of the room. It was true. Not only was she wealthier than anyone else in the village, but she knew how to use her wealth to bring to pass and possess those things that she deemed necessary in her life or that of Stonehaven.

She sat down in a large chair and arranged her blue brocaded skirts and patted her collar. Perhaps her visitor or visitors would come today.

For Elvira knew (for she was indeed aware of *all* happenings of note in the village) of the arrival of Davey Morrison and Malcolm Donnovan in Stonehaven. And she waited with some impatience for them to come calling.

Davey Morrison swung up the pathway that led off the main road to the north of Stonehaven.

He passed between white pillars, where beyond a tall hedge the Elphinstone manor lay open to his view. It was a two-story house of large, gray stone blocks, whose protrusions would indicate that the house had been added onto from time to time. Ivy clung to its walls while rosebushes and azaleas lined the walkway. Above the gabled roof Davey counted chimney flues. Fourteen fireplaces! Obviously the lovely Fiona had no monetary worries.

Davey was not quite sure why he had not come sooner. Perhaps it was a feeling that he might be venturing on a path over which he was not ready to tread? Regardless, the day was fair, and he approached a great paneled door with a steady step. He lifted the brass knocker and let it fall with a heavy thud.

Almost immediately a woman in a long apron and lace cap appeared, inquired as to Davey's mission, told him to wait, and disappeared down a long hall.

A very large cat rose from a patch of sunlight on the floor to check him out. Davey was admiring a black oriental chest with ball feet that stood in the entryway when Fiona appeared beside him.

"Well, Davey Morrison!" she exclaimed with her most engaging smile. "Please come into the parlor."

Davey followed her, thinking her every bit as enchanting as she had been recently in his dreams.

She motioned toward a chair and sat down in another on the other side of a small, ornately carved mahogany table. "I've hoped each day that you would come." She leaned forward just a bit. "And where is Malcolm Donnovan?"

"Actually," replied Davey, "just now Malcolm's out for a walk with Griselda Carmichael."

"I see." Fiona's eyes shadowed but only momentarily. "Auntie will be ready to see you shortly. Meanwhile you and I may use the time to become better acquainted, mayn't we?"

Mayn't we? thought Davey. *Why else does this creature think I'm really here?* However much his thoughts might rush on, he found himself suddenly tongue-tied.

"So tell me, why are you here in Stonehaven, Davey Morrison?" She folded her hands primly and settled back into the daintily brocaded chair.

Davey took a deep breath and told himself that this was an average, run-of-the-mill, ordinary conversation. "Well, in the first place I like the adventure of new things and places. Which is why for the last couple of years I've been a deepwater sailor."

Fiona nodded. "I imagine that *would* be quite adventuresome. How long is it you've known Mr. Donnovan?"

"Not quite a year."

"He's quite humorous, isn't he? I came upon him entertaining some children and passersby in front of a shop the other day."

"Aye," said Davey, "quite humorous."

"So tell me why you and your Malcolm have come to our little village."

Davey hesitated, contemplating the best way to explain. "I've been asked by the Historical Society of Aberdeen to write a brochure on the area. Along with that and because of it, I feel learning more of the fishing industry would be valuable. I may sign onto Duncan Carmichael's fishing barque."

"And Malcolm is to assist you in all this historical research?"

"Aye," replied Davey, noting the number of times Fiona drew Malcolm's name into the conversation and feeling slightly irritated.

"Well, you'll find Auntie an enormous help. She knows everything about anything you'd want to know. No one can really figure out how she learns it all. Auntie's sharp, and terribly healthy, too. Probably *that* comes from all those long walks she takes after dark."

"Interesting," commented Davey.

"She also collects paper sacks, false teeth, and bedsprings. She has many other collections and will show you those, I'm sure. But probably not the false teeth—she's more private about those. And she loves to go to funerals, especially of folks she scarcely knows or doesn't know at all. Some busybodies claim that her going to funerals is somehow connected to her false-teeth collection, but I don't think so, do you?"

"Why are you telling me all this?"

Fiona's eyes were wide and innocent. "It makes a person more interesting to know what they collect, don't you think?"

Davey studied the carpet. "And you, Miss Fiona? What do *you* collect? Let me guess—hearts?"

Davey was not to know what her answer was, for at that moment the servant appeared at the door. "Madam is ready," she said.

Fiona rose. "Follow me."

She led Davey down a long, musty hall of polished stone slabs overlaid with a Persian carpet runner that muffled their steps. Ornate mirrors decorated the walls, and Davey had to duck his head to pass under a chandelier of candles and glass. They reached a heavy mahogany door that swung on great iron hinges.

Fiona paused. "When she's not sleeping or out walking, Auntie spends most of her time in the back parlor."

She pushed at the door, and it swung back to reveal another smaller hall. Fiona veered to the left, and Davey followed her into a large room.

He blinked against bright light from recessed windows that made the rest of the room shadowy by contrast. As his eyes adjusted, he perceived rich brocades—couches, many pillows, and a rug in faded blues and varying shades of rust and red. A peat fire burned in a large fireplace with a hobbed grate. Two black pottery cats on the mantel glared at him with jeweled eyes.

In a high-backed red velvet chair drawn close to the fire sat a woman, erect and perfectly still.

"Auntie," said Fiona, "may I present Davey Morrison."

Elvira Elphinstone nodded almost imperceptibly and gave a half wave toward the chair opposite her. "Please be seated, Mr. Morrison. Fiona, dear, please bring us tea and scones. I told Cook to have them ready."

Fiona left, and Elvira turned her attention to her guest, eyeing him steadily until Davey fidgeted.

"I suppose I should start by telling you why I'm here in Stonehaven," he began.

"I *know* why you say you're here, Davey Morrison. Now let us see if you fit the picture of a deepwater sailor turned historical investigator."

Davey grinned, boyishly he hoped. "I trust I'll pass muster."

"Time will tell on that account, won't it?" she replied. "Ah, here comes our tea."

Fiona placed a full tray on a small low table between them. She curtsied toward Davey. "I shall be attending to other things now. I enjoyed our talk." She smiled prettily. "Please tell Malcolm that I asked after him."

When she had gone, Davey cleared his throat. "I understand your niece is to be pledged to Ian Fraser?"

His hostess lifted the gilded teapot and poured the hot liquid into a porcelain cup. "Fiona? Who knows? What Fiona wanted yesterday is not necessarily what she wants today. Nor is what she wants today what she may want tomorrow!"

Davey took the cup. "She's very beautiful."

Elvira stared hard into his eyes. "Aye. Very beautiful." She poured tea into the other cup and settled back. "Now do have a scone and some biscuits and tell me how I may help you."

Davey took several deliberate sips of the tea. He indicated the large portrait that hung above the fireplace. "I presume the imposing gentleman is an ancestor of yours?"

"Aye. That is my grandfather, Colin Elphinstone, a direct descendant of the sixth earl of Marischal, whose residence during the latter part of the sixteenth century was Dunnottar Castle."

Davey's eyes lit with interest. "Then you must know a good deal of the history of the castle."

Elvira daintily broke off a piece of biscuit. "That I do." She ate it reflectively. "In the past, the extraordinary grandeur of the site made it a place coveted and fought over." Her eyes kindled, and she sat up even straighter, if possible, than she had before. "As has been said, 'Dunnottar speaks with an audible voice; every cave has a record, every turret a tongue; the ear is struck with wandering voices; and words that never die seem at every step to arrest the attention!'"*

Davey ate his scone with delight. His visit was going as well as he could possibly have hoped. "Have you been up there recently?"

"Not for many years. I can walk a good distance on the straightaway, but the descent to the valley and then back up to the castle would be too much."

William Beattie, *Caledonia Illustrated*, vol. 2, (London:Virtue): 168

"The whole place sounds quite dramatic."

"Its most famous incident, other than the defense of the Regalia in 1651, was in 1685. One hundred and sixty-seven men and women were thrown into Dunnottar's dungeon."

"Why?"

"Covenanters—for their religious belief. A most foolish people!"

Davey raised his eyebrows. "Oh?"

Elvira put down her cup. "There are so many philosophies, why hold to any one so stubbornly that it gets you thrown into a place of murder and torture? Certainly it did *them* no *earthly* good!"

Davey grimaced. "Perhaps it was *heavenly* good they were looking for."

"And who has ever returned from *that* region to give us a report?" she asked sharply. She rose and moved to the other side of the room. "Come here, Mr. Morrison, and let me show you a collection I'm quite proud of."

Davey found himself before a tall, dark cabinet. Behind glass doors lay several objects: a pistol, a dagger, several heavy pieces of rope—each with a large knot—an elegant claymore, and a small vial. "The small vial carried a potent poison. It came from St. Andrews. A certain heretic was forced by the bishop to drink it. He died most dramatically!" She pointed to the dagger. "The claymore was used in the battle of Culloden Moor. The ropes are from hangings on Dunnottar Rock, and the other instruments are from murders farther inland."

Davey stared at them. "A rather gruesome collection, isn't it?"

"Surely you *know*," returned his hostess proudly, "that the possession of death instruments brings one great worldly prosperity."

Davey half smiled. "I've heard it. Do you *believe* it?"

Elvira Elphinstone pinned him to the wall with her look. She moved grandly across the room, tapping her cane as she went.

"What do you see here in this room—in this house—but *worldly prosperity?* Of course I believe it!" She reseated herself, holding her gold-tipped cane before her like a scepter. "These things have been *proven,* Mr. Morrison!"

Davey sat down. "Aye," he said affably, reminding himself that he must be more careful with his responses if he wished to keep on the good side of his hostess. He smiled at her warmly. "I don't want to take too much of your time today. You've been most gracious." Davey studied a pattern of sunlight on the carpet. "Can you tell me anything of . . . wreckers?"

"Wreckers?" Elvira slowly measured Davey with her eyes. Then she settled back in her chair. "Those who lure ships to their doom? What do you wish to know?"

"Have you known of any along this coast? Recently or in the past?"

"There are always wrecks! Maritime shipping thrives, and Scotland's rocky coast is full of danger. But as for *wreckers*—not here."

"I see."

She shook her head. "I heard of a church up in Fraserburgh that asked the vicar to pray that if there was to be a wreck, they might profit with the loot by having it happen on their shores." She chuckled. "Hypocrites! Served them right to find out their own vicar was head of a wrecking mob!"

"But you've not known of it near Stonehaven?"

Again she shook her head. "Not here." She eyed him intently. "And why do you ask?"

Davey shrugged nonchalantly. "Such barbarians seem to keep busy along rocky coasts."

"There may have been something of the sort up by Fraserburgh, and perhaps a bit to the south somewhere—"

"A violent lot, wherever they are," commented Davey.

"I presume so," said Elvira slowly. "I've heard they're sometimes

called mooncussers because they operate best in utter darkness."
She paused and tapped her cane thoughtfully. Then her eyes lit.
"Ah, here's a wrecker story, Davey Morrison. 'Twas in the 1700s.
I'm not sure *where* it happened, but it's a true one." She leaned
forward. "A certain Peter Barnes—aye, Peter Barnes was the
name—hung deceptive beacons on fir trees along a lonely point
where he lived in an isolated cabin. Those lights lured a schooner
laden with provisions to a wreck, and the entire crew drowned
on Christmas Eve. Peter Barnes was suspected, but there wasn't
enough evidence to convict him. Well, on Christmas Eve—*exactly*
twenty years later—when he was returning home from a nearby
village, he got confused by a light outside a settler's home and fell
to his death *exactly* where the ship had been wrecked! A fitting
end, don't you think?"

There was a thud against the window. Elvira stiffened. Her
eyes flew wide. She opened her mouth, but nothing came out. "A
bird—against the window," she managed at last, but with great
dignity, "predicts *death!*"

"May I help you somehow?" asked Davey.

"I need *no* help." she responded sharply. She rose, crossed to a
small desk drawer, and drew out a scarlet ribbon. "If I hang this
in the window, there is a *small* chance the curse will be removed."
She looked at Davey, and her eyes glittered. "Things set in
nature are rarely changed, however."

Elvira moved toward the window. A dog howled. She froze.
And from far away came the sound of a cock's crow. "Davey
Morrison," she uttered in sepulchral tones, "just as I thought. It's
no use—there *will be* a death!"

CHAPTER 13

At the Carmichaels'

Margaret Carmichael had done herself proud with the supper for Davey and Malcolm. She had cock-a-leekie soup made from chicken and leeks, fresh herring, boiled potatoes, rumble de thumps, and crusty whole meal bread with jam and a cottage cheeselike spread called *crowdie*. And with great dignity she had laid before them her scones, done to the perfect shade of golden brown.

There was even a bit of decoration in the middle of the table. Meg had insisted on bringing in some heather. Margaret grudgingly admitted that the wiry little evergreen with its purple flowers looked festive—even in an old jar. And she was grateful the incident with Malcolm's flowers was done with and, she hoped, forgotten.

The main part of the meal over, Duncan and Davey had gone to the back shed for more peat. Griselda and the children (including Liza Rafferty, who was often with them) had followed Malcolm to the "sitting" part of the large room that was the setting for all their communal activities.

Feeling that there might be more important matters at stake,

Margaret had refused Griselda's help in clearing the table. She also had decided not to ask Eppie, who was in a high state of excitement over the visitors and in such a frame was liable to drop things. At the moment, Margaret didn't know where Meg was.

Glancing at the little group gathered about Malcolm near the large, gray stone fireplace, Margaret smiled in satisfaction. Griselda was obviously taken with the young man, and Margaret was sure that Malcolm looked at Griselda more than at the others. Davey was the taller and handsomer of the two, Margaret thought; however, Malcolm did have charm and knew how to make a body laugh.

"As sure as I've clawed me way windward in a stiff beat around the Horn, it's true!" he was saying.

Eppie, on the floor, hugged her knees. "Are ye *sure*, Master Malcolm?"

"Aye. It was so *cold* the words froze right there in our mouths. And the upshot of it was we had to wait till spring to find out what we'd been talking about all winter!"

Eppie and Liza giggled. Griselda, sitting on an old stool, stitching, smiled prettily. "Yer so funny, Malcolm!"

Malcolm warmed to his subject and his audience as he strode about the room. "And the wind! I'm telling you, it blew like the furies until we was all leaning one way—like this. And when it stopped, we all fell down on the deck!"

Duncan and Davey entered, with armloads of peat, to the sound of laughter.

"Malcolm's been telling us stories," explained Griselda.

"But," said Malcolm, "I didn't tell them yet about the time I was marooned on one of them isles off of Barbados."

Davey rolled his eyes. "Oh, then, don't let me be the means of stopping you."

Eppie was big eyed. "Was it a *dangerous* island?"

"It sure was! The natives captured me! And I was about to be decapitated." Malcolm made a slicing motion across his neck. "And afterwards hung!"

"Oh, Malcolm," remonstrated Griselda, chuckling.

"What happened?" piped Liza.

"While they was arguing which to do first, I got away!"

Duncan dumped his load of peat into an old bucket by the fireplace. "What was it exactly that Malcolm did aboard the whaling ship?"

Davey dumped his load and answered, "He gave us all our spirit of unity."

"How's that?"

"We *all* wanted to strangle him!"

Duncan took fish lines and hooks from a heavy wooden box in the corner and sat before the fire on a low stool to untangle and mend. Davey joined him in his endeavors.

Margaret bustled toward them with a tray of cups, teapot, and a plate of biscuits. Griselda jumped up, taking the plate from Margaret. "I'll help pass these."

"That was a wonderful dinner, Margaret," said Malcolm gallantly. "Mmm! And so was that jam of yer ma's, Eppie!"

"Did ye like the rumble de thumps?" asked the child.

"Uh—aye!" He leaned toward Griselda as she held out the plate of biscuits. "What were they?"

"That was the cabbage and mashed potatoes mixed together."

"Oh—aye." Malcolm sat up. "Delicious!"

"Then how come ye was slipping them into yer pocket when no one was looking?" challenged Eppie.

Malcolm looked embarrassed and smiled sheepishly.

"Eppie!" remonstrated Griselda.

"Oh, never ye mind!" Margaret poured tea into Davey's cup. "Everyone can't like everything the same. Liza, can ye stay awhile, or are ye to be getting home afore it's too dark?"

"I can stay for a bit," said Liza. "Papa will be coming along for me."

Margaret set her tray down and glanced about the room. "Where's Meg?"

"I don't believe I've seen her since supper," answered Griselda. "Eppie?"

"I dinna ken."

Duncan shook his head. "Do ye mean the child is gone *again?*"

Griselda moved toward the door. "I'll go find her. I know all the places to be looking."

Margaret, hands on hips, watched her go. "I can't abide Meg disappearing like she does. Loses all sense of time, too."

"The sea seems to draw her like a magnet," said Duncan.

Margaret took up a quilt that lay in the corner and sat down in a high-backed chair next to the table. She gave the quilt a vigorous shake to vent her frustration. She was getting right tired of keeping a leash on Meg! It seemed if she turned around once, the girl would wander off. "If I've warned her once it's a dozen times about that undertow when the tide comes in."

Duncan shrugged. "Well, Griselda'll find her. And then we'll scold her—though 'twon't do any good. Worse'n any sailor that goes to sea!"

Davey looked up from the fish lines. "Speaking of which—Duncan, how do you like what you do?"

"Fishing? It's hard work. Puts the broth on the table." Duncan paused to reflect. "Beyond that, there's something about all that expanse of sky and sea—"

"Make you feel lonely? I can relate to that."

Duncan shook his head. "Actually, it makes me know I'm *not* alone. I guess it could be called *awe*—an emotional kind of knowing God's there." He stared at the flames. "Ye believe in God, Davey?"

Davey hesitated. "Well—I—don't think about it much."

Margaret looked up from her quilt. "Well, Duncan does! Reads his Bible and prays every day. I go to the kirk betimes and do my duty. But I ain't what ye'd call *devout*. Not tyin' practically every other thing to Divine Providence. I mean, Duncan thinks the Good Lord is in everything that happens to him—good or bad!"

Davey tugged at a rope. "For myself, I find that hard to swallow."

"Not for Duncan. If Duncan found *death* standing at the door, he'd say, 'Come right on in—what kin we get for you?'" She punctuated her words with a shake of the quilt, feeling annoyed at the direction of the conversation.

"Come now, Margaret!" remonstrated Duncan. "I'm just believing that our times are in God's hands."

"I had a grandfather who felt that way," said Davey thoughtfully. "I even made some kind of commitment at a camp meeting. Thought if I prayed now and then and didn't curse, everything would be all right. And it was—until—" A silence fell.

"Somethin' tough happen, Davey?" asked Duncan gently.

"Aye." A look of deep anger and bitterness came into Davey's eyes. "Then I cursed God! I cursed him and didn't know if he cared that I cursed. Finally I decided it likely he didn't exist. More simple that way." He ran a hand through his hair.

"Simple?"

"I couldn't put the God my grandfather spoke of with what happened to me. For that matter, if you look around at pain and suffering, how can you think there's a *loving* God?"

Duncan spread out a side of the net carefully on the floor. "If ye only believe we're cast by chance like pieces of seaweed to drift with the tide, then it's no problem."

"What do you mean?"

"If ye *do* believe in a loving God, it's only then a body has to wrestle with putting it together."

Davey appeared to be thinking hard. "I suppose that makes some kind of sense. So what do *you* do with it, Duncan?"

Duncan stood, stretching out the net. "Sometimes I don't understand, either. But I can't give up depending on or believing in everything I can't understand." Duncan sat down and leaned toward Davey earnestly. "Beyond that, I believe God *chose* to enter a world of pain and suffering—in Jesus. I don't have any choice whether or not to live in this kind of world. He did. The choice I got is whether or not I'm going to let him walk with me in the pain of it."

The door opened, and Griselda entered with Meg.

Margaret felt a sense of relief over Meg, mixed with gratitude that a discussion that was definitely beyond her had been interrupted.

"I found her out by Bull's Head Rock," announced Griselda as she moved to the fire to warm her hands.

"What's Bull's Head Rock?" asked Malcolm from the floor, where he had been drawn into a game of sticks and jacks with Eppie and Liza.

"Oh, it's a wonderful rock what looks out to the sea. Big enough to lie down on even." Obviously Meg's enthusiasm overshadowed any regret she may have had for her absence.

Duncan crossed toward her. "Meg, we've told you not to be wandering off like that!"

"I'm sorry, Papa. But after supper I looked out the window, and I saw a curlew, so I ran outside. He was hopping along, and pretty soon we was down to the sea."

Margaret stayed in her seat but spoke with forceful shakes of her head. "I can't abide it when ye go out alone—especially near high tide!"

Meg looked contrite. "I'm sorry. I winna do it again. But I just got all caught up in it till I heard Griselda calling me."

Margaret found herself softening. "Well, all right. Never ye mind. Come help me with the quilt. And let's all just git comfy, and maybe Malcolm and Davey would teach us some of their sailor songs."

Before Davey could protest, there was a knock at the door. Duncan answered it to find Rob Rafferty, who announced, "I come for Liza."

Margaret would have said, had she been asked, that Rob Rafferty would be far down on the list of hoped-for visitors. Nevertheless, her hospitable nature rose to the fore, and she nodded affably. "Oh, now do sit for just a wee spell."

"Please, Papa," pleaded Liza.

Rob Rafferty turned his hat in his hands. "I dinna ken."

"Come on now," encouraged Duncan, "Margaret'll give you some tea and biscuits."

Rob Rafferty shook his head. "I dinna ken. Me arthritis is acting up. Means the wind's gonna blow." But he sat down and gratefully took a cup and as many biscuits as he could conveniently get in the other hand. "Yep—yep—gonna blow."

"If ye hang up a dead kingfisher," offered Malcolm, still at his game with the little girls, "his beak'll be pointing to where the wind'll come from."

"Hoot mon. I dinna need a bird to tell me. Me bones do it well enough."

Malcolm stood up. "Ye know, once, out to sea, I counted 136 kinds of Scottish weather in twenty-four hours!"

"Mostly bad, I'll wager," replied Rob Rafferty, who managed somehow to smack his lips over the biscuits and look dour at the same time.

Malcolm turned toward the little girls. "Did ye ever see clouds that look like hens' scratchings and horses' tails?"

Eppie and Liza looked at one another, grinning and hunching their shoulders in a question mark.

"Well," said Malcolm, striking a dramatic pose,

"Hens' scratchings and mares' tails
Make tall ships carry low sails
The lower they get
The nearer wet!"

Liza clapped her hands. "Oh, that's a poem!"

Davey ambled toward Rob Rafferty, hands in his pockets. "Rob Rafferty, you know these parts pretty well?"

"Hoot mon!" exclaimed their visitor, still busy with his biscuits and tea. "Lived here all me life."

"Ever get up to Dunnottar Castle?"

Rob Rafferty set his cup down with a clatter. "Why would ye be asking after sech a place?"

"'Twas a grand sight as the ship came in," Davey countered.

"It's old, Dunnottar is. Nobody goes up there," said Duncan.

"Annie does," said Griselda.

Davey turned quickly. "Does she?"

"Sometimes she goes when she's done teaching in the afternoon. I think she's grieving about her husband. And thinking about her son, Donal, out to sea."

"Seems like a fine place to visit," said Malcolm. "In fact, ye could do some of yer artist sketching up there, Davey."

Davey nodded thoughtfully. "Good idea."

Rob Rafferty got up, moving his hands in great agitation. "Ye kinna go to the castle! It's full of sea demons, it is!"

"Now ye're blethering!" Duncan moved to put a calming hand on Rob Rafferty's arm.

But Rob Rafferty was undeterred. "When the dark comes down, there's shadows—and demon lights! An' iffen there's a storm they're movin' back and forth, back and forth, I tell you!"

Duncan looked at Davey. "He's got a good imagination, he has."

Rob Rafferty wandered about as if in a trance. "I dinna ken where they come from, but they was there! I seen 'em!"

"Sit down, Rob Rafferty!" Duncan ordered. "Ye're working yerself up to a stew!"

Rob Rafferty raised his eyes and pointed toward the rafters. "Once, in a storm I seen a ghost of Duffy Jonas on the side of Dunnottar Castle. Upon me word, I did. He come from the big locker under the seas."

"Papa, please!" cried Liza, running to him in distress.

Duncan sat him down forcibly. "Sit down! Dinna take on so!"

"No! Leave it be. 'Tis a devilish place!" Rob Rafferty shook his head as if to get the awful vision out of his mind. He stood up, looking somewhat calmer. "Best be going. It's gonna be pitch black out there in two minutes."

Margaret wrapped the last of the biscuits in a napkin. "Here— take some biscuits home. Give them to yer ma, Liza."

When good-byes had been said and they were gone, Margaret caught Davey's eye. She lifted her eyebrows and cocked her head meaningfully. "I told you to *fergit* Dunnottar Castle, Davey Morrison!"

Davey shrugged his shoulders and smiled charmingly.

"We were going to have some singing now, weren't we, Mama?" asked Meg.

"Ye could come to the fest and sing, too," piped up Eppie.

"Another fest?" asked Davey.

"This one's in a few weeks, and it's for storytelling and songs," said Meg. "Liza and Eppie and I are going to sing."

"Well," said Malcolm, "that all by itself would be enough to make me come! If I go, ye'd show me around, Griselda?"

"Aye." Griselda blushed happily, which was duly noted by Margaret.

"I say, what's a fest without a bonnie lass to show one about!"

89

Eppie surveyed Davey. "Do *ye* have a bonnie lass, Master Davey?"

"Eppie!" remonstrated Margaret, although she was more than a little curious as to his answer.

"Aye, I had a bonnie lass," he answered after a pause.

"Then what happened to her?"

"Eppie! It ain't polite to ask so much," said Margaret, more as an apology to Davey than a reprimand to Eppie.

"My bonnie lass—" Davey hesitated for a long moment— "died of the fever two years ago."

So that's the reason for the melancholy Davey seems to sink into from time to time, thought Margaret.

"Is that the bad thing ye was talking about?" asked Duncan softly.

"Aye."

"That's a tough one, it is, Davey."

"But life goes on. . . ."

"And ye keep searching."

Davey leaned against the fireplace. "I reckon I'm always hoping that I'll find something that would pull my life together—give it meaning."

Duncan gathered up the fish lines and net and laid them carefully in the box. "Someone once said, 'Our hearts are restless till we find our rest in Thee!'"

"Sounds poetic. But what does it mean?"

"Means God made us so there's an empty space inside. And he's the only one that can fill it."

Davey studied Duncan. "And you think that's why I'm restless?"

"Finding the Lord is like a ship coming home to a safe harbor."

Meg leaned forward, cupping her chin in her hand, the firelight beautiful on her young face. "Master Davey, Jesus is searching for *you* at the same time. Yer bound to run into one another somehow!"

CHAPTER 14

On the Castle Bluff

Davey stood in the cool shadows of Ninian's Den and marveled at the vastness of the rock before him. It had been a precarious descent, and now he eyed his next task.

He had every reason to believe he would find Annie Mackinnon on Dunnottar Rock. Meeting Meg on the path after school had been easy enough—extracting the information he needed, easier yet.

Tucking his artist's pad and pens more firmly under his arm, he began his ascent.

Coming out of the tunnel just past the midpoint of his climb, he at last passed through the ruins of an ancient gate. To his left was a large building, five stories high with crowstepped gables, which he presumed to be the keep. To his right along the southern portion of Dunnottar ran a long, low series of crumbling stone chambers. Stables, probably.

He saw Annie leaning against a stretch of stone wall. She was looking out to sea, and an afternoon breeze gently blew at her skirts and hair. He had already admitted to himself that a certain grace and charm about Annie Mackinnon surprised and interested him. Watching her now, he was struck by her attractive slimness—quite different from most Stonehaven matrons.

Well, here you are, Davey Morrison, he thought as he took a deep breath. *Now to accomplish the next part of your mission.*

Leaning against the stone wall, Annie fingered the filigree bracelet. She had not worn it, nor had she told anyone about finding it. The bracelet had come to seem somehow a gift—something beautiful that represented memories from the past, the carefree times that had been hers when life with the Captain and her tiny son seemed to stretch ahead happily. Had a good angel or a fairy dropped it beside the chapel ruins for her? Since she could not explain it, she would take it as a harbinger of happier days to come.

"Well, as I live and breathe! Annie Mackinnon!" called a voice behind her.

Startled, Annie dropped the bracelet into her pocket and turned to see Davey Morrison striding toward her. Surprise, irritation, and uneasiness fought one another. And still there was that other thread—a quickened pulse that told her she was also attracted to this man. He had a certain breezy outdoor ruggedness and a charm that made him quite unpredictable—one minute surprising her with a bold remark and the next cocking his head and smiling almost shyly. "Davey Morrison!" she greeted.

"And a good afternoon to you!" He stopped a few feet away. "'Tis a bonnie day! And you make a bonnie picture against the sky and sea!"

Annie hoped she wasn't blushing. "What are you doing here?" she asked, smoothing her apron and skirt.

"'Tis public property, is it not?"

"Aye, but . . ."

He swung in beside her, leaning against the wall. "No place grander than a bluff to get sight of the sea in all its splendor. You might say I'm in love with her. Something about her on a day like this all laid out calm and blue and sparkling."

"I find the sea a friend," Annie found herself saying. "It often draws me, fascinates me." She hesitated. "But the sea has been my enemy, too," she added softly.

Davey nodded. "Aye. I've raged at her myself on more than one occasion. But on a day like this, 'twould seem only lofty words are good enough for her.

> 'Whither shall I go from thy spirit? or whither shall I flee from thy presence? . . . If I take the wings of the morning, and dwell in the uttermost parts of the sea; Even there shall thy hand lead me, and thy right hand shall hold me.'

Startled, Annie listened to the resonant voice take the ancient biblical words and breathe life into them until they seemed to hang emblazoned over the sea. "Somehow I'd not expect you to be quoting from Holy Scripture," she finally said.

"I had a grandfather who loved the sea. Many's the time I've listened to those words from him."

Annie gazed out over the water. A great golden eagle swirled above them, turned, and winged its way out over gentle whitecaps until it merged with sky and sea and scudding clouds. "The wings of the morning," she murmured. "I think," she continued slowly, "that for years, in my own way, I've tried to ignore the Presence—Jesus. What I'd once been taught I decided I didn't need anymore. But things change." She glanced sideways at him. "I suppose this all sounds hopelessly unsophisticated to you."

He smiled. "On the contrary—it's quite charming."

"I'm *not* trying to be charming," she returned in definite tones. She turned and studied him. "Then you don't believe them? The words you just quoted from the Bible."

Davey shrugged. "There *is* a beauty and a grandeur in them, but no, I don't. Too much suffering around to believe God's in charge."

"Some claim suffering can make us better than we were before."

Davey grimaced. "Then I'd rather have less suffering and come out less good."

Annie surveyed him. "But then it's not our choice, is it?"

"I suppose you've heard that kind of thing at the kirk. What else does your minister say?"

A bit of mischief glinted in Annie's eyes. "I've not attended enough of late to call him *my* minister. But I have heard him say we need God because we're sinners. Do you feel yourself a sinner, Davey Morrison?"

"No!"

"Sorry. I meant nothing by it."

Davey looked contrite. "Didn't mean to snap. I'm no saint, but there's many a one worse."

Annie arched her eyebrows mischievously. "If you say so."

Abruptly she wondered what she was doing at Dunnottar Castle with Davey Morrison. She found being with this man unsettling though she could not explain why. Her good sense told her it was time to go. She moved toward a lower ledge where she had left a small satchel and a book anchoring a few papers. "Well, enjoy yourself," she said over her shoulder.

"Annie! The last thing I want to do is chase you away!"

"I need to be going," she replied, gathering up the papers and book.

Davey followed. "Annie, please! It'll not hurt for you to sit down and talk to me for five minutes, will it now?"

Annie paused and surveyed him. Tall, handsome, with a charming smile and eyes that pleaded. There was nothing but emptiness for which to rush home; why not stay and pass the time of day? What could be the harm? "I suppose I could." She seated herself and waited. Suddenly he appeared tongue-tied. "What do you want to talk about?" she asked at last.

"Well—" he seemed to be searching—"tell me your philosophy of life, Annie."

She scrutinized his face. Was he joking, or did he want a serious answer? He looked earnest enough. "To be honest about it—to just get through today," she said. She reached down and picked up a small twig. "But I'm thinking more and more if a body doesn't find the Presence—hang on to Jesus—then we may as well suppose we're all cast about by chance, like this twig. Here today, tomorrow blown away." She paused, but the silence only grew. "And you, Davey Morrison?" she asked at last.

He folded his arms across his chest. "You've got me there. At this point, I'm only seeking."

Well, thought Annie, *so much for that topic.* Perhaps it was time to get some of her own answers. "Then let me ask you something you *can* answer. Why are you here—at the castle?"

"I told you. It's a grand place to watch the sea."

Annie shook her head. "There's many another place closer to the village and without such a rugged climb."

"Actually," said Davey, tapping his artist's pad, "I've come to sketch Dunnottar Castle. I'm an artist of sorts."

"Indeed?" said Annie. "Then don't let me keep you."

Davey smiled disarmingly. "Oh, but now that I find you're here, the other can wait."

"You'll shortly lose the right shadows."

"Well . . . I . . . "

"So, sketch." Annie stood up and pointed to the ledge. "I'll watch. I've never seen anyone do Dunnottar Castle before." She found she was enjoying herself.

Davey sat down and with reluctant slowness, opened his pad, and selected a pen.

"You'd best hurry," coached Annie, standing behind him and

watching over his shoulder. "The shadows are fast going to swallow it."

Davey proceeded to give it his best and most determined effort. "I'm a bit rusty," he conceded finally.

"You may as well stop."

The pen poised in midair. "Stop?"

"Davey Morrison, you're no more an artist than I'm a deepwater sailor!" She pointed to his efforts. "My schoolchildren on the first level can do better than this."

Davey swung around and contemplated her in solemn silence. Then he grinned charmingly. "You've found me out."

"I've found you're not an artist." She frowned. *"Who are you? And why are you here?"*

Davey stood up and rested one foot on the ledge. "All right. I came to the bluff because I found out *you* often come up here about this time. Now, do you believe that?"

Annie sat down, thinking Davey the most puzzling person in the world. "Aye, I believe it, though the *why* of it escapes me."

Davey sat down beside her. "You're someone I'd like to know."

"You'd be better to spend your time with Fiona Elphinstone or Mary McIver or—"

"I'd like to be *your* friend, Annie."

"That's unlikely."

"Why?"

"We're so different."

"Makes a good balance."

Annie took his measure thoughtfully. "I've lived longer than you, Davey."

"Ah, but not by much, I'll wager. Anyway, in my thirty-two years I've run around more of the world than you—and at a faster pace. So that makes us even, doesn't it?"

Annie shook her head, smiling, and thinking that there was no way to not want to be the friend of this rather fascinating and certainly charming individual. "You surely know how to make your point, don't you?"

He smiled. "I try." After a pause he asked, "Why do *you* come up here, Annie? It's quite a climb."

She stood and turned, shading her eyes against the sun, which had begun to hang lower behind the castle. "There's something about the castle that draws me. I wouldn't come at night, of course. Some think it's haunted."

"Rob Rafferty certainly goes on about it."

"He does, doesn't he? But in the day there's something about it that looks so solid and unchanging. Somehow that comforts me."

A silence fell as clouds covered the sun. Annie shivered.

Davey folded his arms across his chest. "Dunnottar has memories for you, doesn't it? Perhaps it's the place you come to mourn for your husband?"

"Aye," she replied solemnly. "And to think about my son, Donal, out to sea, and to worry about him." She looked up at Davey and saw something in his eyes that made her uneasy. Whatever else, she had no doubt spent enough time with him. "I'd best be going. I have things to care for in the village."

Davey blocked her path. "Mourning for your husband must be hard," he said coldly.

Annie stepped back, puzzled at the change in Davey's tone. "Aye. You would know that. Meg tells me you've had your own grieving to do."

"Perhaps you have more than one reason to mourn the Captain." His eyes filled with dark anger. "Or perhaps you know that it is indeed better that he's dead!"

Annie instantly recoiled from him. "What do you mean?"

"You must grieve that the Captain left you for another."

"That's not true!" she cried as panic poured over her.

"It *is* true!"

"No!" She clutched her throat.

"It is!"

"No one knows!" Annie's head pounded. She felt as if she were choking.

"And they won't," he said more quietly.

"You—you can't know."

"But I do."

"How?" she asked in almost a whisper.

Davey moved a step toward her and glared down at her. *"It was my wife, my bonnie lass,* that the Captain ran away with!"

Annie stared at him, terrified. She felt that she might faint. One thought pounded through her—to leave him, to get away. She turned to run.

Davey grabbed her arm and swung her toward him. "When he tired of her," he said through his teeth, "he went away to sea again. I found out later that she and a child had died in a tenement, of the fever."

Annie pulled away, her mind reeling. "Please!"

"Isn't it better that the Captain's dead?" he bellowed.

"I loved him!" she cried.

"He wasn't worth it."

Annie sank down on the ledge and covered her face with her hands, sobbing. "Please! Please, just leave me alone."

Abruptly Davey reeled toward the sea. He threw his head back and raked his hands through his hair. "I'm sorry. Suddenly all the anger and the pain were there again."

"You aren't the only one who suffered!" came Annie's muffled voice.

"I know that. I do know that." He turned back toward her. "Annie, I'm sorry. I never meant to tell you this way."

Annie fought for comprehension. Her life, which had felt somewhat rocky anyway, had just been turned upside down and rearranged. And this heretofore stranger had suddenly become connected with its most intimate details! "It—it was—*your wife?*"

"Aye."

"I've never been able to accept that it happened," she offered weakly.

"I can understand that," said Davey, facing the sea again.

"The Captain had a charm about him. And—and your lass was no doubt bonnie as well as young."

"Aye."

Annie shook her head, trying to clear it. She gazed at the broad back of the man who had sent her world spinning. Was he friend or foe? She didn't know anymore. "Is that why you came here?"

Davey seemed to have his eyes on the far horizon. "I've hated the Captain these years. I had to come. It seemed the only way to close the door on that part of my life." He paused. "I came expecting to hate you as well."

"Because—"

"Because you had let him go."

Annie felt weak. "And *do* you—hate me?"

"No."

"Why not?"

He turned back and regarded her intently. The anger was gone from his eyes. In its place was pleading and respect—and admiration. "Truly, I don't know *how* he could have left you." He sat down beside her. "I've no more reason to hate you than you me. Annie, *please* forgive me. I've found there's something about you—a kindness, a genuine spirit that's true and deep—I truly want to be your friend. This other—which I shall never tell anyone and which we need never mention again—makes a bond between us. We've been through the same kind of grief."

Annie looked at him in silence. "Aye, we have," she said finally.

"And there will always be a sense in which we understand each other better than anyone else does."

"Aye." She gazed at him, and her eyes grew puzzled. "But why is it, Davey, that I have the feeling there's still *something* that you're not telling me?"

"You'll have to trust me, Annie." He held out his hand. "Friends?"

Annie hesitated, taking the measure of Davey Morrison. Then she put her hand in his. "Friends."

CHAPTER 15

The Song

Liza stroked the kitten's fur gently as they both lay atop the old quilt on Liza's little bed, which was separated from the rest of the house only by a heavy curtain. She touched the kitten's nose softly. "I missed you, Dusty. I did!"

Two days ago she had brought the kitten home with the promise that she would come back every few days to let Thomas check on Dusty's health. The prospect of that pleased Liza.

The kitten purred, and Liza nuzzled it. But at the same time her eyes clouded, for the tempo and level of the conversation on the other side of the curtain had risen.

Rob Rafferty had returned in an ill humor just before supper. All during the meal he had lain sullen and unresponsive while Liza and her mother ate quickly and quietly. Now she heard her mother's reasoned pleadings followed by her father's curses. There was a thud and shattering of glass, a cry, and a volley of louder curses.

Liza gathered the kitten up in her arms and crept out, looking neither to the right nor the left. With tears running down her cheeks, she stood just outside the house.

She nuzzled her wet face into the cat's fur. "Poor, poor Dusty. Ye can't want to hear all that, can ye?" After pausing uncertainly, she started down the path. "I'll take you to Master Thomas, that's what I'll do. It's time he be checkin' you over."

Reaching Thomas Blacklock's shed, she stopped and brushed at her tears as best she could with one hand. She was about to knock when she stopped, stock-still, listening.

From inside came the sound of a voice singing—a voice deep and melodious. The sound of a hymn. *Who* could it be? As the hymn died, she knocked, and Thomas opened the door.

He looked sheepish. "Liza—ye haven't been here long, have ye?"

Liza entered, looking curiously about. An old oil lantern cast patterns of light and shadow into the corners. But no one else was there. She eyed Thomas in wonder. "Master Thomas, it was *ye* singin'?"

Thomas almost hung his head. "Aye. I wasna knowing anybody was hearing."

"Ye sing like what'd gather a body right in!"

Thomas flushed. "Ye brought the kitty?"

Still holding the cat, Liza gazed at him. "We sing that down to the curing shed."

Thomas took the animal from her and carried it to his workbench, where he appeared absorbed in his examination.

"But ye've not been there." She moved closer. "Have ye?"

He set the kitten on the floor, where it limped a few steps and lay down. "I've not been in the curing shed," he answered honestly.

Liza sat down on the floor next to her pet, and Thomas sat on a stool close by. She stroked the kitten's fur, then looked up at her friend to find him studying her.

"Ye had somethin' bad happen, Liza?" He handed her the least dirty cloth closest at hand. "Ye could wipe yer face iffen ye want."

Liza did so. "Papa was yelling up a storm, and I didn't want Dusty to get all bothered. So we come away."

Thomas nodded sympathetically, and for a time the only sounds were crickets outside the shed.

"I been *outside* the curing shed by the window listening a time or two," he said finally. "The music's real soothing."

Liza brightened. "Ye *have*?" A companionable feeling settled upon her. "I like when Brother Turner says Jesus is thinking 'bout us all the time. And he says God's music wraps around us and smoothes out our hearts when Jesus knows we're needing it." Liza touched the kitten's nose softly and wiped at one more tear. "And do ye know which song I like the most best?" she added more cheerfully.

"Which one?"

"The one ye was singing before."

"'Amazing Grace,'" said Thomas slowly.

"Could ye sing it again?"

There was a silence. "I dinna ken."

Liza regarded him earnestly. "But I'll sing it *with* you, Master Thomas."

Thomas tugged at his collar and moistened his lips nervously. But he nodded, almost imperceptibly, and began to sing, joined by Liza.

> *"Amazing grace—how sweet the sound—*
> *That saved a wretch like me!*
> *I once was lost, but now am found—*
> *Was blind, but now I see."*

The wonderful melody filled the old, rough shed as lantern light played over the gaunt man with the slouched shoulders and the little girl with a tear-streaked face who sat beside him.

CHAPTER 16

A Strange Object

Annie sat quietly on the ledge. Gray clouds hovered far to the southeast, but the breeze blew gently off the North Sea over Dunnottar.

She had been drawn to Dunnottar Castle like a homing pigeon to its roost. She needed to think. The last few days in Stonehaven, when she had time to ponder amidst other duties, had left only a dreadful jumble of thoughts, emotions that had seemed hopelessly tangled.

Meanwhile, she had caught sight of Davey Morrison nowhere.

Now she forced herself to stillness. The sweep of sea away to the horizon was vast, the movement of the waves steady and predictable. She smiled wryly. *At least for the moment it is!*

The sea breeze seemed to blow through her mind. Surely here she could sort things out—make at least some vague semblance of order.

Two days ago Davey Morrison, a relative stranger, had become something else. But what? He was the only one in Stonehaven to know her secret—something she had been careful to keep from all others, something she even had tried to convince herself could not have happened.

The Captain's death on the high seas had ended part of the pain. She need no longer picture him with someone else. But it also meant he would never return to her. She had tried to concentrate all her hurt and sorrow into the fact that he was dead and gone. Wasn't that the way any widow would grieve?

Now this newcomer to Stonehaven had changed all that. He had raked up the whole agonizing past. And it was his wife! She couldn't hide from the fact. If only Davey had never come, had never found her.

And yet he had.

He seemed to be a basically kind person, she told herself. And she knew instinctively that she could trust him not to reveal their secret. Beyond that, he had suffered in the same way she had— and he wanted to be her friend. Better that than her enemy.

"Annie," said a voice just behind her. She turned. It was Davey Morrison. "I knew you'd be here," he said.

"And I think I knew you'd come."

"May I sit?"

"Of course."

Beyond them an osprey skimmed the water, its great brown wings spread to full breadth. Abruptly it dove and came up with a fish in its talons. Immediately it soared off toward the land.

"Sometimes I feel like that fish in the osprey's grasp," murmured Annie. "Like I'm caught by things I can't do anything about."

"I know the feeling."

Abruptly Annie stood, hardly knowing she did so. She twisted her hands nervously. "I—I don't want to hear anything about— about your wife—or—or any details—"

"I told you we need never speak of it again."

"But if we don't, it will always be between us." She paused.

"Unless you plan to leave Stonehaven soon." Annie realized with a start that she wasn't sure if she wanted him gone or not.

"No. I won't be leaving. Not yet. Not now," he answered quickly.

Annie took a deep, calming breath. She almost smiled. "Then we shall have to think what to do with you, won't we?"

Davey grinned. "I suppose. Because I'm not going to stay away from you, Annie. I meant what I said—about knowing you better."

Annie gazed at him. How strange, how unreal all this seemed. She turned away toward the sea. "Then tell me—I don't mean details or anything like that—but tell me how you got through all this."

There was a long silence with only the sound of the waves below and the calls of a few seagulls circling above. "At first, I guess I denied it could be happening," Davey finally said slowly. "When it *did*, I was filled with rage against the Captain. If I could have found him, I believe I would have killed him!"

Annie stood perfectly still, her eyes on the water.

"Shall I stop?"

"No. Go on," she said firmly.

"I cursed God until I decided it was futile because he didn't exist. Finally—and this *was* hard and took a long time—I came to the conclusion that my lass, who was very beautiful, lacked character, that her soul was somehow empty. Then I hated them both for causing me such pain. Because I did love her. Maybe I hated myself some *because* I had loved her." There was a long, stretching silence. Finally he said, "Actually, I think Fiona Elphinstone reminds me of my wife."

Annie swung around. She stared hard into his eyes. "Oh," was all she could manage to say.

Davey looked down, studying his hands. "Fiona is the most beautiful girl I've ever seen. But I think she may be empty, shallow like . . ." He looked up. "Perhaps it's why I'm drawn to *you*, Annie."

Annie blinked. What did he mean? Did he mean more than

friendship? Given the past two days, *nothing* seemed out of the realm of possibility. Her heart gave a small lurch. A sudden gust of wind swirled past them, and Annie's eyes were drawn to the south, where clouds were darkening. "Perhaps we'd best start back. It's a long way down and then up, as you now know."

Davey made no move to leave. "Has coming up here to the castle always been your special thing to do, Annie?"

Annie forgot the storm clouds and leaned back against the wall reflectively. "I've found solace since I was a wee lass. But it has been especially comforting since the Captain went away." She took a deep breath. "Left me." There. She'd said it. Voicing it seemed like a triumph. "I guess it seemed the only thing I could do. When you have grief prisoned up inside, it seems one would go mad if there wasn't some way to let it out! By the time I got up here, I'd be physically exhausted, and it helped with the pain inside. There was no cemetery, no grave to go to and mourn the end of—happiness." She half smiled at Davey. "Actually it seems strange to be with anyone up here."

"You never brought your son?"

"Donal understood that I wanted to be alone." Annie sighed. "And now he's out there, somewhere on the sea."

"And you worry."

"I can't help it." Annie knit her brow in deep thought. "It seems like all of this up here has come to be *mine*. As I had this terrible battle with humiliation and anger and loneliness, the solid unchangingness of the castle came to be some strange sort of comfort to me." She paused. "Perhaps *God* gave me this place. If I had remembered Jesus through it all, it would have been easier, I should think."

Davey glanced about. "It *is* a wonderfully wild and dramatic place." He stood up. "Which, I'm afraid, is about to become *more* dramatic. Look at those clouds."

A lowering sky moved closer, and the breeze became a wind.

Davey swept her books into the satchel and reached for her hand. Annie lifted her skirts, and they ran toward the gate.

Once through it, they began the descent. Not speaking, they turned all their attention to their footing on the precarious path as Davey, going before, steadied her.

Suddenly a rock tumbled, and Annie lost her balance and fell into Davey's arms. He held her longer than was necessary before he set her on her feet. "There now. Are you all right?"

"I think so," she said, smoothing her skirts. She looked down at something glinting at her feet.

Davey, seeing it at the same time, quickly picked it up. "A bracelet."

Annie held out her hand. "It's mine. It fell out of my pocket."

Davey handed it back. "Looks foreign. From the Captain, I suppose."

"No, actually I found it recently up by Dunnottar Castle. I can't imagine how it possibly got there." She smiled. "Even though I *say* I'm not superstitious, I've kept it as a good omen."

Davey looked serious. "May I see it again?"

Puzzled, she gave it to him. He turned it over in his hand thoughtfully. "Looks to be from India or someplace thereabouts, I would say." He handed it back. "And you found it up by the castle?"

Annie nodded as she slipped it into her pocket. "It's strange, isn't it? Oh, Davey! Here comes the rain!"

A few bright drops quickly turned into a pelting rain as they fled downward at as fast a pace as possible and into the tunnel that marked the midpoint of their descent. They shook and wrung the water from their clothes as best they could in the damp and now partially darkened shelter.

They stood near the opening, listening to the downpour. How strange and utterly unforeseen the recent events of her life had been, Annie thought. Looking into her heart, she unexpectedly found more peace than she had had in a very long time.

She glanced sideways at her companion. "Davey, I wouldn't have known it would help to talk to you. But it has, and I feel better."

Davey swung around toward her. In the tunnel opening she couldn't see his eyes, only his strong silhouette. But he reached for both her hands and squeezed them, hard. "Me, too, Annie. Me, too."

The rain tapered off and stopped as suddenly as it had begun. As they stepped out of the tunnel and again on a downward route, Annie held tightly to Davey's hand.

Wind had blown the clouds away, and the sky was as bright a blue as it had been dark before. Life, like the weather, had the ability to change very quickly, Annie thought. She also reflected that along with living through most peculiar and emotionally shaking days, she had liked being in the arms of Davey Morrison.

CHAPTER 17

A Question and an Odd Request

Cock-a-leekie soup simmered on the cast-iron stove, sending up the mouthwatering aroma of chicken and leeks. Meg's eyes followed Annie as she bustled about the kitchen. "Griselda said she'll be over to help just as soon as she can." She sank onto a chair next to a small table with a sigh. "Oh, it's so romantic!"

Annie, at the counter kneading a large pan of barley dough, raised her eyebrows. "Oh? And what's that?"

"*Davey Morrison*, Miss Annie! To have him come to Stonehaven right outta the blue and just clean sweep you off yer feet."

Annie gave the dough a great, vigorous thump. "How you talk, Meg! Mr. Morrison is just a good friend. That's all!"

Meg leaned her arms on the table, her eyes dreamy. "Maybe he'll take you all around the world and show you them huge deserts in Arabia with camels going across them and porpoises playing in the Persian Gulf and the pyramids in Egypt rising up clean to the sky!"

Annie lifted the dough into a baking pan and moved toward the stove. "Dear Meg, I do believe you're impossible!"

Meg, in her own world, appeared not to hear. "Wisht I was old enough to come to a romantic supper like Griselda. She's hemming up her best dress is why she ain't here yet."

Annie closed the oven door and pushed her hair back with a floury hand. "It's just a neighborly supper Griselda and I are having for Mr. Morrison and Mr. Donnovan. Not a romantic occasion, as you call it."

Meg got up and wandered about the room. "Well, Griselda has that look in her eye. And Mama says the last couple weeks ye been walking around with a lilt in yer step." She paused, eyeing Annie. "I think ye *are* happier, Miss Annie, than ye used to be."

A faint smile played about Annie's lips. She had to admit that life had taken on a rosier tint. Davey Morrison knew how to do charming things at unexpected moments. He had become a friend who understood her, and the pain of the past had begun to fade. Her worry over Donal's safety was deep within her, but the days seemed more normal now. Normal, she thought, was a wonderful way to feel. As for romance, friendship was all she needed just now.

Annie moved to the counter where a ginger cake stood and began to cut thin slices and arrange them on a plate. Meg followed her, and Annie put her arm around the young girl's shoulders. "I love you, Meg! You know that, don't you?"

Meg nodded happily. "Miss Annie, did ye hear that Doory Wilson's girl, Gillian, is getting married to Ritchie Mealing from over to Banchory? And there's to be a big party after the wedding in the Wilsons' barn so long as Thomas Blacklock gets done fixing it up. Griselda's all excited about Master Malcolm maybe taking her."

"I wouldn't be surprised if he does." Annie pointed to a slice of ginger cake. "Have a bit of cake, Meg."

Meg munched happily. "Only I think Griselda's worried about Fiona on accounta Fiona ain't actually *pledged* to Ian Fraser yet, and she's so pretty and all and makes a play for Master Malcolm every chance she gets. And Griselda ain't sure but what Master Malcolm likes it. Oh dear, ain't life awful complicated sometimes?"

Annie, opening a crock of jam, paused. "Aye, that it is," she answered fervently.

Meg toyed with a crumb of cake. "Ye know down to the curing shed where Papa and Griselda and I go?"

"Aye."

"Brother Turner says the Lord's maybe calling him to go on down to Montrose in a few weeks so's folks can get all fired up for Jesus down there, too. Anyhow, Brother Turner says God knows who it's best we romance with and get married to and that iffen we pay good attention he'll show us who. Do ye think that's true, Miss Annie?"

Annie gazed thoughtfully at Meg. She thought back to her prayer the night before she'd first laid eyes on Davey Morrison. She had asked for something or someone to come into her life—to show her that Jesus had not forgotten her. Could Davey Morrison be the answer to that prayer? Annie frowned. Davey wasn't exactly the kind of person Annie would picture the Almighty sending. She was also struck by the thought that she had waited mostly for what Jesus would *do* for her rather than turning her thoughts, her heart toward him. She sighed. It was too much to ponder just now.

Thomas Blacklock was almost to his door before he saw her. Returning late from his work on the Wilson barn, head down and collar turned up against the chill of the night air, he stopped dead in his tracks.

There she stood beside his door like a sentinel. Elvira Elphinstone.

He knew who she was. Didn't everybody in Stonehaven? But he'd never spoken to her, nor she to him. Nor did he ever wish to do so. And so, finding her standing there, all he could do was stare with wide, startled eyes.

"Mr. Blacklock," she intoned imperiously, "I would have a word with you."

"With me?" Thomas asked in some amazement.

"Why else do you think I would wait at *your* door?"

"Aye, mem," he murmured obsequiously.

Elvira tapped her cane. "It's much too chilly to carry on business out here," she observed pointedly.

"Aye, aye. Ye be coming in." He pushed the door open, and she followed him into near total darkness. She waited perfectly still while he fumbled to light an oil lantern.

"Shall I make a peat fire for you?"

Elvira glanced about the shed and folded one hand upon another over the cane. "You have not the proper ventilation. I'd rather deal with the chill than be asphyxiated by fumes and smoke."

Thomas nodded, casting his eyes about for something for her to sit upon. He moved toward the only chair with a back but decided against it as it was rickety and couldn't be depended upon. Apologetically he placed a stool near the lantern, and she sat down.

He waited patiently.

"Sit down, Mr. Blacklock. I cannot speak with you towering over me."

Thomas seized upon a nearby stool and sat.

Elvira's gaze traveled around the shed and finally rested upon its owner. "You are to make a coffin."

"Mem?"

"A *coffin*, Mr. Blacklock. Certainly you have the ability?"

"Aye."

"Then what is the problem?"

"Nay. I have no problem. No doubt ye'll be telling me if it be for a tall man or mebbe a lady what's small. Though I've not heard of anyone dying hereabouts."

"No one has," she said.

114

"Mem?"

"No one has died in Stonehaven that we have not buried," she explained almost patiently. She appeared in deep thought for some minutes. "But someone *will*," she said finally. "Therefore make it large. That way we shall be prepared for any contingency."

Puzzled, Thomas watched her every move, her every flickering of eyelash. At last he asked, "Of what would ye be wanting it? Pine?"

Elvira rose. "No. Let us do it up right. Cedar. Aye." She nodded in satisfaction. "That will last longer as well as give a better impression." She moved toward the door, holding the cane aloft as if to avoid its contamination with a mud floor. She turned, her eyes steely. "I shall pay you, of course, when it is finished. Not before. Make it immediately. We cannot tell *when* the Fates will move." Her eyes suddenly glittered with what seemed to Thomas an otherworldly intensity. An *eerie* world, he thought.

Then she was gone.

Thomas stared after her. He was not given to overanalysis, but he did sense that if he were, it would be no use to try to figure out the woman, ramrod straight and cane aloft, who had just marched out of his door.

Anyway, whatever else, one did *not* go against Elvira Elphinstone. Probably no one in Stonehaven would dare. Least of all Thomas Blacklock.

CHAPTER 18

An Escape and a Picnic

The two men strode along the narrow causeway, heading back toward Stonehaven. Behind them, Reef Point Light swung in a steady arc over the sea, reaching into a haze of fog, clouds, and a quarter moon.

"Kind of a strange fellow, that Jonathan," commented Malcolm. "Like one thing about him don't fit with another."

Davey paused and turned back toward the lighthouse. He seemed to analyze every detail of the tower against the sky. "Whatever else, the keeper of this lighthouse seems both careful and organized," he murmured, thinking on his own track.

Malcolm thrust his hands into his pockets. "And don't it strike ye somethin' peculiar—all that pent-up energy like it's gonna burst out somewheres? Not to mention his reaction to a simple question about wreckers that other time ye was out."

"Maybe living alone so much makes him a mite peculiar," rejoined Davey, eyes still on the tower. "Can't be a much lonelier job than a lighthouse keeper."

"The village children seem to like visiting him."

"Aye. First time I came out here was with little Liza, Rob Rafferty's girl."

"Griselda seems to be a special friend of Jonathan's. I get the impression she talks to him a lot. Maybe that Jonathan confides in her."

"What kinds of things?"

"Haven't the faintest idea. Thought she was gonna tell me once. But she clammed up, wouldn't say a thing. We was on the subject of what makes a body feel guilty." Malcolm paused. "Could be our lighthouse keeper feels guilty about something, Davey."

"Well, keep your eyes and ears open." They turned from the lighthouse and continued to make their way back along the causeway. Davey's lips curved faintly into a smirk. "Speaking of Griselda, you're quite the man-about-town, aren't you?"

"No more'n what I see you with Miz Annie Mackinnon lately," returned his companion.

"Ah, but you have Fiona Elphinstone vying for your attention, too."

"Oh, pshaw," said Malcolm. "Fiona'd flirt with anybody. Ye can't tell me she hasn't tried her wiles out on you."

"Aye, she has, but *only* when you're not around. The minute *you* show up her eyes are only for the charming Malcolm Donnovan!" Davey jabbed his friend playfully in the ribs. "Better watch out, or Ian Fraser'll have your head—or run you through with a claymore. . . ." Davey's voice trailed off. "Keep walking. Looks to me like someone's been keeping a bead on us."

"I don't see anyone."

"Just past Willow Row, where the road turns off by the marine station."

Malcolm peered ahead through the shadowed evening. "Don't see—wait—leaning up against the station? That Blacklock person?"

"Aye."

"Nothing so big about that, is there?"

118

"He was there in the same spot when we went out to the lighthouse to see Jonathan about forty-five minutes ago. Before that I had the feeling we might have been followed. Caught sight of someone tall and skinny. Thought it might be my imagination."

"Thomas Blacklock's a strange bird, anyhow. Always lookin' like he's afraid of his own shadow."

"He's managed to speak up pretty good—with questions if I come upon him at the Wilsons' though. Like he's *real* interested in whatever I have to say."

Malcolm instinctively quickened his pace.

Davey tugged at Malcolm's arm. "Hold it. Walk casual. When we get to shore, we'll give him a run for his money."

As they reached the shoreline, they quickened their pace, suddenly veering southward, then struck inland and around the walled gardens of Low Wood Road. Skirting Dunnottar Woods, they ran southward over the Bervie Braes, then slowed to a casual walk and meandered toward the sea.

Davey looked back over his shoulder. "I'm sure we lost him long ago—if he was indeed even following us."

They stood on the rocky shore. At their feet, small wet pebbles glistened in the faint light from a banana moon. Malcolm reached down, selected one, and sent it skimming out over the water. "So ye were up at Dunnottar Castle this afternoon?"

"Aye."

"Alone?"

"Aye. And found nothing. Except dusty, crumbling buildings. An old dungeon. It's a dank and rather fearsome place."

Malcolm picked up another stone but held it, contemplating the castle on the bluff to the south. "I have an idea. Maybe one day soon I'll try my luck approaching the castle from the sea— along this shore—rocky and forbidding though it may be." He hurled the flat stone over the sea and counted seven skips before it sank from sight.

The moon had disappeared behind clouds as Davey and Malcolm turned homeward toward the Wilsons'.

As they neared the curing shed, Davey abruptly stopped in his tracks, peering ahead.

"Now what?" whispered Malcolm.

"Shhhh—look there." They crept forward in the shadow of bracken and mountain ash. Then they saw clearly. Thomas Blacklock knelt beside the shed, holding his head in his hands. He was sobbing.

Davey and Malcolm looked at one another. "What'll we do?" asked Malcolm.

Davey pondered. "Come on," he whispered. "We better find out what's going on."

They paused a few feet from the man on his knees. Davey cleared his throat. Thomas looked up and leaped to his feet.

"Thomas, may we help you some way?" Davey asked.

The man's eyes filled with terror. "Nay—nay!" He turned and ran as if the Furies were after him.

Annie tucked a stray curl behind her ear and smiled at Davey. They knelt on the ground, an old tattered picnic cloth between them. Davey was lifting items from a large wooden basket.

"You know what this picnic is, don't you?" asked Annie. "It's called high tea."

Davey grinned. "High tea, is it? Out on the high seas the most genteel we sailors ever got was cockles eaten right out of the shell or winkles turned into soup. Mostly it was oatcakes and water. Now and then raw milt of herring thrown in between the cakes."

"Sounds awful," responded Annie, settling herself and tucking her skirts comfortably. She leaned back contentedly against a stone wall. The crumbling crofter's house behind shielded them from an east breeze, and the late afternoon sun was still high enough to be warming.

When Davey had appeared on her doorstep a half hour before with a basket of food packed by Doory Wilson, Annie couldn't resist his charming invitation for a picnic. Now she watched him, busy with preparations against the green of the forest just beyond. "Are you sure I can't help you?" she asked.

"I'm sure. Doory and I have this all planned." He laid tin plates and bowls on the picnic cloth, followed by a heavy earthenware pot. "Now this is stew and tatties, Doory says." He took the cover off to sniff the savory meat and small potatoes and nodded approval as he served Annie and himself and then clapped the lid back on.

"How does Doory find time to cook for you with Gillian's wedding coming so soon?"

Davey shrugged. "Beats me what you ladies do to make ready for those occasions." He opened a tin of bannocks and passed the small, flat cakes to Annie.

"From what I hear, Doory's worried about the barn being done in time for the wedding feast."

"What do you know of Thomas Blacklock?" Davey asked suddenly.

Annie paused over the stew Davey had ladled for her. "Not much. He was in Edinburgh for a time studying veterinary medicine. Seems things didn't work out. He keeps pretty much to himself as far as I can tell. Though Liza tells me she goes to see him with her kitten."

"Liza has a way with hurting or strange people, doesn't she?"

"Aye, that she does," said Annie thoughtfully. "I wonder how much Liza herself hurts, with Rob Rafferty for a father."

Davey stood up holding his mug of freshly poured tea. "Life sometimes seems full of hurts, doesn't it?" He looked down at her, and his eyes were full of tender concern. "How 'bout you, Annie? You all right?"

Annie took a pastry from a small container. She ate it thoughtfully. "Better," she said. "It's nice to have a friend who . . . who knows what I've been through. And understands."

Davey moved to the wall and lowered himself to sit beside her. "I feel the same way, Annie." He contemplated the lengthening shadows of late afternoon. "I've never had someone like you— someone I could trust, who I felt was a *true* friend. Even . . ." His voice trailed off. He finished his tea and set the mug down. "You know, I find myself wanting to be with you all the time."

Annie felt the color rise in her cheeks. Davey Morrison had restored a kind of sanity to the inner core of her life. She felt that a healing had taken place. That this dashing adventurer would pay this much attention to her was flattering to be sure. But did she return those feelings? She wasn't certain. Davey Morrison had charm, but there was also some sort of mystery. He had admitted that she was not his only reason for coming to Stonehaven. But *what? Why?* Why did he choose to be secretive? She took a deep breath, determined to be careful with her heart. "How long do you plan to stay in Stonehaven?"

"I don't know. It depends on several things."

"Will you soon be going with Duncan on his boat?"

"Possibly. I'm not sure."

Annie wrinkled her nose. "You're quite evasive, Davey Morrison."

Davey moved closer. "Well, I—Annie? What are you staring at?" His eyes followed hers to the forest.

"Far back in the thicket—do you see? Is it a candle? I think it's moving."

Davey squinted. "Maybe a small torch of some sort—"

"It's a pale bluish color. I almost hate to say it, but it looks like what folks call a death candle." She shivered. "The superstitious believe it means someone will die—soon."

Davey put his arm about her and pulled her close. "Well, I won't let anything happen to you."

"I told you—I'm not superstitious." But she didn't pull away from him.

Davey grinned disarmingly. "Well, death candles or not, it feels good to hold you close to me, Annie."

CHAPTER 19

A Threat in the Forest

Thomas Blacklock leaned against the tree in Dunnottar Woods trying to look casual. But in reality he felt anything *but* casual.

The man who moved restlessly back and forth in front of him seemed to mirror Thomas's own emotional state. From the time he had first prayed for forgiveness outside the curing shed, a sense of consternation had been growing within him.

For the greater part of his existence, he had not been given to introspection. He had simply accepted life's blows as his lot in life. The inner pain that came with them would finally even itself out into a dull ache that he would come to accept as normal.

But ever since he had heard James Turner speak of Jesus and had listened to the songs and the earnest prayers, it was as if a door had been opened—just a crack, it's true—and a small ribbon of light had shown on the bleakness of his soul. A conviction had been growing, even though a part of him wished to escape it, that the Almighty did indeed have a claim on his life and that Jesus Christ was reaching out to him, to that lonely void within.

All had drawn him back to the meetings at the curing shed.

He arrived after the meetings had begun, listened secretly in the shadows outside the window, and left before they ended.

Meanwhile, revealing the activities of Malcolm and Davey to the unknown masked individual had continued. But not without increasing dismay. Thomas's reimbursement for his reporting was now received with more discomfort than gratitude. He had come to feel quite devious about the whole affair. He still had no fondness for Davey Morrison, but gradually he not only intellectually *knew* but also *felt* his deeds and thoughts to be under the scrutiny of almighty God.

However, a way out of this entanglement had not presented itself. The deeds themselves and his own timidity had caught him in a web.

The masked figure quit pacing. "Tell me again," the usual muffled voice rasped, *"where* Davey Morrison has been asking his questions."

"At the market, down to the marine station, and when he be at the Wilsons'. Mebbe at Elvira Elphinstone's. Leastways he went calling there. But I dinna know what was said."

"And was it *only* about the castle?"

Thomas shifted on his feet and thrust his hands into his pockets. "Nay. He asked about the lighthouse keeper some. But about Dunnottar Castle most."

There was a long pause. "And the lighthouse—he was at the lighthouse?"

"Aye. With the Rafferty child. I already told you."

"And have ye come up with any more of what he asked?"

"Nay, the child has said no more."

"Now what else have ye to tell me?"

Thomas hesitated. He kicked at a stone with the toe of his shoe. "Davey Morrison was out to the lighthouse again, this time with Malcolm Donnovan," he said at last.

"When?"

"Three nights ago."

"Why?"

"I dinna know."

"How long were they there?"

"Three-quarters of an hour, mebbe."

"At night?"

"Aye."

The masked figure folded his arms. "And when they came back, ye followed them."

There was a silence. Thomas moistened his lips and tugged at his collar. "Nay," he offered finally.

The figure moved a step toward him. "And why not?"

"When they be reaching shore, they run."

"But did ye *try* to follow?"

Thomas felt his face twitching. "I dinna. That's all. I dinna." He took a deep breath. "Isn't it enough I tell you already?"

The hulking figure grabbed Thomas's arms with strong hands. He leaned close, and for a moment the voice lost its rasp and sounded strangely familiar. "Nay! Nay, Thomas Blacklock. Ye shall tell *all* ye know, and ye shall find out more than this if ye want payment." The voice dropped into a menacing whisper. "Ye have no choice, Thomas. If ye do not, Stonehaven will have to find another coffinmaker, for *ye* shall be in one!" With a mighty thrust he threw Thomas from him against the tree.

With a cry Thomas went down, twisting his knee. He pulled himself up to a sitting position as jabbing pain shot through from knee to ankle. He watched the man disappear into the forest's thicket.

He was not sure if seconds or minutes had gone by when he staggered to his feet. Then he limped home, not at all sure where the mental agony left off and the physical pain began.

CHAPTER 20

Ninian's Courage

Thomas laid his tools down and surveyed the coffin. It was not done, but he had made good progress, considering the fact that he had to spend most of his time at the Wilson barn, where Doory Wilson was in a frenzy over last-minute preparations for Gillian's wedding.

As he had beveled edges and polished the cedar, he had reflected only occasionally on Elvira Elphinstone and her odd request. A strange lady, indeed, but if she was willing to pay, why should he question it?

Now he turned from the coffin and grabbed a wool jacket against the chill of evening and went out. His destination: the curing shed.

He had continued to go occasionally, always alone and always unobtrusively stationed outside the window in the darkness. But now Liza, who still happened by frequently with her kitten, had told him that next week Brother James Turner would be gone to Montrose. Therefore, tonight was not to be missed.

He limped along as rapidly as possible, grateful that the pain in his knee from the incident in the forest was subsiding. Of course, he had lied to Liza about it when she asked. It struck him as odd that telling a lie to Liza bothered him when it never would have done so formerly.

Reaching the curing shed, he lowered himself to the ground in his usual spot. He had just settled when a small shadow fell across him. "Master Thomas?" said a soft voice.

"Liza?" He pulled himself to his feet and glanced about. "Ye be alone?"

Liza's eyes filled with tears. "Mama—"

"Yer mama's sick?"

"She's leastways a wee bit sick . . . because Papa . . ." The tears rolled down her cheeks.

Thomas felt the muscles tighten around his heart. "Yer papa hit yer ma?"

Liza nodded. "So Mama's lying down to get her strength back, she says. And Papa's gone out. He'll be gone a long time. He always is after . . . after he hits Mama. And I wanted to stay with Mama, but Mama says I must go to the meeting and listen to every word Brother Turner says and tell her on accounta this might be Brother Turner's last time. Mama wanted to come, but . . ."

Thomas laid his big hand awkwardly on Liza's shoulder as the child wiped at her face with the corner of her apron.

She looked up at him. "Would ye come inside with me, Master Thomas?"

Thomas shifted uneasily on his feet. "Liza, I dinna ken—"

"Ye needna stay iffen ye dinna like it."

Thomas tugged at his collar. "I'd no be fittin' with all those people. I'd best be here."

Liza's eyes pleaded. "Please, Master Thomas." Her voice sank to a whisper. "I dinna want to be alone."

Thomas regarded the child for a few moments, then he held out his hand. "And I'd not want you to be. Come."

When they entered the curing shed, it was easy to see that

word of Brother Turner's imminent departure had spread, for it seemed every available space was taken. Some had probably brought stools and boxes from home. Children packed the dirt floor. There was not even space for men who had no seats to lounge casually against the walls. Instead they stood shoulder to shoulder.

The last strains of a hymn drew to a close as Thomas cast about nervously for some place to be other than prominently in the doorway. Fortunately a kind-faced lady on the bench next to him scooted over and looked down the row of what must have been her family with a look that said "make way and squeeze together," which they did.

Thomas sank down gratefully on the bench with Liza beside him. Griselda Carmichael and Meg waved and smiled at Liza from across the room. Peat smoke and fish oil mingled with the odor of perspiration from the packed-in company. Thomas wished to be out in the clear, cool air rather than where he was.

James Turner rose to speak, clutching his Bible in one hand. Thomas and the others settled themselves and gave their earnest attention to the evangelist, whom they had come to respect. "There be a man," Brother Turner said quietly, "who lived in gentleness and solitude beside the sea. Nay, he had no distractions, no conflicts. But almighty God spoke to him in the quietness, in the inner part of his soul, and said to him, 'Ye must take my Word—my gospel—my light—into a place of darkness. Ye must go up yonder and *be* light in that darkness, with my power!'"

His voice had risen but now dropped again to softer tones. "So the man set out, with one companion, unarmed and with no supplies, to confront an unknown and strange people with the great love and gentleness of God in Christ."

The evangelist paused, and his eyes scanned the room. "His name? Ninian! Aye, ye know the name! For it is Ninian's Den ye know of between the great bluff and Dunnottar Rock." The audience stirred and glanced at one another, nodding.

"But what ye may *not* know is that fourteen hundred years ago Ninian climbed Dunnottar Rock for Jesus' sake!

"'Twas dark that night." James Turner laid his Bible on a small stand and stretched forth both his arms. "The wind blew, and the waves pounded on the rocks. And Ninian climbed until he stood in the midst of a people who worshiped the moon that rode high in the sky and to which they prepared to offer human sacrifice!"

James Turner lowered his arms. All eyes were upon him, and no one moved. The evangelist's eyes were on fire. He pointed a finger before him. "They screamed for Ninian to go, but he stood his ground. Because he was a courageous man? Nay! He had not his own courage. *But in the strength of Jesus he stood!* And stayed.

"He stayed, and in kindness he loved the people until he could tell them of Jesus who had loved them enough to die for them." James Turner's face lit with joy. "And upon Dunnottar Rock Ninian left a witness—a Christian church to be a beacon of light in the darkness."

Liza leaned toward Thomas. "Ain't that grand?" she whispered. The people stirred, pondering.

Brother Turner picked up his Bible and held it high. "Fourteen hundred years ago there was a witness on Dunnottar Rock! Has it disappeared into nothingness? Nay! Two hundred years ago, 167 men and women were thrown into the castle dungeon for their faith, and the dark dungeon was *lit* by their faith in the midst of grievous circumstances! But now—here—today—where is faith? Where is courage?"

He stopped, scanning his audience with intensity. "Ye are *here*—in Stonehaven—to be the Savior's light. Ye must have yer own faith. But courage? That must be his."

Thomas Blacklock wrinkled his brow. Courage? He had none.

And to appropriate anyone else's? He shook his head. For him this was quite impossible.

The evangelist was walking back and forth, one arm flailing the air like a pump. "Faith and courage for what?" he asked. "Faith in Christ and courage to stand against the powers of evil, the gods of superstition." He fixed his audience with his eyes, and the shed grew very still. "My people, when ye harken to the old superstitions, ye worship other gods! For it is Christ and *Christ alone* who saves!"

Abruptly he stood very still. His arms dropped to his sides. "Now it's time for ye to pray. Everyone. Ye know what prayer it is *ye* need to pray, and whether it be aloud or silent within yer own heart, the Lord will hear you."

The shed was still, and then voices murmured here and there. Thomas shut his eyes tight. His lips moved silently. He could not have said what he prayed. He only knew that in some way in his heart he had reached out to God with his heartache, his guilt, his timidity.

Thomas had no idea for how long this went on. Eventually the evangelist raised his voice once again. "It says in the Scriptures that they sang a hymn and then went out. And that's what we shall do.

"But first I have one more story to tell ye. One hundred years ago there lived an immoral, rough, blaspheming seaman. He forsook God and sought every kind of evil. It wasn't enough for the man to throw God and morality out of his own life. He set about to destroy the faith of everyone around him! He did a good job of it, too—until God got hold of him—until this book—" he held his Bible high—"got through to his soul and Jesus became the center of his life.

"He quit his old job of hauling chained slaves on his ships to be sold at market. And God gave him a new courage. Courage to stand for Jesus right in the middle of the most awful corrupt society of folks.

"At the end of his life, his last words were: 'My memory is nearly gone. But I remember two things—that I am a great sinner, and that Christ is a great Savior.'"

James Turner stopped and surveyed the people gathered around him. His eyes grew moist. No one stirred. "Soon I must leave you. But the Savior dinna. For he has said the same thing to ye as he did to the former blaspheming trader, *John Newton*—'I will never leave you nor forsake you!'"

The evangelist spread his hands out in blessing over his little flock. "The Lord bless you and keep you. The Lord make his face to shine upon you and give you peace."

Some of the people wiped at tears. A big man in front of Thomas blew his nose noisily.

Brother Turner nodded, tried to smile, and wiped his own eyes. "Now let's sing the song written by the old slave trader after he met Jesus.

> *"Amazing grace—how sweet the sound—*
> *That saved a wretch like me!*
> *I once was lost, but now am found—*
> *Was blind, but now I see."*

The voices of young and old fell upon the words and the melody and grew in earnestness and volume until the shed was filled with it. Some sang as tears coursed down their cheeks. Others lifted their hands in praise or penitence.

But Thomas Blacklock stared straight ahead, not moving, not singing. He could hear Liza's sweet voice beside him and could feel her eyes resting upon him in concern, no doubt because of his silence.

Thomas thought he could feel the Spirit of the Almighty move over the little company, seeking, calling.

Still, he could not sing.

CHAPTER 21

The Wedding

Doory Wilson nodded in satisfaction. A chest of drawers, four pairs of white sheets, blankets, two bolsters, four pillows, one dozen towels, a tablecloth, hardware, cups, bowls, and tubs sat in a corner of the parlor and overflowed in all directions. These, along with a feather bed, would be transferred to Gillian's new home in the late morning.

Gillian, not yet in bridal attire, tripped in the door and made a beeline for the one window. She was followed by Great-Uncle Henry and Great-Aunt Emma, just arrived that very morning up from Montrose for the festivities.

The wedding was taking place on Friday—exactly as dictated by Great-Uncle Henry—for Friday was the day dedicated by Norsemen to the goddess Frigga, believed to be the bestower of marital joy and happiness. (Since Great-Uncle Henry had some Norse heritage, he felt strongly about it.)

Gillian, having eyed the arrangement of sky and clouds outside, pronounced it "a beautiful, lovely gem of a day, Mama!"

"Well, let us just hope it'll *stay* that way for more than ten minutes," intoned Great-Aunt Emma, who was given to a pessimistic disposition.

Doory Wilson patted her shoulder. "Now don't ye be worrying, Aunt Emma. It's September, the time of the new moon, and good weather to boot. What more can we be asking? Not to mention the wedding cakes have been baked, and not a single one cracked!"

Great-Aunt Emma raised her eyebrows significantly. "I knew of a bride where the cakes cracked and the ale wort boiled up on the far side of the pot. The girl was sickly from the day of the wedding on, and her young man was thrown by a horse and died five years later to the day!"

"Oh, my goodness!" Doory clapped her hand over her mouth. "We 'most forgot a sixpence for yer shoe, Gillian!" She dove out of the room, returning almost immediately with the desired coin. "There, darling, now we needn't worry." She beamed in motherly fashion. "Yer first wee bairn will be healthy and as robust as the day is long!"

"Unless Gillian, in days past, has made a vow to any other," offered Great-Aunt Emma with a doleful expression.

"Oh, now, Emma, 'tis not the day for dour predictions!" Henry sank into the one chair available, as all others were stacked with goods of one kind or another.

Doory drew her daughter toward the door. "Come, come, Gillian. It's time ye are getting into the things laid out for you."

"But first—" Great-Uncle Henry smiled benignly from his chair—"Gillian, my dear, may you have a long, happy life, a sound and healthy body, a cottage that does not leak, and a meal chest that is always full!"

Gillian nodded and smiled happily.

Great-Aunt Emma drew herself up to her full height, which was considerable. "However, it is only practical to remember: 'Marriage is like a bee. It contains both honey and a sting!'" She then followed Gillian and Doory out of the room.

Griselda was doing her best to stand still despite a highly pronounced state of nervous excitement. "But what if it's not done in time? Or what if the tear still shows?"

Margaret, crawling around on the floor with pins in her mouth, answered as best she could. "Well, ye kinna be anybody's best maid with yer hem dippin' down like this!"

"I can't see any tear in it from here," said Eppie from her perch on the bed, where she and Meg were watching the proceedings.

"Of course not!" snapped Griselda. "It's on the other side. And if ye hadn't been so careless, it wouldn't be there at all!"

"Oh, now, never ye mind," soothed Margaret, pulling herself to her feet. "Slip out of it, and I'll have it all evened out and mended up in no time." She gathered the dress up in her arms. "Eppie, hold the mirror for Griselda so's she kin fix her hair," she called as she left the room.

Griselda, in her slip and a ruffled and flounced petticoat, seated herself. She leaned forward, eyeing herself critically.

Meg, still on the bed, looked dreamy. "Just think, being someone's best maid. All the eligible men'll be looking at you and lining up for a kiss. How romantic!"

Griselda concentrated on pulling a comb through her brown hair.

"Or do ye maybe wish ye *weren't* best maid so's Master Malcolm could've asked you to go with him?" asked Eppie, holding the mirror.

"Malcolm's a good friend. There's no big ruckus about that," Griselda retorted, working on a recalcitrant tangle with vigor.

"Brother Turner says we should be careful who we romance with on accounta Jesus wouldn't want Christians to get joined up with folks what's not," observed Meg thoughtfully.

Griselda put the comb down on the chest with a clatter. "I'm *not* thinking of marrying Malcolm Donnovan."

Meg was not to be deterred. "But ye got that look in yer eye, and so's he!"

"And a wedding's awful fun and romantic, ain't it?" added Eppie.

Griselda stood up, smoothed her petticoat, and gave a little twirl. "Aye, Eppie, it is!" she admitted.

Eppie laid the mirror down. "And do ye wish Fiona was across the sea in Ireland or maybe even Africa?"

Griselda stood still, pondering. Her lips curved softly upward. "Maybe I do," she said.

Fiona tossed a gown of deep blue satin toward the maid. "No, it just isn't quite right!"

"It looked perfectly fine to me," observed Elvira Elphinstone, ensconced nearby in a velvet high-backed chair and elegant in a brocaded dress of soft greens and lavender.

"Well, it's *not*, Auntie. Bring me the pink, Nora."

The maid complied and was then dismissed, leaving Fiona to turn back and forth before the full-length mirror in the upstairs bedroom. Soft pink muslin swirled about her and highlighted her flushed cheeks. "Aye," said Fiona at last, "he'll like the pink."

Elvira tapped her cane. "I presume you refer to Ian Fraser."

Fiona turned to look at her aunt. "Ian Fraser thinks I'm perfectly enchanting no matter what I wear." She paused, then arched her eyebrows. "But there just may be someone else at the wedding who takes to the pink."

"Malcolm Donnovan?"

Fiona turned back to the mirror, gazing at herself intently. "One never knows just how the circumstances of one's life will fall out. Actually, that's part of the fun of it."

Elvira rose. "You seem to march to your own drumbeat, Fiona."

"As do you, Auntie," Fiona retorted.

Elvira pressed her lips into a straight line. "Well, no more of this. If you'll wait here, I shall lend you my rose-colored pendant."

"I have something else in mind." Fiona opened the top drawer of the dresser.

"The pendant is from my Egyptian collection, Fiona."

"Thank you, Auntie, but—" Fiona removed a rectangular carved box and drew out a gold filigree necklace. In each gold leaf lay chips of ruby and agate. With a deft motion she fastened it about her neck. "*This* will be just the right finishing touch," she said with a flourish.

Davey Morrison stood, arms akimbo, in the shadows to the right of the main entryway. He found himself possessed with an odd feeling of foreboding as his eyes scanned the wedding revelers.

The newly married couple—particularly the bride, resplendent in layers of muslin, lace, and ribbons—was currently the center of attention, with a mixture of congratulations, mocking condolences, and raucous laughter.

The barn was lit with lanterns of all sorts and festooned with streamers above tables laden with every kind of food imaginable—scones, crumpets, biscuits, shortbread, gingerbread, ginger cake, currant loaves, butter and jam, meat pies, mince pies, and slices of fresh mutton. The ladies of Stonehaven had done themselves proud, thought Davey.

At the far end of the barn, where the volume was rising, bottles of ale and whisky were being passed freely, with buttermilk provided for children and teetotalers.

He spied Annie Mackinnon serving herself ginger cake at one of the tables and moved quickly toward her.

"Ah, Davey Morrison! And don't you look splendid," she greeted him.

"And you, Annie Mackinnon—" Davey's eyes took in her gown of green muslin with flowing sleeves and rows of lace about the neck. "You look a lovely picture, Annie!"

Annie blushed prettily. "Thank you, sir. And where is your friend Malcolm?"

Davey helped himself to a plate and a slice of mutton. He nodded in the direction of the drinking. "He's over there imbibing. And I'll wager it's not buttermilk."

"I might have thought you'd be engaged in the same activity," responded Annie coyly.

Davey put several breads on his plate, and they moved away from the table. "Tonight I feel I need a clear head."

They paused close to a small raised platform where two wee girls were singing "Brochan Lom" in Gaelic. Annie gazed at him with a look of puzzlement. "Why? Is anything wrong?"

Davey grinned. "Strange that we should think something's amiss if one prefers a clear head." He grew serious. "Actually, I don't know what it is. Maybe like something ominous hangs over the barn—as festive as it all seems on the surface. Like I must be careful—but of what, I'm not sure."

Annie finished her last bite of ginger cake and daintily licked her fingers. "You seem to be one who usually hits life with whole-hearted abandon."

"Aye. You're right. Though sometimes my abandon, as you call it, has gotten me into trouble." He wrinkled his brow thoughtfully. "Maybe my talks with Duncan lately are changing the way I look at life. . . ." His voice trailed off.

Annie followed his eyes to the barn's entryway. Fiona Elphinstone, a vision of pink loveliness, was entering on the arm of Ian Fraser. Annie leaned close to Davey. "Aye," she said softly. "Fiona Elphinstone is very, very beautiful."

With a courtly bow, Malcolm held a deep coral-colored rose toward Griselda. "To the most bonnie lassie of all!"

Griselda took the rose and sniffed at it. "It's a lovely fragrance,

Malcolm." She smiled coquettishly. "But ye haven't seen all the lassies here, or ye couldn't say it."

"Aye, but I could," returned Malcolm gallantly, "for ye have beauty both inside and out."

Griselda had seen Fiona enter with Ian some minutes earlier. Now she saw Fiona making her way toward them and found herself disturbed by the fact and equally cross with herself that it should make any difference at all. "Come, Malcolm, have ye tasted Doory Wilson's scones?" She led him toward the other side of the table, away from Fiona.

In the center of the barn two fiddlers and a piper began to tune up for the usual strathspeys and reels. Griselda swept up a scone and held it toward Malcolm. "See, Malcolm? Doesn't it look wonderful? And here's some of Mrs. Riley's grape preserves. If ye hold the scone, I'll just—"

Griselda felt a little jostling next to her and then a bump of her arm, and a generous spoonful of grape preserves cascaded down the white muslin front of her dress. Griselda stared at it in horror.

"Oh, my goodness!" exclaimed a sweet voice beside her.

Griselda turned to gaze into Fiona's very innocently distressed eyes.

"Oh, I'm so sorry!" Fiona warbled. "Folks are crowding in so getting ready for the dances. Someone must have bumped you. Oh, dear, it may even have been myself. Here—let me get a serviette, and we'll dab at it."

Griselda shook her head. "No, that won't do. I'll take care of it. Mama will help me."

Fiona smiled fetchingly. "Then my part shall be to keep Malcolm from being too lonesome while he waits for you." She took Malcolm's arm and drew him toward the fiddlers.

Griselda turned away, trying desperately to keep her eyes from filling with tears. She must find Mama.

Eppie swooshed in beside her. "I saw what Fiona did!"

"Eppie, quick, take me to Mama."

They found Margaret busy slicing a large currant loaf in a makeshift kitchen area in the back of the barn.

"My stars!" she exclaimed when she caught sight of Griselda. "Whatever happened to you?"

"Fiona Elphinstone bumped Griselda on purpose and made her spill," offered Eppie. "I saw her with my own eyes, I did!"

"The little witch," muttered Margaret. "Come on. We've got a bucket of water here, and we'll have it out, or nearly so, in no time."

Margaret scrubbed while Eppie watched and Griselda sniffled into her hanky. Finally, Margaret had done all she could.

"I'm so embarrassed. How can I ever go out there? The stain isn't gone," wailed Griselda.

"Well, it's mighty close to gone," countered Margaret. "The only way a body could see anything is if they was hunting for it."

Griselda continued to sniffle.

Margaret observed her for a moment, then took her firmly by the shoulders. "Now ye listen to me, Griselda. Ye are goin' to dry yer eyes and blow yer nose. And ye are goin' to go right out there with yer head up high. That Fiona Elphinstone may think she's a princess, but she ain't got as much class as a backstairs scullery maid!"

Griselda couldn't help but smile as she dabbed at her eyes. She took a deep breath. "Come on then, Eppie, let's go back out."

"And believe me," Margaret called after them, "that Malcolm knows when he sees *real* class!"

They moved slowly toward the barn's center. "Oh, just look at her!" Eppie pointed to where Fiona dipped and twirled—in and out with one partner after another. "Fiona knows how to flounce so elegantly—at least she *thinks* she does!"

As the reel came to an end, Fiona clung to Malcolm's arm,

laughing merrily. Before Griselda could stop her or know what she was doing, Eppie darted out toward them. She tugged at Malcolm's coat and whispered something in his ear and then ran off in the opposite direction.

Malcolm disengaged himself from Fiona, nodding and smiling. Then his eyes sought for Griselda.

"Ah, ye look bonnie as ever, my lady!" he said when he had found her.

"Oh, dear. Whatever did Eppie say to you?" asked Griselda, feeling rather flustered.

"Just that ye were all fixed up and looking for some fun." He grinned disarmingly.

Griselda felt the color rise in her cheeks. She glanced toward where she had last seen Fiona, but she was lost in the crowd. Hopefully with Ian Fraser!

The party progressed with much hilarity. Fiddlers played, stories were told, and anyone able to entertain did so, along with an unending supply of food and drink provided by the folk of Stonehaven. And all the while Malcolm was by Griselda's side. In fact, she even ceased to notice where Fiona was and with whom.

The sun had long since set when at least three-fourths of the company, along with every fiddler, accordionist, and piper in the barn, were engaged in one of the faster reels. They were whirling and snapping their fingers and shouting till the rafters fairly shook.

Next, the fiddlers and pipers swung into a Caledonian fling. By this time most dropped out to watch and catch their breath, leaving about two dozen of the more hardy. Fiona, Griselda noted, was one of these.

Griselda found she could not help but admire Fiona's energy and precision as with the others she twirled, "heel and toed," and raised her arms gracefully to depict the antlers of the red deer.

As the last note sounded, Fiona collapsed in a heap of pink

muslin and satin at the feet of Malcolm and Griselda. She did not get up.

"Fiona?" said Malcolm. "May I help you?"

Fiona looked up, her face contorted with pain. "I don't think I can walk," she whispered. "I've turned my ankle."

"I'll get Ian," Malcolm said, starting away.

"No!" The voice was no longer whispering. "That's just it—he's gone! Hector came looking for him. Ian said there was some sort of emergency with the sheep and he had to go." Tears began to roll down her cheeks. "Oh, whatever shall I do?" she wailed softly.

Griselda watched helplessly as Malcolm knelt beside Fiona. "Oh, now don't worry none. I'll help you," he soothed.

The tears stopped. "Oh, would you?" she breathed. "I'm so sorry! I don't know what made my foot turn so suddenly. If you could just help me up and let me lean on you, it shouldn't take too long to walk home."

She struggled to her feet with Malcolm's help.

"There now. Just hang on, and we'll make it fine." Casting an apologetic look at Griselda, he put his arm firmly around Fiona's waist with the look of one who saw his duty before him and would rise to the occasion and do it—but who also, try as he may, could not conceal the fact that various aspects of that duty might be *very* pleasant indeed!

Griselda watched them go, trying not to look miserable and noting that Fiona was getting along especially well for someone who had so recently been in tears of pain.

CHAPTER 22
The Body

Even a wedding celebration did not keep Elvira Elphinstone from her usual late-night walk. She slipped away from the party in the barn long before it was done. She changed her velvet slippers for sturdy shoes and her finery for a light wool skirt and shawl. Next, she seated herself and opened a small black book. She sat reading intensely for some moments. She shut the volume with a clap and stared into space murmuring, "Aye, the spirits *will* move." Then she arose and set off.

She wandered slowly through the back garden, past bushes and ferns shadowy in the starlight of a sky half full of clouds. Silver birch and giant oaks cast ghostly silhouettes around her.

She turned to gaze at the house behind, its two stories massive in great gray granite. Then she moved toward a stone wall, where she let herself out of a small iron gate.

She climbed the path up the northern brae until she moved along the cliff top, sometimes at a leisurely pace and at other times quite briskly.

It was just past midnight when she made her way toward the shore on the southern edge of Stonehaven. The tide had receded, leaving a shoreline of round, wet pebbles. She bent down absent-mindedly to pick one up.

Suddenly her eye was caught by a strange shadow to her right. She straightened up, staring at it fixedly, hardly daring to breathe.

It was the body of a man lying facedown upon the pebbly shore. The body did not move.

Although it was past midnight, Thomas Blacklock had not retired for the night.

Instead he strode restlessly back and forth across the length of his shed. Ever since he had gone inside with Liza to the meeting in the curing shed, his agitation had been growing.

What he did or did not do with his life had not been much pondered by him in the past—beyond what practical things must be attended to or changed in the wake of whatever circumstances befell him.

Now he wrestled with his *inner* life.

A hymn from the curing shed insisted on singing its way through his head, even when he wished it would not.

I hear the Savior say, "Thy strength indeed is small." Well, he could relate to that.

"Child of weakness, watch and pray, find in me thine all in all." Surely he was a child of weakness. In fact, he could think of no one who was any weaker than he. And he had prayed—sometimes, though falteringly and with only a little faith. But how could one find the *all* of the hymn in Jesus? *How?*

He stood still in the center of the shed. Finally he shook his head and blew the lantern out, kicked off his shoes, and fell upon the cot that was his bed.

He had just pulled the blanket up over himself when there was a sharp rap at the door. He waited, his heart beating faster. The knock was repeated, definite, and louder than the first time.

He sat up. "Aye?"

The voice behind the door was sharp and demanding. "Thomas Blacklock, it is necessary I see you. Open immediately!"

Thomas thrust his feet into his shoes and fumbled to light the lantern. Then he pulled the door open and stared, perplexed, at Elvira Elphinstone.

She pushed past him unceremoniously into the shed. She turned slowly about until her eyes rested on the coffin. "Well, it appears to be finished. Is it?"

"Aye, mem. It is."

Elvira nodded in satisfaction. "I shall pay you, of course. But first, we have a more important matter to attend to."

"Mem?"

"I have the body," she stated matter-of-factly.

Thomas stared at her, dumbfounded.

"Oh, of course, I don't mean I have it *with* me! But I will show you where it is. It's by the water."

Thomas picked up his coat, all the while eyeing Elvira and wondering if he were dreaming. They went out into the night, and he shut the door behind them. "Who is it, mem?"

"I can't tell. You don't think I'd *touch* it, do you? It's a man lying facedown on the pebbles next to the sea." Without more ado, she set off in rapid strides, and Thomas followed her through a field and down several deserted and darkened streets. When they reached the waterfront, she led him southward.

Finally she stopped and pointed. "See there."

A few feet ahead lay a man, facedown as she had said, one arm thrown out. Thomas knelt beside him and felt the man's arm. There was no pulse, and the body was growing cold.

In the half-darkness, Thomas rolled the body over. The shirt was torn and full of blood. "Looks to me like he's been stabbed," muttered Thomas.

He peered at the face. It was Malcolm Donnovan.

CHAPTER 23

Elvira Takes Charge

Thomas held the body in his long arms and peered at Elvira Elphinstone, whose eyes glimmered in the ghostly light like the pebbles under their feet. She folded her hands in front of her, and Thomas had the feeling he stood before a magistrate or a judge.

"Mr. Blacklock," she intoned, "you will bring the body to *my* home. You will lay him out there. Moreover, that is where we shall have the wake and the funeral."

"But, mem, he's been staying at Doory Wilson's, and Davey Morrison may—"

"I shall take care of Davey Morrison. As for Doory Wilson, she's in the midst of a wedding party. Besides, she has no room. Her barn may be large, but the house has rooms no bigger than a cracker box. She'll be most relieved not to have a dead body arrive the same night her daughter is married."

Thomas opened his mouth, but Elvira cut him off. "And the sheriff must be contacted. I'll see to it." She turned on her heel. "Now follow me!"

The body grew heavy in Thomas's arms as he accompanied

149

the tall lady whose cane made an occasional rat-a-tat on the path before them.

Reaching the home, Thomas followed Elvira up the steps to a bedroom, where a wide-eyed servant lit a lantern and spread a heavy canvas on the bed and on top of that a sheet.

Elvira pointed to the bed, and Thomas laid the body down. For some moments a heavy, sepulchral silence hung in the room, invaded only by the ticking of a large clock.

Another servant appeared in the doorway, and Elvira gave commands in low, intense tones with staccato rapidity. "Nora, get me a candle." "Mary, wake the gardener, and have him unlock all the doors and throw them open. And before you return, pour all the milk in the house on the ground."

The servant started out.

"And cast out all the onions and butter," Elvira called after her.

Thomas had begun to loosen the blood-matted clothing from the victim's body.

Elvira stopped him. "Not now. There will be time enough for that, and the servants will help you with the washing and laying out." With great care she lit a tall candle brought by the servant and placed it on a stand next to the bed. "This must be kept burning night and day until the funeral is done."

She straightened up. "Now, Thomas, open all the windows at once. Hurry with it! I *feel* the evil!"

Thomas stared at the body on the bed, thinking that he, too, felt the evil in the room.

Elvira glared at him angrily. "Don't just stand there! Do as I say, or the evil spirits cannot leave!" Her eyes seemed to glisten with dark portent.

Thomas moved toward a window and opened it.

"Nora, cover the mirror and every picture!" Elvira yanked open the drawer of a dresser and lifted out several linen cloths. Then she moved toward the clock, which stood on a long, narrow table. She stopped its movement.

A cat wandered into the room, mewing.

"Take it out of here and shut it in a pen until burial," she ordered.

"Aye, but we've no pen," Nora objected.

"Then find one or put a tub over it, but get the cat out—now!" She fixed the servant with her eye. "If you do not and the cat jumps over the body, the first person the cat meets will be blinded by evil spirits—eventually. *Move*, or it will be your fault!"

The woman caught the cat up and left, the echo of mews sounding down the hall.

Elvira turned her attention to Thomas. "As I said, Mr. Blacklock, the servants will help you. You know what the appropriate procedures are, and I trust you to do them. I shall also send the gardener around with the death bell." Only a hint of a smile played about her lips. "We shall need neither the sexton nor indeed *anyone* representing the kirk for Mr. Donnovan's funeral." She eyed Thomas more intensely. "Mr. Blacklock?"

Thomas, almost in a trance, gawked at the body. He was only vaguely aware of Elvira's continued commands, except for the fleeting thought that the lady seemed to be enjoying the whole situation.

A sudden whiff of breeze from the open windows ruffled the curtains. Or was it evil spirits? He stared at the blood-matted body on the bed. Could it be that he himself was in any part responsible for the death of Malcolm Donnovan?

"Auntie?" Fiona appeared in the doorway, looking sleepy and disheveled in a satin robe. "What's the commotion? I heard the cat mewing, so—" She caught sight of the body, and her eyes widened in horror. With a scream she collapsed on the floor in a faint.

Davey fought a sense of uneasiness.

He had long since walked Annie Mackinnon home from the

wedding festivities in the barn and then returned to his room. Having seen Malcolm leave earlier with Fiona, he expected him to be back at the Wilson house. He was not.

He went outside and paused uncertainly. He started toward the Elphinstone manor, deciding at least to walk past it to look for a sign of his friend. No lights were visible from the front of the house, and all had no doubt retired for the night.

He turned back toward the Wilsons'. Surely by now Malcolm would be there. But when he checked inside again, Malcolm was still gone.

Restlessly Davey strode toward the waterfront and then southward. Dunnottar Castle was silhouetted against clouds in the distance. He stopped and thrust his hands into his pockets, gazing at it thoughtfully.

A large figure ambled unsteadily out of the shadows toward him. It was Rob Rafferty. "Davey Morrison! Out and about a wee mite late, ain't ye?"

"As yourself, Rob," returned Davey.

From under his shaggy brows, Rob Rafferty seemed to study Davey as well as could be expected in an inebriated state. "Wal, tonight must be the night fer wanderin' about at the 'witching hour,' as they calls it." One long finger scratched at his ear. "I told yer mate, Malcolm—"

Every sense within Davey became alert. "Malcolm? Where did you see him?"

"Oh, somewhere about where ye are right now. Seemed to be about to take himself off on a walk. Down that way." He pointed southward along the shore.

Davey turned and bolted on a run back toward the Wilsons'. *Could Malcolm have been so foolish as to start out for the castle along the sea on a night as dark as this?* thought Davey. He would change into his boots, find some sort of torch, and then he would do his best to find Malcolm. There was nothing else to do.

At first he paid no attention to the rhythmic tolling of a bell, so busy was he with his thoughts. But as he drew nearer to the Wilsons', he sensed it came from behind the house toward the barn.

Rounding the bend he saw a man standing in light streaming from the open barn door. Two dozen or more of the revelers had gathered outside to hear his news.

The death bell. Davey knew of the custom, especially in east-coast fishing villages, to announce death. Although he told himself there was no reason for it, his heart began to beat unnaturally.

Abruptly the tolling ceased, and the messenger, leaning into the light, began to read from a small scroll. "Brethren and sisters, I hereby let you to wit that Malcolm Donnovan departed this life tonight, according to the pleasure of almighty God, and ye are invited to attend the funeral two days hence at the home of Miss Elvira Elphinstone." He began to ring the bell again while raising his voice in singsong fashion above the din. "And may all evil spirits be held at bay by the sounding of the bell!"

With a low curse and a pounding in his head, Davey Morrison fled in the direction of the Elphinstone manor. Thoughts refused to formulate. His brain could only scream, *No!*

When he reached the house, he found the front door ajar. A lantern burned dimly in the hallway. There were no sounds.

He strode down the corridor to a stairway, where he paused and looked up. Light filtered down, along with muffled sounds.

He bounded the stairs, two at a time. At the top and to his left was an open door. Inside a large room, candlelight cast long fingers over the walls.

He entered.

A man was bent over the bed. On hearing Davey, he straightened and turned. Thomas Blacklock stepped back awkwardly.

In a trice, Davey was beside the bed, his eyes riveted on the figure who lay with a sheet pulled up to the neck. There was no escaping the awful fact. *Malcolm! Dead!* He felt light-headed.

Thomas coughed and cleared his throat nervously. "He's been washed. And of course I'll be gettin' the coffin and his better clothes. We be doing all decently."

Abruptly, Davey grabbed Thomas's shirt with both hands and yanked him closer. He spoke through clenched teeth. "I don't care if he has copper coins on his eyelids or a saucer of salt on his chest. *What happened?*"

Thomas's eyes grew large and frightened. "Stabbed he was. In the chest."

Still Davey held him. "Who did it?" he thundered.

Thomas shook his head. "I dinna ken. Miss Elphinstone found him—facedown by the sea."

Davey let go of Thomas so suddenly that Thomas staggered backward.

"I be sorry about yer friend," he murmured obsequiously.

Without sound, Elvira Elphinstone appeared regally just inside the door. "I, too, offer my condolences, Davey Morrison. Try not to fret. Unfortunately, death is deaf and will hear no denial." She smiled faintly, then stirred to action. "The magistrate has been sent for. The sheriff from Kilamon will come tomorrow."

She moved across the room to where a second candle flickered wildly next to the silent clock. She blew it out, trimmed the wick, and relit it. "Of course, the funeral will be here. Doory Wilson's is much too small—you and Mr. Donnovan have made so many friends." She turned and smiled, warmly almost, then glanced at the body. "As well as an enemy or two, it would seem."

The late morning sun beat down on Thomas as he approached the Carmichael home and knocked uncertainly at the door.

A wide-eyed Meg answered it.

Thomas turned a black felt hat in his hands. "I come to see Miss Griselda."

She opened the door for him to enter. "I'll git her for you," she said and disappeared.

Thomas stood in the middle of the room, holding his hat and staring at the floor. Shortly, Griselda entered in a dark skirt, her eyes red and puffy and a handkerchief crumpled in her hand.

She nodded toward a chair and sat down herself, peering at him in puzzlement.

Thomas tugged at his collar. "I be right sorry for you, Miss Griselda." He stared at the floor for some moments, then shook his head dolefully. "Death is no particular who it takes away."

Griselda dabbed at her eyes. "Thank you." Still she watched him, puzzled.

He licked his lips nervously. "I have somethin' fer you." He looked down again. "When we found Mr. Donnovan, he had somethin' clasped tight in his fist, he did." He looked at Griselda earnestly. "Nobody saw it but me, so's I put it in me pocket and kept it fer to give you." He fumbled in his coat and drew out a small brown paper package.

Slowly Griselda opened it and drew out a ring. She gazed at it in wonderment. A small gold circlet enclosed a gold leaf with chips of ruby and agate.

"It's very pretty, but—"

"I be knowin' Mr. Donnovan had a real shine to you, Miss Griselda. He'd like you to have it. I feel it in me bones."

Griselda fingered the ring thoughtfully. "I wonder where it came from."

CHAPTER 24

The Funeral

Thomas threw another heavy spadeful of dirt behind him and stopped to lean on the handle and catch his breath. The grave behind the Elphinstone manor was almost three-quarters dug.

Thomas shook his head. A strange lady, Elvira Elphinstone. For the past two days she had displayed the emotional energy of a general in battle. Thomas was used to seeing her firmly ensconced at every funeral he had ever had anything to do with, her eagle eyes taking in every detail. But this was different—she obviously felt *this* funeral belonged to her and had taken charge with a vengeance.

Thomas had not even completed laying out the body when she declared that the burial would not be in the kirk yard but on *her* property, in the southeast corner, as evil influences came from the north.

Candles had been carefully trimmed and relit at all hours. And she had kept contingents of two to four persons at watch beside the body night and day so that the devil could not carry off the corpse or put a mark on it.

Thomas dug deep into the soil and threw out another spadeful of dirt. A breeze from the east ruffled the leaves above him. He shivered, although it was not cold. He glanced at the sky—it was blue enough with only a few clouds to the east—and wondered at the feeling of foreboding that had seized him upon awakening.

Why this apprehension? The funeral would take place in the afternoon, and then he would be done with the whole business. Done with Elvira Elphinstone, done with her glittery eyes watching his every move, done with her wild superstitions.

He was aware that a goodly number in Stonehaven believed in the old wives' tales, but the lady of this house appeared to *live* for them. While most added superstition to whatever else in Christianity they believed, Elvira seemed to hold fiercely *only* to paganism. And paganism is what Thomas now believed these superstitions to be. Of late, and especially in his dealings with the Elphinstone woman, he could hear the words of Brother Turner in the curing shed, ringing in his ears, "It is Christ and *Christ alone* who saves!"

Recently he had tried to pray—sometimes at night as he returned from work on the Wilsons' barn. Something about the vault of stars and clouds overhead made him feel that the Almighty was indeed listening. But he had never prayed on the way to meet the masked figure in the forest—nor upon his return.

As for any part he may have had in Malcolm's final misfortune, he had convinced himself that either there was no connection between the murder and the strange individual in the forest or at least the murder had nothing to do with himself, as he certainly had had no knowledge of Malcolm's whereabouts on the fateful evening.

But something was definitely in the air today, something ominous.

He attacked the dirt with a vengeance, determined to bury his tension in physical activity. If only it were as easy to do away with this gnawing anxiety as it was to bury a body. Besides, it was high time the grave was finished and he move on to the next step.

A small shadow fell across the grass. "Master Thomas?"

He turned to see Liza standing before him, dressed in her best clothes. "Liza! Now ain't ye a bonnie thing in all yer finery!"

"Everybody else is in black, but I didn't have any, so Mama said to wear my Sunday dress on accounta the funeral."

"Yer ma here?"

"Aye. And Papa, too. They went out to the shed over on the other side of the house. There's all kinds of things in there to eat and a lot of noise. But I wasn't one bit hungry, so I came out, and Miss Elphinstone was standing by the door talking out loud to herself—something 'bout spirits, and her eyes looked kinda funny. And so I come back here to see you."

Thomas, frowning, kept at his work.

"I didn't much like going in the house to see Master Malcolm's body. All the men took their hats off, and a lot of people talked to the body just as if Master Malcolm could hear 'em. And Papa said I had to touch Master Malcolm's body or I'd have powerful bad dreams, and I didn't want to but Papa made me, and Master Malcolm felt cold and funny. And there was bread and water next to him. Papa told me Master Malcolm's spirit would come back every night and eat it and if they didn't put the bread and water there, Master Malcolm's spirit couldn't never settle down and rest *nowheres!*" Liza leaned as close to Thomas as she could. "Do *ye* believe that, Master Thomas?"

Thomas's frown deepened. He took out the last spadeful of dirt and began to smooth the sod carefully around the edges of the grave.

Liza followed him. "'Cause Brother Turner would be powerful upset for folks to believe it, wouldn't he? And ye know what, Master Thomas? I'm thinking Jesus might be crying to see folks thinkin' about everything else exceptin' him."

Thomas contemplated the child, whose eyes were large and troubled. "I speck he might, Liza," he said at last.

The large shed on the west side of the Elphinstone manor was packed with tables groaning with every kind of food and drink brought by the village ladies and around which clustered the greater part of Stonehaven's inhabitants.

Davey had tried to eat but found he could not. At present he stood silent and brooding beside Annie Mackinnon.

Griselda, on Davey's other side, was dressed in white with a black ribbon at the waist, as was the custom for the women closest to the deceased. Davey had tried to comfort her, somewhat awkwardly and probably to no avail. She stood like a statue, white-faced, dark circles under her eyes.

The level of noise within the building was rising in direct proportion to the amount of ale and whisky being imbibed, which was considerable.

Annie, glancing up at Davey, read his thoughts. She leaned closer. "They say a Scot's funeral is merrier than an Englishman's wedding."

Davey contemplated. "It may be that the rest of life in the north country is so dour that it only seems so by contrast. Or the Scots just drink more." He sighed.

His eyes were drawn to the door, where Fiona Elphinstone, wearing a dark navy blue dress and a pensive expression, was just entering. Of course she was with Ian Fraser, who, it seemed to Davey, must be a patient sort. Did Ian *expect* someone as beautiful as Fiona to flirt as she did?

Fiona's eyes quickly scanned the room. She tugged at Ian's arm, and they moved toward Griselda and Davey.

"Oh, my dear Griselda," Fiona crooned, clasping Griselda's hand, "how terribly sad for you—for all of us! You look so lovely, dressed as a widow might. But, of course, you almost were, weren't you? Oh dear, one can get so mixed up in one's words, can't one? Especially at an occasion as awful as this." She stopped momentarily to catch her breath and dab at her eyes with a hanky. "When last I saw him, Malcolm was so full of life and energy and charm." She sniffled. "And had been *so very* helpful in my poor plight."

Griselda closed her eyes, as if she could scarcely bear to look at Fiona. "Malcolm was a fine person," she murmured.

Ian nodded briefly toward Griselda. He glanced uncomfortably in Davey's direction and seemed about to move on but paused. "I reckon Malcolm's death was a big loss to you," he said.

"Aye," returned Davey. He watched Ian's quickly retreating back thoughtfully.

Fiona had not followed him. She was staring wide-eyed at the front of Griselda's dress. "That ring—on the chain around your neck—where did you get it?"

"Excuse me?" said Griselda, angry color creeping into her cheeks. "It was given to me!"

"By Malcolm?" When Griselda didn't answer, a smile played momentarily about Fiona's lips. "It must have been—or you wouldn't wear it today." She grew serious again. "How very strange, though. Your ring matches in every detail the necklace that Ian gave me." She gathered herself together to move on. "But then, life is full of unexplained oddities, isn't it?"

Aye, thought Davey, finding he had one more thing to ponder.

The procession moved slowly from the front of the manor where the coffin, covered with a mortcloth, had been lifted off two chairs and was now being carried by Davey, Duncan Carmichael, Jonathan (who had an older man take his duty at the lighthouse), and three others. Servants immediately overturned the chairs, as custom—not to mention Elvira Elphinstone—dictated, so that the spirit might not return from the unseen world. The rest of the men walked before them, and the women came, two by two, behind. The gardener followed them all, tolling the death bell.

Davey noted that the overcast sky of late afternoon was darkening, considered by most to be a bad omen for the welfare of the soul. As they rounded the back corner of the manor and struck off for the grave at the far corner of the grounds, four pipers with bagpipes hung with black crepe streamers set themselves to a mournful dirge, "The Dead March," accompanied by drummers, whose thudding rolls completed the atmosphere of gloomy lament.

Reaching the grave, the coffin was immediately lowered into its final place of rest. Thomas Blacklock stepped forward to offer "consolation to you, the friends of the deceased." He dropped a wreath made of heather intertwined with bracken on the coffin lid and stepped back to his official position behind the grave.

The company fanned out noisily over the yard as a lady Davey had never seen before sang "Time Wears Away," a soulful number. The more inebriated guests made unseemly remarks, while others blew their noses and women dabbed at their eyes with their hankies.

Davey stood beside the grave with Annie and all of the Carmichael family. He eyed the mourners strewn over the yard. *Mourners?* he thought. Probably very few mourned. Most likely the greater part had come out of curiosity to this unorthodox funeral behind the Elphinstone manor. Not to mention a feast and an excuse to get drunk, a consequence of which was that many a grudge would be settled with violence and blood on the way home.

Standing just a step or two in front of the main gathering was the lady of the manor. Dressed in flowing black, Elvira Elphinstone drew herself up in ramrod majesty.

She held in her hands two small dark books. One of them Davey supposed to be a Bible. There were only two things Davey had insisted upon—indeed the only two he cared about.

That Duncan Carmichael be allowed to give the eulogy and that
someone should read from the Psalms.

Casting a wary eye at the darkening sky, Elvira gave a signal to
the gardener, who immediately set about placing torches in the
cleared space before the grave.

Pipers and drummers swung into "The Flowers of the Forest."

> "The prime o' our land, are cold in the clay.
> Sighing and moaning on ilka green loaning,
> The flowers of the forest are all wede away."

Davey shifted on his feet. If there was anything needed to
complete the melancholy of the day, "The Flowers of the Forest"
surely took care of it.

As the last note died, Margaret Carmichael threw her arms
around Griselda, moaning aloud, "Ah, me dearie, the death cloud
was on his eyes! I knew it! I knew it!"

Elvira turned toward Duncan. "Mr. Carmichael—now, please."

Duncan stepped forward for the eulogy. He glanced about at
the guests, only half of whom might listen, Davey surmised, for
there was a rumbling murmur of talk here and there. One who
had fallen down, drunk, staggered to his feet, helped by his
neighbors.

Duncan cleared his throat. "This here ain't the kind of thing
I'm used to doing, but I'm honored to say a good word for
Malcolm Donnovan. Seems to me he was helpful and kind, and
he knew how to get a good laugh outta anybody he met." He
stopped and looked toward the grave. "One thing I know, sure as
sure, is Malcolm ain't in that grave over there. He's got called
away, and one day he'll give an account to his Maker."

There was a sudden rustle from Elvira. She stood up taller, if
that were possible, and her eyes darted everywhere.

"I reckon," continued Duncan, "that an occasion like this is a good time for all of us to be lookin' into our own selves because one day we'll *all* be standing before Jesus, who died for us."

Elvira had noisily flipped open one of the books she held. She moved toward Rob Rafferty, who stared back drunkenly. Seeming to think better of that, she turned toward Jonathan, the lighthouse keeper.

Duncan's voice reached to the edge of the crowd. "Our final destiny's gonna depend on what we done with Jesus' gift of salvation to—"

"Thank you, Mr. Carmichael!" Elvira said in strong and dismissive tones. "Jonathan will now read the Scripture." She thrust the open book into Jonathan's hands. "Here—it's marked, and I expect you to read *only* what is marked. If you'll just move toward a torch, you'll see well enough."

Elvira returned to her former station of command while Jonathan moved uncertainly toward the light. A breeze had come up. The giant oaks and silver birch swayed in ghostly rustlings above them.

Davey studied Jonathan, wondering just what Elvira Elphinstone had selected from the Psalms and remembering that Annie had said the most superstitious were liable to mix parts of the Bible with their beliefs.

Jonathan stared at the open book in his hand. "From Psalm 90," he began uncertainly. "'Thou turnest man to destruction. . . . They are as a sleep: in the morning they are like grass which groweth up. In the morning it flourisheth, and groweth up; in the evening it is cut down, and withereth. . . . Thou hast set our iniquities before thee, our secret sins—'"

Jonathan coughed. He opened his mouth, and nothing came. He frowned and began again. "'For all our days are passed away in thy wrath: we spend our years as a tale that is told—'" Jonathan's eyes glazed, and he dropped the book.

Suddenly Liza stood beside the lighthouse keeper. Her voice, to the obvious amazement of the crowd, rang out clear and sweet. "But that ain't the whole of it! Jesus died for all the bad things we ever done, and if we thank him and join up with him, we can live with Jesus forever and ever!"

Elvira moved swiftly into the torches' circle of light. "Enough!" she said sharply.

Thomas could feel it coming even before Elvira Elphinstone said it. "Mr. Blacklock! You will come here please!"

Thomas's heart beat like a trip-hammer as he dutifully moved toward the woman. After all, she was the one person in Stonehaven that *no one* defied.

She held out another book with a scarlet ribbon in it. The Bible that Jonathan had held still lay on the ground. "Take this," she commanded, "and open it to the scarlet ribbon."

He did so and stared at the words. His eyes widened. He felt the blood rush to his face, his heart thudding even faster.

"Read them," she prodded, stepping back a bit and folding her hands grandly before her.

Thomas glanced about him. Was there no place to flee? Jonathan stood as if in a trance where he had dropped the Bible. Liza moved close to Thomas, her big eyes gazing into his with complete trust.

The breeze became a wind, pulling a black canopy of clouds over the yard. He gazed at Elvira Elphinstone, who remained utterly still even as the wind whipped at her skirts. The string of white pearls she wore against black brocade matched the glitter in her eyes, just as the pebbles on the beach had done the night he had found the body of Malcolm Donnovan.

"Nay," he said at last. "I kinna read these words."

The wind suddenly ceased as a silent prelude of the storm to come. And with it a straining hush as onlookers, too, stood immobile, waiting.

Elvira moved a step toward him. "But you *will* read!" she ordered.

Thomas was trembling violently. "Nay! For these are—are incantations—to the devil!" His voice shook, and for a moment he thought he might faint.

"*Read!*" she screamed.

Thomas had barely the strength to shake his head and reiterate, "Nay."

Elvira moved backward as if she had been struck. Her face twisted in violent rage. "Then I shall call all the curses of the spirit world down on you!" she shrieked. She let forth a volley of shrill curses, staggering as two men led her to a bench and helped her sit.

It was the first time the people of Stonehaven had seen Elvira Elphinstone lose her composure.

Thomas, dazed and only half aware of what was going on, still trembled. Abruptly he felt Liza's hand in his. "We could sing, Master Thomas," she whispered. "We could sing about God's grace."

Thomas stared into the child's bright eyes. What was it that Brother Turner had said? *Yer own faith—but the courage must be his.*

He looked up and briefly took the measure of his audience. Many in varying stages of inebriation, others bowed with care or the power of evil.

Again the words of James Turner rang through him: *Courage to stand against the powers of evil—for it is* Christ *and* Christ *alone who saves!*

He looked again at Liza, who still gazed at him earnestly. "Aye. We'll sing, Liza," he whispered.

He took a deep breath. "Amazing grace—how sweet the sound—" His voice, though definite, was not strong, and he looked at the ground. Liza's voice joined his. He could feel all eyes upon him and yet his voice gathered strength: "That saved a wretch like me!" He looked up then, threw his head back, and sang for all he was worth: "I once was lost, but now am found— was blind, but now I see."

A new boldness entered his soul, and he gave himself to the music and its meaning in a wonderful and nearly wild abandonment.

The wail of the pipes and the thudding roll of the drums joined him and reached out to the furthermost parts of the strange scene, the plaintive pipes representing the sorrow and sin of the human condition even while the words and melody counterpointed the message of God's grace.

One by one the funeral company added their voices to a song that most knew but few understood or had experienced. It swelled on the air and changed the atmosphere of the manor, previously charged with the forces of evil. For God's Spirit was present, seeking—and hearts, here and there, were responding.

Davey watched and listened in amazement. The entire atmosphere was altered. The coffinmaker was transformed. His voice, deep and melodious, rose above the others. His face, lifted to the sky in spite of raindrops that had begun to fall, had a look of peace—maybe even of triumph—and Davey thought that if he were religious, he might even say that the glory of God shown upon Thomas Blacklock and the little girl who clung to his hand.

CHAPTER 25
Annie and Davey

The sun shone warm, and the breeze blew gently over Dunnottar Castle as Annie leaned against its stone wall and looked out to sea. Again there were things she needed to sort through in her mind.

Life at the present moment was puzzling, to say the least. It had been a week since Malcolm Donnovan's funeral, and she had not seen Davey since that same evening when he had left her at her door, seemingly distracted and saying nothing of significance.

A few days later she had seen Doory Wilson and had tactfully extracted whatever information she could. Davey had left early the morning after the funeral, telling Doory only that he expected to return. He had said nothing about where he was going or why.

It unsettled Annie to realize how much she missed Davey. More and more of her days had begun to center about this man who had dropped into her life with his shocking disclosure, followed by his declared intent to further their relationship. Further it to what extent Annie could not guess, especially now.

There was no way to keep thoughts about the Captain and Davey's wife from her mind when she was with him, although they had not spoken of it since that time two days after the initial revelation. On the other hand, she continued to find a certain comfort in the fact that someone else knew all about it—someone who had suffered as she had.

Mostly though, in recent days Davey Morrison's charm had driven any disturbing thoughts away, and she found herself fascinated—or was it bewitched?—by this daring, adventurous, partly mysterious individual.

Only now, the mysterious part of him had resurfaced with a vengeance. Where was he? And why? And what was he really doing in Stonehaven in the first place? His other explanations had seemed weak, and he had as much as admitted that he had not told her everything.

Perhaps it was high time to assess things carefully in the light of day, to put out of her mind things that were probably foolish or that someday might cause more pain than pleasure.

She drew Donal's letter from her pocket, sat down on a nearby rock, and spread the letter before her.

> *I think I'm almost used to life in the merchant marine now. My new ship is a three-masted schooner named the* Brighton, *and we are just now docked at Liverpool, but if you send letters to the old address, I'll get them.*
>
> *It seems that your last few letters have had a great deal in them about Davey Morrison. Is this a new romance, Mother? Perhaps you should tell me more about him.*
>
> *As always, your loving son,*
> *Donal*

Annie folded the letter, frowning. If even Donal had sensed enough to question—

A familiar figure striding toward her interrupted her thoughts.

Davey! Quickly she stuffed the letter into her pocket as she felt her heart begin to beat unnaturally.

"Annie! It would seem a magnet draws us both to Dunnottar Castle at the same time!" He smiled broadly.

She felt herself flustered, ill at ease. "I didn't see you along the way, and I haven't been here that long." Abruptly she eyed him more dispassionately. "In fact, I haven't seen you *anywhere* for the past week," she said with just the hint of an edge in her voice.

Davey looked almost, but not quite, contrite. "Sorry. I—I met with the sheriff and—and had other—business that needed tending."

"I see," said Annie, thinking that no, she did *not* see.

"I missed you," he offered.

Annie looked away, making a conscious effort not to see whatever was in his eyes. Perhaps the conversation should be taken in a safer direction. "Did you find out anything from the sheriff about Malcolm's murder?"

"Nothing," returned Davey thoughtfully, "but I haven't given up. That's why you didn't see me just now. I came the other way, along the shore."

"Why?"

Davey sat down on the grass beside her. "Because Rob Rafferty said that Malcolm started off that night along the shore toward the castle. Besides, Malcolm had said—" He broke off, staring into the distance. "Anyway, I came along the water. Annie, do you know of any passageway up here from the sea?"

"I've never heard of one."

He was silent for a few moments. Then Davey asked, "Ever heard of anything to do with wreckers hereabouts?"

Annie eyed him quizzically. "Wreckers? Why would you ask that?"

He stretched casually. "Oh, just that sometimes castles— places like that—become places to store pillaged cargo."

"I've heard of wreckers, especially off of Cornwall. Of course, there have been wrecks in bad weather. Perhaps several in the past year up or down the coast and some rather close to the castle. But surely not wreckers here!" She frowned thoughtfully. "Do you think Scotland and the Scottish more violent than other peoples? In the days of the clans it seemed no clan was respectable without a feud. And in some places still, the ones most admired are those who drink the most and fight the most fiercely."

Davey chewed reflectively on a piece of grass. "Maybe it's the wild and barren terrain—the stretches of moor and shadowed valleys. The unpredictable weather—sunny one minute and lowering the next. And always the sea close by—mostly in varying degrees of fierce!"

"Good description."

"I once told you I was in love with the sea. Maybe I'm in love with Scotland the same way. Partly because she's unpredictable."

"You have some wildness in you, don't you, Davey?" But she smiled at him, not disapprovingly.

He twirled a small twig, then broke it in half. He leaned back on his elbows. "I was born a Scot, and we Scots are adventurers. At one time—or maybe several times in my life—adventure is what I lived for!" He stared at the sky pensively. "Now perhaps Duncan Carmichael has made me at least begin to look at things differently."

"How's that?"

He sat up, leaning his arms on his knees. "I think I've prided myself on being a searcher. And maybe a searcher only thinks he sees the whole picture. A searcher never needs to settle down, defend anything, invest in anything. I don't know, perhaps I don't want to live that way anymore."

"Then what *do* you want, Davey?" Annie asked softly, wishing almost immediately that she hadn't.

Davey looked at her directly. "What if I said—you?" There was a hint of mischief in his eyes.

Annie felt the color rise in her cheeks. "Then I should have to tell you that your thinking must be out of kilter—that in my opinion, in this regard, you're still searching."

"Maybe not." Davey stood up, grasping Annie's hand as he did so. He pulled her gently to her feet, facing him. "I missed you this past week, Annie. I missed you dreadfully." He drew her to him and kissed her. At first gently, then long and hard.

Annie did not resist, and her heart was beating wildly. When he released her, she stammered, "Davey Morrison, you certainly know how to surprise a body!"

He regarded her earnestly. "Did you mind?"

Annie could not look at him, afraid of what might be in her eyes. "No," she said softly, "but don't take it to mean too much."

"Ah, then we shan't worry about it!" he replied more jauntily than Annie wished. "Come! It's time to explore! Ever been inside the castle buildings?" He struck off at a fast pace toward the row of stone chambers that ran along the north, just past the keep.

Annie followed, thinking this man was a good bit like Scottish weather—unpredictable. "Only a few times. It's mostly bare, crumbling, gray stone," she called after him. "There's a dreadful dungeon that faces the sea."

Suddenly he swung about toward her. "Where exactly did you find the bracelet that you kept?"

She pointed. "Over there. By the corner of the chapel. Just lying on the ground."

Davey stared toward the ruins of the building.

Another thought struck Annie. "Do you remember the ring Griselda was wearing on a chain at the funeral?"

He nodded.

"Griselda told me it was clasped in Malcolm's hand when he was found after the murder. Thomas Blacklock gave it to her."

Davey blinked at Annie, frowning. "Malcolm had the ring?" he repeated slowly. He froze in deep thought for so long that Annie began to wonder if he had forgotten where he was or what he was doing.

She waited quietly until he roused.

"Come, Annie! What am I doing here like a statue? One would think I'm part of the ruins! Come, you must be my tour guide."

They entered a series of small, dusty chambers with tiny windows, or lookouts, high in the walls. Finally they passed through a door to a spiral staircase that brought them to a large room with good-sized dormer windows on both sides and a large, imposing fireplace at the end.

"I believe they called it the Great Hall," offered Annie. She stared at the high vaulted ceiling and ancient darkened timber carved in the elegance of a bygone day. "Can't you just see the great lords and ladies entering for a feast?"

"Ah, what I see," returned Davey grandly, "is you, Annie Mackinnon, entering on my arm! There we are—a fetching couple—and you the loveliest lady of them all!"

Annie laughed. "Now what I'm hearing from you is blarney all the way, Davey Morrison!"

"Nay!" stated Davey soberly. "You *are* a bonnie lass, Annie Mackinnon!" He folded his arms and held her with his eyes. "And I'm thinkin' I may be fallin' in love with you."

Annie, blushing in the shadows, could think of no suitable reply.

Davey stirred to sudden action. "Come! We've seen the Great Hall. Now let's find the great dungeon!"

Annie followed him out of the room thinking, *Aye, Davey Morrison and Scottish weather! Two of a kind!*

CHAPTER 26

Ready for the Fest

The large clock, imported from Jamaica by the Captain and standing on the Mackinnon mantel, struck the hour of three as Annie painstakingly pinned the lace on the hem of Meg's best dress.

"You must stand quite still, Meg, or we'll not be making it come out even. And stand up straight, too."

Meg drew herself up as tall as possible. "Oh, Miss Annie, I just thought I was about to clean die when I saw how it was hanging so dreadful. And then when Mama got out the lace from Great-Aunt Mabel, it was like a bolt of light pierced clean outta the heavens to light up my darkness!"

Annie smiled. "Meg," she scolded fondly, "do you mean to tell me the fest would have been ruined? Or that you wouldn't have been able to sing with Eppie and Liza?"

"Maybe not quite. But when a body knows she's not looking right, she cain't do her best. And the fest is one of my most favorite days what with ever'body all dressed so festive and banners and flags flying." Meg stopped to catch her breath and to frown. "Griselda said she wasn't going to sing 'John Highland

Man' with us, and sometimes she looks so sad on accounta Master Malcolm. But I think Master Malcolm wouldn't have wanted the fest to get ruined—him being so jolly and all."

"I think you're right, Meg. Only sometimes feelings don't do what we wish. Is Griselda at home with your ma?"

Meg shook her head. "She was going to go out to the lighthouse to see Master Jonathan. Seems like if Griselda gets all churned up inside, she goes out to the lighthouse."

"There now!" Annie stood back, eyeing Meg's hem. "Take it off, and you can start sewing the lace on where I've pinned." Annie analyzed the lace she still held in her hand. "I believe there's enough here to put a row on your apron."

"Oh, Miss Annie!"

"And give me your kerchief. There just might be a bit left over for that," said Annie, giving Meg reason to sigh with happiness.

Meg settled herself contentedly. "Miss Annie, didn't ye think at the funeral it was just the most surprising thing? I mean, of a sudden there was Liza right out in the middle of things, speaking out for Jesus!"

Annie continued her stitching. "Liza's a special little girl."

"And then I just almost couldn't believe when Master Thomas began singing and then the bagpipes and drums and practically ever'body was singing. It was like 'Amazing Grace' was everywhere!"

"It did change the flavor of things," Annie murmured.

"And all the way home Papa kept saying, 'Praise the Lord,' but Mama didn't say much exceptin' she thought maybe folks had got most carried away and they shoulda not done what'd make Miss Elphinstone powerful angry. It was kinda like Miss Elphinstone *owned* Master Malcolm's funeral and Master Thomas took it away from her. And ye know what? Nobody's seen Miss Elphinstone since!"

Annie finished the lace on the kerchief and gave it a little shake. "Whatever else," she commented thoughtfully, "it all gives one more than a bit to think about."

Annie sat quite still, pondering. She found herself again in the darkening Elphinstone garden, feeling the power of evil and the drama of Elvira's angry, flashing eyes.

And then in the midst of it all, Thomas Blacklock and little Liza Rafferty had shown like beacon lights! Thomas—timid, beaten by the circumstances of his life, to whom most folk paid scant attention. And Liza, the sturdy little daughter of the town's most drunken drifter. It was *these two* who were lights in the darkness, clearly surrounded by the Presence and power of Jesus.

Annie frowned. Nothing about their lives, either of them, was any seal or sign of pleasant circumstance. And yet their faces were lit with joy—coming from some sort of depth, a strength *within*.

Annie, still deep in thought, gathered her sewing things and laid them in her sewing basket. Thomas and Liza had the Presence of Jesus while she, Annie, had been looking for the gifts.

A gust of wind blew over the causeway to Reef Point Lighthouse, catching Griselda's bonnet and blowing it across the rocks. Scurrying, she retrieved it. She paused uncertainly. She was at the midpoint between Stonehaven and the lighthouse. It would be easy to turn back.

She had not seen Jonathan since the funeral, now almost two weeks ago. Perhaps it was time to talk to someone. She turned resolutely toward Reef Point and continued on, although not too quickly.

She needed to sort out her feelings with someone, and she felt more comfortable with Jonathan than with almost anyone else, possibly because Jonathan had chosen to confide in her.

She saw him ahead of her up on the catwalk. He waved and started down.

Shortly she found herself seated across the old oaken table

from the lighthouse keeper. "Kin I get you anything, Griselda? Tea? Maybe a biscuit, though I have to say they ain't the most fresh."

Griselda shook her head, and a silence settled into the room.

"It's been a strange kind of time, ain't it?" he asked finally.

Griselda stared hard at her hands folded on the table. "I'm not sure if I can think of things right in my head, let alone explain 'em to you."

"Want to try?"

She nodded. "Aye." Again quiet ensued as Griselda stared past Jonathan to the window, murky with clouds beyond. "I just get so tired of life sometimes," she sighed. "All the endless cooking and mending and helping Mama with the fish cleaning and curing. Seems like it never ends!" She paused and glanced at Jonathan apologetically. "It don't sound very helpful or Christian or anything."

"Sounds human," returned Jonathan.

"Anyhow, along come Malcolm like he was from a whole different world! Maybe I'm not sure if I was supposed to get quite so fond of Malcolm on account of I don't know if we looked at life the same way. Leastways, we never talked about anything that wasn't silly or fun. But he was so charming, I began waking up in the morning wondering what good thing was goin' to happen that day." She smiled ruefully. "Exceptin' when Fiona came around."

"She's one to be reckoned with, ain't she?"

"I have to work real hard sometimes to not hate her. Don't it sound awful? But if she hadn't hurt her foot—or pretended is what I think she did—Malcolm might still be alive."

"Aye," murmured Jonathan sympathetically.

"But ye know something, Jonathan?" Griselda's clear eyes looked into his. "I been going weeks and weeks with Papa to hear Brother Turner from Peterhead, and it's like 'specially since

Malcolm was killed, God has been playing Brother Turner's words over and over in my mind."

"That so?"

"Brother Turner said if we belong to Jesus, we ain't never walking around all by ourselves—even if it seems like it."

Jonathan wrinkled his brow. "Ye believe that?"

Griselda searched through her mind. "Aye," she said at last. "Papa keeps saying we don't have no choice about whether to live in a world where all sorts of hurtful things happen."

"No doubt of that," said Jonathan fervently.

"The choice comes in whether we're going to let Jesus walk *with* us in the pain of it."

Jonathan stared hard at her in silence.

"When I was a wee girl, I asked Jesus to come into my life—though it's been easy to forget about it as far as everyday things—ye know, *after* ye leave the kirk."

"So now?" prodded Jonathan.

"I been talkin' to Jesus as I go about and 'specially when I'm hurting real bad." She smiled ruefully. "Which is most of the time lately."

"Does it help you?"

"Aye. It helps not to be alone and to have someone with the power of Jesus listening to you. Sometimes if I still feel bad, I just got to grab on to him in faith. Papa's been helping me and reading Bible verses to me to hold on to."

Jonathan stood up. Thrusting his hands into his pockets, he strode back and forth before her. "Seems to me there's some things clean beyond even the Almighty!"

Griselda's eyes clouded. "Papa says nothing is. *Nothing*, Jonathan!"

Jonathan stopped pacing and slumped to the chair, his head in his hands.

Looking at the broad back and bowed head of her friend, Griselda was reminded that the lighthouse keeper carried a great burden as well, and her heart ached for him. "Will ye think about it?" she pleaded.

Jonathan sighed. "Aye."

"One more thing. Will ye get Charlie for the duty and come with me to the fest?"

"I'd not be good company."

"Please, Jonathan. I know Papa and Mama won't let me stay at home. Besides, Eppie and Meg and Liza would be crushed if we didn't hear them sing."

Jonathan smiled faintly. "Ye make a good case, Griselda. Aye, I'll come with you."

CHAPTER 27
The Fest

It looked to Davey as if every Scottish banner and flag imaginable fluttered in the breeze that swept across the village square. The only objects presently with more movement were Eppie and Liza, who cannonballed their way from one festive table to another, sampling as many of the offerings of Stonehaven's cooks as possible until their mothers bore down upon them and led them off to less gastronomical pleasures, fearing, no doubt, for their offsprings' stomachs.

Davey's eyes swept the tables laden with black pudding, mince pies, currant loaves, crumpets, and scones. If he did not have other things on his mind, he would be tempted.

Even the barques and square-riggers in the harbor joined the festive mood, with flags hung from their masts, though the sailors had deserted them for the amusements on shore.

A platform for a stage had been erected in the middle of the square, and around it harpers and fiddlers plucked at strings, and bagpipers and drummers tuned and warmed up.

On a grassy area next to the square, men and older boys played at hammer hurling and caber tossing. And everywhere the folk of Stonehaven, in their most festive garb, greeted one another, exchanged gossip, admired their young, and anticipated festal glories yet to come.

Ian Fraser, having deposited Fiona beside a table filled with baskets and flowers, moved toward Davey.

"Well, Davey," he said jovially, "how's it going?"

"I'm holding my own," returned Davey.

Ian leaned close. "Then best not to change a thing, my man, not even yer socks!" Ian laughed loudly and moved toward Rob Rafferty, whom he clapped on the back. "Rob Rafferty! 'Tis a fine day!"

"Hoot mon!" responded Rob. "Skies may be clearish for the moment, but me bones and me nose tell me a storm's brewing." He pointed. "See, yonder, them little harmless-looking puffs? Means a backing wind'll be starting any moment."

Rob Rafferty wandered off, looking his usual gloomy self, and Ian headed in another direction. Davey reflected that Ian appeared to be in an almost strangely good humor. Perhaps Fiona Elphinstone had finally promised to be his?

Jonathan hurried toward him. "Davey! Griselda and I've been looking all over for you." He waved an envelope. "Letter for you. Came in the last post."

Davey took it, glancing at it carefully.

"Looks official," commented Jonathan, obviously hopeful for information.

Davey put it in his pocket. "I'll read it later. By the way, how are things out at Reef Point?"

"Oh, about the same as usual, I'd say." Jonathan paused and frowned. "No, wait. There was something strange. I was cleaning the glass up in the tower yesterday—takes me a good three hours to do it—and when I come down again, sure as sure the lock on the closet where I keep the kerosene drum had been tampered with."

Every sense within Davey became alert. "Oh?"

"And night before last, Charlie, the one what spells me, Charlie was sure he heard strange noises outside. Calm night, too, so it warn't the wind. Never could find nobody though."

"Things like that ever happen before?"

"Can't say as they have." Jonathan pulled out his pocket watch. "Time's a-going, and I can't stay too long. I'd best go find Griselda. We promised we'd hear Liza and Eppie and Meg sing. Looks to me like Miss Annie's gettin' 'em ready over there."

Annie straightened Meg's kerchief. "You look lovely as can be, Meg. The lace we added is perfect. And Eppie and Liza—don't you both look festive!"

Eppie fairly danced up and down. "We're going to sing soon!"

"I can't wait to hear you," Annie reassured her. She glanced at Meg. "Meg—*Meg!* You've got that faraway look in your eye. What are you thinking about?"

Meg stared dreamily toward the sea. "I saw the prettiest little petrel bird. Flew off before I could get a good look. Had the cutest long legs. Petrels just look like they're dancing when they land on something!"

Rob Rafferty, passing by, leaned toward the little group. "Stormy petrel's a *sure* sign of bad weather," he intoned.

Annie gave Meg a hug. "Just don't you be flying off with any of them!"

"Come, come, girls." Duncan, the appointed master of ceremonies, cried. The three girls bounded onto the stage. "I think we're going to let Eppie tell you what they're going to sing. Eppie—"

Eppie drew herself up proudly. "We're going to do 'John Highland Man,' and it's written by Robert Burns."

As the girls sang, Annie glanced toward Davey, who stood a little distance away. They had talked—indeed, Davey had

183

accompanied her to the fest. He had been charming, as usual, but at times appeared preoccupied and almost distant. Now she watched him remove a letter from his pocket, scan it intently, frown, and shove it back into the jacket.

The girls finished their song with curtsies, followed by applause from the onlookers. Annie hugged them and then watched Liza run off to Thomas Blacklock, who hovered back by the market. As for Elvira Elphinstone, Fiona, when asked, had replied that "Auntie has taken to her bed with a dreadful headache." No wonder, thought Annie. She probably had not yet recovered from the confrontation with Thomas and the funeral's strange ending.

Duncan clapped his hands to gain the attention of the crowd. "Time for Ian Fraser and 'The Sheep-Shearing Song'! Find yer partners and make yer circles!"

Almost instantly Davey was at Annie's side, drawing her to where circles were being formed. Bagpipes and fiddles tuned up, and Ian, who had quite a decent voice, burst forth with

> *"Come now, step it along*
> *Cum t' bravely heel and toe*
> *Fill th' air with happy song.*
> *To the clippin' on we go!"*

This was met with much stomping, heel-and-toeing, twirling, circling, and the enjoyment of both participants and watchers.

"That was fun," exclaimed Annie, her cheeks flushed as she tried to catch her breath.

Davey smiled down at her. "Everything with you, Annie, always is." His eye was caught by the lighthouse keeper, who was standing close by, looking fixedly at the sky. "Jonathan?"

"Strange haze in the sky," he murmured. "Maybe things are a little too still."

"I told you! I told you!" proclaimed Rob Rafferty.

"Think I'd better get back to Reef Point." Jonathan started off. "Tell Griselda for me, Miss Annie," he called back over his shoulder.

Annie moved toward Griselda, who was being joined by Margaret, asking, "Now where's Meg?"

Annie shook her head. Meg gone *again?* It seemed no use to think that the child would *not* be lured to wander off—no matter how much she was admonished.

"I haven't seen her since her song with Liza and Eppie," answered Griselda.

Margaret looked alarmed. "Duncan!"

Duncan strode toward her. "Don't tell me Meg's gone off again."

"Well, I don't see her. Eppie! Where's Meg?"

Eppie pointed toward the harbor. "I seen her go that way."

"Don't worry," said Duncan. "She'll be back when she's ready."

"I'll go," offered Griselda. "I can always find her. Besides, a walk will do me good."

Margaret looked at the sky. "Gettin' some rain clouds yonder," she commented. Annie's eyes followed Margaret's. Dark clouds were moving in, and the air had taken on a yellow haze. A strange feeling of presentiment caught at Annie's heart, and she shivered, although the day was warm.

Duncan shrugged. "Well, we've warned her and warned her. If she gets soaked, that's the consequences!"

"Griselda'll find her, Mama." Eppie tugged at her mother. "Come, Mama, Miss Annie. Ian Fraser is about to tell one of his stories."

Annie settled herself between Eppie and Liza, who had joined them, but her eyes kept scanning the edges of the crowd for Meg and Griselda.

On the stage, Ian appeared to be in high spirits. "So," he boomed, "King Montcreiffe of the ancient royal house of Munster was done in—murdered! And then his wife, Queen Isobel, was taken out and *left*, mind you, on a rock out to sea to be *swept away* at high tide and drowned!" Ian paused and scanned his audience for desired effect.

"That's scary!" commented Liza.

"People was *awful bad* a long time ago, warn't they, Miss Annie?" whispered Eppie.

"Sometimes they still are," replied Annie solemnly.

"But!" proclaimed Ian. "Along comes me great-great-grandfather, Ronald Ritchie Fraser, on his pirate ship. And a fine pirate he was, too!"

Eppie frowned. "I thought pirates was always bad."

"He was handsome and strong, he was. And there warn't nothing he wouldn't do if he took a mind to it. He was on his ship, and he saw the rock over yonder." Ian pointed dramatically. "At first he thought he seen a mermaid on it. But when they got closer—thar she was, Queen Isobel—though he didn't know who it was at the time." Ian gestured with a flourish. "He ordered the ship at full sails as the tide was comin' in, and he managed to save the lady just before the waves was goin' to sweep over the rock!"

He paused and folded his arms grandly. "And the end of it is he married her! And that's how come I got a real queen for me great-great-grandmother!"

"Isn't it romantic?" sighed Eppie.

Ian motioned to the fiddlers, who immediately began to ready their instruments. "Ah, the pirate ships had a glory in them as the pirates sailed to riches or to death! And I'm dedicating this next song to me great-great-grandfather, Ronald Ritchie Fraser!" Ian swung with great gusto into a song of pirates on the high seas.

"Wisht I could be a pirate," sighed Eppie at the song's conclusion.

"I'd like to be a queen!" countered Liza. "How 'bout you, Miss Annie?"

Annie murmured something vague in reply. As jolly as it all was, she couldn't stop thinking about Meg.

Ian started down from the platform but stopped and grinned ebulliently. "The Frasers probably had more royalty in 'em than any other clan from these parts."

There was a stirring behind Annie as Davey stood up. "Indeed? Well, let me tell you of Clan Morrison!"

Ian raised his eyebrows. "Aye? Yer not but a hodgepodge of lily-livered dunheads with a yellow stripe running up yer plaid!"

Davey strode onto the stage, and Annie held her breath. "Lily-livered? At least we're not bouncing around the seaside falling in love with everything we see sittin' on a rock!"

Annie relaxed. Both men were smiling broadly and immediately launched into leading the Stonehaven folk in cheers for Frasers and Morrisons, ending with much hilarity and slapping each other on the back before they parted.

Hector, Ian's sheepherder, strode toward him. "Take a look at that sky, Ian. Don't look good. The sheep will shortly be running every which way."

Ian nodded. "Let's go." And they hurried off.

Margaret, too, was assessing the heavens. "Duncan," she said, "I don't like the looks of that sky. I wish Griselda would get back with Meg."

"Aye," commented Rob Rafferty, "she's gonna blow. That she is."

"I can't stay here! I've got to look, too." said Annie, starting off.

Just then Griselda appeared, looking disheveled and out of breath. When she caught sight of her mother, she ran toward her, dropping a small bundle she carried. She threw herself into Margaret's arms. Annie froze in alarm.

"Griselda," remonstrated Margaret, "where's Meg? Isn't she with you?"

But Griselda could only sob.

Duncan laid a hand on her shoulder. "Griselda! Ye must tell us!"

Griselda tried to swallow her sobs. "I went home, but she wasn't there—and then to the sea—"

"Ye should have *known* to go there first!" cried Margaret, distraught.

"Margaret!" scolded Duncan.

Griselda's eyes were wild. "I didn't catch sight of her anywhere, and then I ran toward Bull's Head Rock. The tide had already gone out, so I went down below it and—" She began to sob again as the villagers gathered around the little group.

Annie froze, panic washing over her. Not Meg! Not dear, sweet, dreamy-eyed Meg—as dear to her as if she were her own! Not swept out to sea! *Please, God—no!*

From the corner of her eye Annie saw that Eppie had picked up the bundle Griselda had dropped. "What's this?"

Duncan took it from her and shook out a torn, bloody cloth and a small scarf. Annie's heart contorted. Both contained the lace she had sewn on for the fest.

"It's Meg's!" screamed Margaret. "Meg's apron and her kerchief!" She covered her face with her hands and sank down upon the ground. Annie, shaking, fell on her knees beside her, her mind reeling with horror.

"Griselda!" Duncan ordered. "Where did ye get these? *Tell me!*"

"Below—below Bull's Head Rock."

"Come! There's no time to lose!" shouted one of the men. "Duncan, see if ye can find out anything more—then meet us at the Rock!" He ran toward the sea with at least two dozen of the men following.

Rob Rafferty shook his head as he followed more slowly. "I knew evil was a-comin'. It's the sea demons. I kin feel it."

Duncan turned his attention back to Griselda. "Go on, Griselda!"

Griselda's eyes were full of misery. "The clothes were caught on something in front of the rock. I picked them up and ran toward the water screaming and calling. But all I could see or hear was just the waves and the wind."

"She's gone!" shrieked Margaret.

Annie heard the words, saw the men as they ran. But she felt disconnected from it all. Instead she had been caught up and whirled into some awful dizzying pit where she only screamed, "*Meg! Meg!*"

Duncan knelt on the other side of Margaret. "Lord Jesus, keep her!" he cried in agony.

Margaret turned toward Duncan with sudden agonized ferocity. "Don't pray, Duncan! We're *alone!* God doesn't hear us!"

"Margaret," he remonstrated, "wherever she is—Jesus is with her."

"No! She's drowned!" sobbed Margaret. "I don't believe anything anymore. It's all lies! Lies!"

Duncan stood up. "Annie, stay with her. I've got to go." And he ran toward the sea.

Annie tightened her arm around Margaret. Frantically she searched her mind for something, *anything* appropriate to say. "Margaret, they'll find her—you know how plucky she is." Annie didn't believe her own words. But maybe, somehow, *saying* them would make them true.

"No! No!" shrieked Margaret.

Griselda and Annie helped Margaret to her feet. "We'll go home, Mama, and wait for news," said Griselda.

"I want to go to the sea," sobbed Margaret.

"No, Mama," said Griselda firmly. "The wind is going to come up worse. We'd best be home. That's where they'll be bringing her."

Annie watched the sorrowful group go, Eppie and Liza in the rear, clinging to one another. She was only dimly aware that in the crisis and prelude to the storm, the square was now nearly deserted. Darkness seemed to be closing in on her; there was nothing to which to cling. She thought fleetingly of Jesus, of his Presence, but *only* fleetingly, as her heart screamed within her. Her legs felt as if they were about to give way. She sank upon a nearby bench.

"Annie?" Davey's hand touched her shoulder. Heartsick as she was, there was comfort in his touch. "You love her very much," he said.

"Aye."

"They'll find her."

"I'm so afraid they won't!" She covered her face with her hands and began to cry great heaving sobs.

Davey dropped to the bench beside her and pulled her into his arms. Annie found herself clinging to him, his warmth, the feel of his strong arms about her. In her wracking fear for Meg it seemed only Davey could be a rock—a source of comfort. He held her, murmuring to her until her convulsive heaving subsided. "We *have* to believe she'll be all right," he said softly. He stroked her hair tenderly and sighed. "The day seems full of tragedy."

"There *can't* be anything more," she murmured.

"Shipwreck north of Liverpool."

Annie's heart skipped a beat. She sat up, rigid. "How do you know?"

"Jonathan brought me a letter. A three-masted schooner in the merchant marine came apart on the reefs, and all were lost."

Stark terror seized Annie. "The *merchant marine?* What ship? What was the name of the ship?"

"I don't remember." He fished the letter from his pocket and opened it.

Annie seized his arm in a frenzy. "Tell me the name of the ship, Davey!"

"Annie, if you're thinking of Donal—it can't be—"

"*Tell me!*"

He scanned the letter. "The *Brighton.* It was the *Brighton.*"

Annie rose. She backed away from him. "Donal!" Her voice sank to a whisper. "Donal's ship! All were lost?"

Davey stood. "Aye, but are you *sure*, Annie? Are you sure it was Donal's ship?"

She felt as if she were in a trance. She nodded woodenly. "It was Donal's ship."

Davey threw his arms around her. "Oh, Annie! I'm sorry!" He led her back to the bench and helped her sit.

Nothing seemed real. Everything about her blurred. "Why didn't they tell me?" She looked at Davey strangely. "Why did they tell you? You don't know Donal."

"A letter must be coming to you. I have a friend in the coast guard who writes me." Looking miserable, Davey knelt before her. He took her hands in his. "Oh, Annie! Please! Let me help you—somehow."

Annie stared at him, eyes glazed.

"I'll help you, Annie. Please!" Davey pleaded. "We'll see it through together—somehow."

"Where did it happen?"

"Off the coast of Cornwall."

His answer triggered Annie into a different frame of mind. She pulled her hands away and stood up. "Cornwall? On the reefs off the coast of Cornwall?"

"Aye," said Davey, looking puzzled.

Annie's eyes kindled in sudden knowing. Of course! It all fit together! "Wreckers! It was wreckers!"

"We don't know that."

"But we *do* know it!" she shrieked in near hysteria. "There are more of them in Cornwall than anyplace else! *You* know that!" She stopped and looked at him with new eyes. Things began to fall into place with sickening thuds—the questions, the evasions—she knew with a terrible comprehension that Davey, her last bulwark, her place of refuge, was not to be trusted. Her eyes blazed with anger and betrayal. *"You!* You know that! You've been going around Stonehaven asking your questions about wreckers. Why? Who are you, Davey Morrison? *Who are you?"*

"Annie, you're not thinking right—please!"

Annie turned and walked away a few steps. The frightful dawning continued. Had she not heard tales of so-called respectable people being part of a wrecking operation? Thoughts raced through her. She whirled back to confront him. "Revenge! That's what it is. You hated the Captain! You only pretend not to hate me. And you've killed Donal for revenge!"

"How could I kill Donal?" he cried.

"Because you're a part of it all—the whole cowardly, murderous bunch! You're part of the wreckers!"

Davey moved toward her. "Annie, upon my word—"

She backed away from him. "No! Don't touch me! You're not a friend, Davey Morrison! You're a revenge-seeking scoundrel!" She turned and fled into the gathering dusk.

CHAPTER 28

Thomas Pays a Visit

Thomas had been at the fest. He had heard Liza sing, had complimented her, and had gratefully slipped away.

He had never been comfortable with large gatherings, especially festive ones. Besides, he needed time to think about Elvira Elphinstone.

She hadn't been there. He was sure of this, as he had taken time to carefully scrutinize every area of the village square. Which meant she was more than likely at home.

He stopped by a bend in the road. His head ached, and he felt a weariness behind his eyes. It would be so much easier to just go back to his shed.

Nevertheless, with all the determination he could muster, he planted his feet firmly on the path to the Elphinstone manor.

The maid, Nora, answered the door. "You wish to see Madam? She's resting just now. However, I shall tell her you are here, Mr. Blacklock. Please wait."

Thomas waited, feeling lonely and strange, although the

house had become familiar enough as he dealt with Malcolm Donnovan's body and his funeral.

Presently, having been told that Miss Elphinstone would see him, he followed the maid down the long hall to the back parlor, feeling his dread grow with each step. By the time the maid swung the great mahogany door open, Thomas wished himself to be anywhere but where he was.

The maid left him, and there was nothing to do but enter.

A low fire in the fireplace cast its light on Elvira Elphinstone, who sat close by in an enormous chair, her arms resting on its sides. She reminded Thomas of a queen upon her throne. She was wearing black brocade and pearls, as she had at the funeral. Her expression was inscrutable.

"Well," she intoned, "Mr. Blacklock."

He nodded. "Good day to you." He moved diffidently to the center of the room, where he stood turning his hat slowly in his hands.

"I presume you have come to say something to me," she said finally.

"Aye."

"Say it then!"

Still he turned his hat. "Seems like it'd be a sight easier iffen I could sit."

Elvira's eyes flickered in disdainful amusement. "Then sit." She pointed to the appropriate chair on the other side of the fireplace.

Thomas sat, turning the hat and moistening his lips.

"You may place your hat on the floor," she said, as if to a child.

He dutifully did and followed that motion with an uncomfortable silence.

Finally Elvira stirred in her seat. "You may as well get your apology done with."

"Mem?"

"You did come for that purpose, did you not?"

Thomas tugged at his collar. "Nay, I dinna."

Elvira's eyes widened. "Indeed!"

Thomas coughed and cleared his throat. This was even harder than he had thought. He sent up a brief prayer for help and took a calming breath. Staring at the floor, he began. "I been reading in the Bible, and I come to where Jesus said, 'Ye kinna serve two masters—elsewise ye'll hate the one and love the other.'"

"Mr. Blacklock," said Elvira severely, "I fail to see why you should waste my time with quotes from your religious book."

"But ye see, mem," returned Thomas, feeling more courageous, "that's just it—the funeral, I mean. I wouldna want to go agin you or to bring distress to you, so I needed to tell you *why* I couldna read from yer book." For the first time since he began his "confession," Thomas looked directly at Elvira. "I been surprised the Almighty would want me, but I done give myself to Jesus on accounta he died fer me and loves me. So I kinna read from a book what has incantations to the devil."

He looked down at his hands and waited for the wrath of Elvira Elphinstone to fall on him. But when there was only silence, he finally looked up. She was gazing at him with a strange mixture of disdain and admiration. "I *paid* you, and you turned my funeral into a shambles!" she said. "However, your singing voice is . . . admirable."

He was about to mumble some word of thanks, but she cut him off. "A most foolish song, however! 'Amazing Grace'! What is *amazing* is that so many Scots sing it! I doubt they have an idea of any meaning in those senseless words."

"Mayhaps they'll be learning of its meaning," returned Thomas with an influx of courage.

Elvira picked up her cane, which leaned against the chair. She tapped it thoughtfully on the rug in front of her. "Tell me, Mr. Blacklock, does your Jesus approve of your spying activities?"

Thomas froze inside. How could she possibly know? After the

incident when the masked man had thrown him against the tree, he had only been to the forest once, at which time he was grateful he had had little to divulge. Thomas had done his best to push this involvement out of his mind, hoping that somehow time or circumstance would take care of the thing and hoping the Almighty understood the difficulties of extricating himself.

He stared in distress at the woman. "How is it ye—?" He fell silent. Could it be her well-known night walks? What did it matter how? She knew.

Elvira leaned forward, her eyes dancing in anticipation. "How does your so-called God feel about your involvement with a—" she paused—*"wrecking operation?"*

The color drained from Thomas's face. "Wrecking operation?" he stammered. "Wreckers?"

She smiled maliciously. "Aye."

"But—but they be violent! They pillage! They *murder!*"

"Surely you must have known *something* was afoot of which the law would not approve!"

Thomas got to his feet. "Then—there be no choice! We must be telling a sheriff—or—"

"Sit *down*, Mr. Blacklock!"

He slumped to the chair.

"Actually, it's a rather large and well-run operation."

"How are ye so sure of—of all of this?" he asked miserably.

Elvira stood. She drew herself up proudly, holding her cane before her. "I know *everything* that takes place in Stonehaven and its environs." She began to pace slowly back and forth in front of him. "Let us just say that I came upon this—this operation in the dark of the night. Normally, I might feel it my duty to report it." She smiled. "However, those involved felt it would be mutually helpful if in exchange for my silence and a bit of money now and again, they would give me items to add to my collections."

Thomas looked puzzled.

"Come here." Thomas followed her to a glass cabinet on the far side of the room. She pointed with her cane. "See there—ivory carvings from India. Worked silver from Philistia. And upstairs I have silks and tapestries from Damascus."

Thomas turned, walked back to the chair, and retrieved his hat. He stood regarding her earnestly, almost sternly. "How can ye live with yerself? Being involved in what's violent and murderous? Having what's *stolen* in yer house?"

"It is *you* who are not seeing this in true perspective. Any ship the wreckers lure in to reefs conveniently close to Stonehaven is in so severe a storm it would have been wrecked anyway—somewhere."

"I don't see it like that, mem."

She moved toward him until she stood quite close. Her eyes gleamed wickedly. "Ah, but you'd best see it *exactly that way*, Mr. Blacklock. For if you do *not*, you'll not live to give any allegiance at all to your God."

Clutching his hat, Thomas turned and bolted out and down the long hall to the front door.

He was shaking as he strode from the house. He had accomplished nothing by his visit except to find himself part of a wrecking operation. Why had she told him? He suddenly realized that Elvira Elphinstone had been *pleased* to reveal his involvement in such a notorious activity. She had reveled in watching him squirm. Was it revenge for the funeral? Or did she hate him anyway? Thomas supposed why didn't really matter.

He shuddered. What was he to do? To whom could he turn?

CHAPTER 29

Annie and Griselda

Griselda hurried out and down the path.

Davey had come to the Carmichael home with news of Donal's ship. He had said little and seemed anxious to leave. When Griselda had been bold enough to ask why he was not with Annie, he replied that he had done all he could.

And so she had left her mother surrounded by her grieving neighbors and set off, puzzled and worried.

Reaching the path to Annie's home, she quickened her steps. She noted that although late afternoon storm clouds had turned everything gray, no lamp shone from any window. A sense of foreboding settled over her.

She lifted the brass door knocker and let it fall with a thud. There was no answering movement within. She raised it again and rapped several times. Still nothing. She turned the knob, pushed the door open slowly, and stepped inside.

She stood motionless, listening. The large room, cast in deep shadows, was still and silent but for the ticking of a clock on the mantel. As still as death, Griselda thought.

She was about to turn away when she caught sight of Annie—sitting barely discernible in a deeply shadowed corner.

Griselda drew in her breath. "Annie?" There was no answer. She moved toward a small table on which was an oil lantern. "May I light the lamp? The sky is darkening so." There was no response. She fumbled with a small box, found a match, and lit the lamp.

She turned toward her friend, who sat on a high-backed chair, hands in her lap, immobile. "Annie?"

Annie's eyes flickered. "Why are you here?" she asked woodenly. "Have you news of Meg?"

"No. They're still searching—"

"Then what are you doing here? You ought to be with your mother."

"Annie—" Griselda crossed to the chair—"I had to see you! Oh, Annie! Davey told me about Donal. I'm so sorry!" She threw her arms around her friend.

Annie remained rigid. "There's nothing anybody can do."

Griselda knelt beside her. "I want to be with you, Annie. I want to help you. There must be something—"

Annie, staring straight ahead, seemed not to hear. "That monster out there—the sea. Every day I've feared it. Feared for Donal—and now it—it's happened. And Meg gone, too." Annie's eyes glazed. "Tomorrow I won't have to fear because there won't be anybody to fear for. And I've *nothing* to fear with. My heart's all gone."

"Oh, Annie!" Griselda had never seen her this way. It was as if she, too, had died.

Annie rose and took a few steps distractedly. "Donal was so fine and steady. He could stand straight and tall because his heart was honest and good. And he loved me, Griselda."

"I know. I know he did." Griselda found herself relieved to see Annie show some emotion—any emotion at all.

Annie stood very still. "I don't know how to—to get through it."

Griselda jumped up and threw her arms about her. "I'll stay by you. Go ahead and cry, Annie. It'll do you good."

But Annie turned away. "I can't. Something's all horribly dried up and sick inside, and I can't cry."

"Only Jesus can heal you, and he'd be wishin' for you to ask him," Griselda said softly.

"My heart is human! How would God know how I feel?" Annie returned, suddenly angry.

"Jesus knows. Even though he was God, he took a human heart so he could feel—suffer with us. Do ye think his heart bleeds and suffers for you any less now than when he was on earth?"

"How? How can Jesus help me bear it?" Annie cried in frustration.

"Because if ye have him, ye aren't walking around alone—ever. And he hurts right alongside you."

Annie slumped to a chair. "Do you really think he knows how I feel?"

Griselda searched through her mind desperately. *Please, Jesus,* she prayed, *give me the words to say!* "He was once deserted by everybody."

There was a long pause. "I'm all alone, Griselda. Everybody who could have been special has gone away—or been taken away— or—or turned out to be different from what I had thought." Annie's eyes were full of pain.

"I love you Annie." There seemed nothing left to say or do but to pray. And pray she did.

A silence settled into the room. The ticking of the clock on the mantel sounded louder than usual and its chimes mournful as it struck the hour.

Finally, Annie stirred. "You must go, Griselda. Thank you for coming—and caring. I need to be alone now. Please—go. And don't worry about me."

Griselda moved reluctantly toward the door. "I'll go, but I'll be praying and praying for you. And—I'm not leavin' you alone, Annie—because Jesus *is here,* and he's loving you and hurting for you."

Griselda closed the door softly as she went out.

Annie stared at the door through which Griselda had gone. The only sound was the ticking of the clock. She gazed about the room. She felt oppressed, closed in. Suddenly she could sit no longer.

She glanced out the window. There was only one place that had ever offered her any solace. There was still some light. Certainly enough to find her way.

She snatched up a shawl and went out.

CHAPTER 30

The Village Square

Griselda paced back and forth across the room. In one corner Margaret, with her apron thrown over her head, wailed piteously. Several women gathered about, plying her with comforting words and hot food—all of which she refused. Eppie and Liza watched from a wooden settee, silent, eyes wide and frightened. Duncan had not returned.

Along with terrible anguish over what she now believed to be Meg's fate, something else had been growing within Griselda— fright over what Annie might do. She had never seen her friend this way. What if in her despair Annie planned to harm herself? She should never have left her alone, even though Annie had told her to go.

She could not remain at home any longer. There was nothing she could do here. Annie needed her. She flew out the door and ran almost all the way back to Annie's house.

The lantern burned low in the parlor, but the house was empty. Could Annie have gone to Dunnottar Castle? A terrible place in the dark and storm and in Annie's present state of mind! Griselda knew she must find Davey.

The Wilsons'—she would go there. But when she arrived, all was dark and empty. *Where* could Davey be? She ran distractedly toward the village square.

Rounding the bend, she came upon Rob Rafferty standing in the middle of the square, staring at the heavens as lightning pierced the sky and rumbles of thunder grew louder. The storm was worsening.

"Rob Rafferty!" shouted a voice behind him.

Rob whirled about. "Jonathan! Hoot mon! Ye give me a start, ye did."

Griselda watched the lighthouse keeper race toward him, his coattails flying in the wind. He seized Rob's shirt in both his hands. "A man's got to do what he's got to do!" he bellowed.

"I'd not be stopping you—whatever it is."

Griselda ran toward them. "Jonathan, Rob, have ye seen Davey Morrison?"

"Naw," drawled Rob, smoothing his shirt and dusting himself off even while he eyed Jonathan in some puzzlement. "I ain't seen him. But I tell you what I *have* seen. Strange lights and shadows up to Dunnottar Castle, that's what. Lights movin' back and forth on the bluff. It's a night for the sea demons, it is!"

"I can't find Davey—at the Wilsons' or—"

Rob shoved his hands in his pockets and rocked on his feet. "Well, it's the kinda night fer folks to be vanishing, it is."

"Please, Rob, would ye be finding him for me?"

"Heh! Where to be looking I dinna ken. But fer you, Griselda, I'll try me best."

"Tell him to come quick. I'm worried about Miss Annie!"

Rob Rafferty took off at a fairly good clip, muttering, "Sea demons is busy, they is!"

Griselda turned her attention to Jonathan, who was pacing back and forth. His clothes were rumpled, and he raked his big hands through his hair till it stood on end. Altogether his appearance, augmented by storm and wind, was definitely wild. Suddenly she realized how strange it was for him to be there. Was the whole world upside down? "Jonathan! Why are ye not at Reef Point? Is it Charlie has the duty?"

"Naw. He's gone for supplies."

"Then why are ye here? It's a storm besides!"

Jonathan looked at Griselda as if seeing her for the first time. Slowly he shook his head. "The lighthouse—it ain't no use."

Griselda gaped at him. Jonathan was often enigmatic—sometimes strange. But something about him tonight alarmed her. "What can ye mean?"

"Ship's passing soon, round Kinnaird's Head Reef."

"Then why are ye *here?*" she asked in exasperation.

Jonathan gazed at her with glazed eyes. "I tell you, Griselda—it don't make any difference—I got to do what I must do!" He paused as if he were listening. "In the dark and the storm I hear them calling me."

"I know! I know you do, but *what about the lighthouse?*"

Lightning lit the square, and loud rumbles of thunder rolled in from the sea. Jonathan stood quite still, regarding her earnestly. "Griselda, ye've been a good friend to me."

"Aye."

"And ye know about me what no one else knows—"

"Aye." Griselda moved a step closer. "And I promised you I'd not tell it to a living soul."

"While I live ye'll not tell it."

"I promise."

"When I die, ye can. May chance it'll take away some of the guilt."

"Jonathan, ye are *not* going to die!" cried Griselda, wondering how much more agony she could absorb on this awful night.

"A man must do what he must do."

"What is it ye speak of?" she asked frantically.

Jonathan frowned. He looked toward the sea, now only a dark mass. "Guilt is such a thing it eats away at a man like the waves eat at the shore."

Griselda tugged at him. She had to make him understand! "But if ye pray to God to forgive—"

His voice rose to an agonized pitch. "Some things is *done!* And the print of it will always be."

"Jonathan! Ye must listen to me. There's nothing—*nothing* that's too much to be forgiven. Jesus'll hear you."

"I hope ye may be right." He pulled away and started off, but stopped. "Griselda, remember I love you as if ye were me own daughter."

The night swallowed him, leaving Griselda alone. She stood uncertainly, her head pounding. The day had started as normally as any day had since Malcolm's death. Then, so suddenly, the festive air in the village had turned tragic with Meg's disappearance— and now Annie's Donal. Griselda looked toward the sea but could only hear wind and the crash of waves. It was all too horrible to contemplate.

Rob Rafferty materialized out of the darkness. "Griselda, I've looked, but I ain't seen Davey Morrison nowheres."

Just then Duncan appeared from the other direction. Griselda ran toward him gratefully. Surely he would know what to do! "Have ye seen Davey Morrison?" he shouted.

"I tell you," replied Rob Rafferty, "folks has been running in and outta the square like so many minnows in a bucket. But him I've not seen—and can't find."

Duncan was wild-eyed and out of breath. "Go! Round up the men of the village! There's work to be done!"

"Hoot mon! Ye best be catching yer breath and tell me what."

"Is it Meg?" cried Griselda.

Duncan put his hands on his hips, breathing hard. "Nay. She's not been found. But now the light's out! Reef Point Light is out!"

"It's never out!" Griselda gasped.

"It is now. Someone blew up the fuel drum—or lightning struck it. But it's out. And if any ship's out there, she'll wreck herself in this storm with no light."

"Then what's to do about it?" asked Rob Rafferty.

"Reef Point's past help for now. And I'm afraid—afraid my Meg is, too." His eyes filled with tears. "But we can do our part to see that no ship's lured in to wreck herself on the reefs!"

"What can you mean?" cried Griselda.

"Wreckers!"

"*Wreckers?*" Griselda's head spun. She had heard tales of murder and pillage but not near Stonehaven.

Rob Rafferty scratched his head. "That's serious business!"

"I haven't wanted to think it," said Duncan, "but tonight I saw lights moving up on the bluff by Dunnottar Castle."

Rob nodded vigorously. "I seen 'em! I been tellin' you I see 'em, but folks don't pay me no mind."

"Go!" directed Duncan. "Find who ye can. Bring yer pistols. We'll meet this side of Bull's Head Rock. Go!" he shouted. "Fast as ye can!" He turned to Griselda. "Griselda, the storm's going to be a wild one—"

"Papa! Please *listen!* Annie found out Donal is lost at sea! I'm worried about her. She's acting strangely. I'm afraid she's gone up to Dunnottar Castle! It's where she always goes when she feels bad."

Duncan shook his head miserably. "How much more can *any* of us take? Go home, Griselda. I'll look for Annie—if I can." And he left as quickly as he had come.

"If there's wreckers up there, the sea demons is helping 'em, sure as sure," Rob declared firmly. Then he ran for all he was worth.

Griselda stood uncertainly in the square as lightning flashed around her. Her mind whirled with questions. And with fear. *Oh, Annie! Meg! Reef Point Light is out! And what did Jonathan mean—"A man must do what he must do"?*

CHAPTER 31

Storm on the Bluff

The night wind from the North Sea blew furiously over Dunnottar's bluff. Annie pulled her shawl more tightly about her as windy gusts pulled her hair into wild wisps and tugged at her skirts.

Her head and heart had pounded as she had made the precarious descent followed by the arduous climb upward. But this time the physical exertion had not diminished the pain in her heart.

Below, to her left, lay Stonehaven, shadowy, with only pinpricks of light here and there. Farther to the north, Reef Point Lighthouse was illumined only occasionally by a moon that fought a losing battle with gathering clouds.

Reef Point Light was out. No reassuring beam swept the turbulent sea. Annie noted this. At any other time it would have been the cause of wild alarm. But not tonight. Tonight the storm within her caused everything else to pale in significance, for to the other losses of her life was now added that of Donal, her son so fine and strong. And Meg too. Meg's body was somewhere out there, tossed by the cruel sea.

She reeled about as if forsaking the sea could blot out the appalling visions in her mind. As she did so, the ruins of Dunnottar Castle rose before her—shadowy, massive, and mysterious against the starless sky.

Another pang shot through her. It was here, by the castle, that Davey Morrison had confronted her, had revealed the strange and terrible secret that had become a bond between them. Davey, warm and charming, who had finally won her friendship and perhaps her heart as well.

Now even that was over. Davey was no more than a revenge-seeking scoundrel!

There was *nothing* left in her life to hang on to—to trust in. Her childhood faith, her mother's words, the Presence of Jesus—all seemed long ago and far away.

She whirled back to the sea, dreadful now in a roar of wind and waves. Clouds had covered the moon, leaving a yawning, awful dark. She moved closer to the edge of the bluff. Her heart was at one with the black chasm before her. If there was a God, he certainly was not *here* and had nothing to do with *her*. Perhaps there was only one way to end the horrible pain within—

Her eye caught a moving light to her right, on the bluff. She peered through the darkness. No, there were two lights—lanterns. A sudden flash of lightning illumined the scene. A mule with two lanterns tied to it was being led by a man. Two others walked beside him. They had been walking away from her but now turned the mule and moved in her direction.

Annie drew in her breath and froze at the sudden, terrible realization. *Wreckers!*

CHAPTER 32

A Decision

Elvira, lifting her long skirts, strode steadily through the night southward over the Bervie Braes. She was not intimidated by the storm that worsened by the moment. On the contrary, its very wildness energized her, warmed her blood, quickened her anticipation.

Finally she stood on the bluff looking across the chasm to Dunnottar Castle, her dark cape streaming in the wind behind her. The great sentinel was lit periodically with lightning flashes against the turbulent storm clouds. But it was smaller lights for which she sought.

Then she saw them—two lights moving along Dunnottar's bluff in the distance.

Abruptly the rain came sweeping toward her over the landscape. She pulled her cape around her and its hood over her head. She nodded in satisfaction, turned, and hurried back the way she had come.

Thomas Blacklock sat on his cot, his knees drawn up, holding his head in his hands. The drumbeat of rain on the roof, punctuated by crashes of thunder, seemed only to echo the storm within him. How long had he sat thus as anguished thoughts assailed him? He did know his misery grew with the passing of time.

His horse, outside under a rough lean-to, whinnied in fear. Perhaps he ought to bring Blacky inside.

An urgent rap sounded at the door. Thomas's heart lurched.

He opened it to find a tall black figure dripping in the rain. Elvira pushed past him without invitation. He shut the door only to block out the din of the tempest.

Elvira regarded him, her expression unfathomable. "It's *time*, Mr. Blacklock."

Alarm rose within him. "Mem?"

Her lips curved in a malicious smile. "You may now *prove* where your loyalties lie!" Her eyes lit as she spoke in a rapid-fire staccato. "A wrecking operation is under way. Now." She motioned with her head. "Out there, in the streets, the pitiful foolhardy are making ready to launch some sort of foray against the wreckers. It's time for you to fight *for* the wreckers."

Outside, the horse gave a dreadful whinny.

Elvira pinned him with her eyes. "And don't even *think* of going for help. The road between here and Kilamon will be a raging river." She moved closer. "Moreover, if *any* disloyalty on your part surfaces, *you* will end up *in* a coffin rather than building them."

She marched out the door, slamming it behind her.

Thomas stood in the middle of the shed, his heart pounding. "Oh, God!" But could God hear him? Could he? "Ye be telling me!" he cried out. "What's a man to do?"

Rain drummed on the roof, and the wind slammed a loose shutter. But it seemed he could hear Liza's soft voice, see her earnest, trusting eyes. He thought of Ninian's heroic climb to Dunnottar's unknown dangers. And he heard those in the curing shed lift their voices: *Child of weakness, watch and pray. Find in me thine all in all.*

"Dear Jesus," he prayed, "I got nobody to hang on to exceptin' yerself!"

Abruptly he grabbed a heavy jacket and went out. In blinding rain he saddled his horse.

Then he mounted Blacky, pointed the horse's nose westward, and galloped off through the downpour in the direction of Kilamon.

CHAPTER 33

The Long Night

Annie fought through a haze of terror as she was propelled along a dark passageway within Dunnottar Castle by a man she could scarcely see and did not know. He held her arm in a grip that sent shooting pain into her shoulder and down to her fingertips. The lantern he carried cast bizarre shadows over the walls and only added to the unreality of the night.

She wondered if she were having a nightmare. If only she could waken! Her mind reeled with the horrors of the day, unable to sort out Donal's death, Meg's drowning, the perfidy of Davey Morrison, and this last horror—wreckers at work at Dunnottar and their seizure of her on the bluff. What fate did the present hold? She cried out in panic and yanked at her arm. But in vain.

Her unknown captor paused before a great wooden door. He put the lantern on the floor and fumbled with the bolt. It finally slid, and the door swung back slowly on large rusty hinges.

Annie was thrust roughly inside. She fell to her knees as the door swung back and was bolted. Footsteps faded down the hallway. She covered her face with her hands and shook violently. Was she in utter darkness?

There was a small skittering sound behind her, and she leaped to her feet, her heart thudding. Who knew what creatures might be close at hand?

A flash of light illumined the darkness, and she caught sight of an opening at the far side. It must be toward the sea, as the sound of wind and waves came from that direction. More lightning flashed, followed by faint light from the opening. But as her eyes adjusted, she knew she was in a vaulted dungeon—the one famous for its prisoners of a long-ago day.

She moved warily along the dirt floor. Reaching the long, low window, an indistinct mass of black sky and sea seared by intermittent lightning flashes met her view.

She leaned out momentarily. It was a sheer drop to the sea. She thought irrationally of screaming for help. But no one would hear, and if they did, what good would it do? Or jumping to her death. Hadn't that been her thought on the bluff?

Her eye was caught by a pile of rags on the floor in a corner to her left. As she peered at them, the rags moved. She stifled a scream.

There was a soft moan, and an arm flung up as a figure turned on its side. With her heart in her mouth, Annie watched, scarcely daring to breathe.

Then came a flash of sheet lightning. No! It couldn't be! Annie moved closer and fell to the floor on her knees beside the figure. "*Meg!*" She touched her arm gently. "*Meg! Oh, Meg!*"

Meg moaned. Her eyes flew open, full of terror. She sat bolt upright, and gaped at Annie. "Miss Annie?" she asked, incredulous.

Annie threw her arms around the young girl. She rocked her back and forth, trying to deal with this latest astonishment. "Oh, darling! My darling girl!"

Tears flowed down Meg's cheeks. "Oh, Miss Annie, it's so terrible. I been so scared."

"We thought you'd drowned. I thought you were gone. Oh, Meg! Meg!" Annie sobbed.

"I didn't think anyone would ever come for me."

Annie continued to rock her and stroke her hair. The night had been horrible, but Meg was alive. *She was alive!* "I'm here! I'm here!" Finally Annie gently held Meg at arm's length. "Meg, *how* did you get *here?*"

"Well," began Meg, still sniffling, "I saw a stormy petrel, and I followed it. I *know* ye said not to, but I was only going to go a little ways—I know I lose all track of time. And when I couldn't see it anymore, there was the sea all laid out starting to churn in the wind. And the sky just looked like it was coming right down to the water."

Annie shook her head gently. "Oh, Meg!"

"So I went along past Bull's Head Rock close to the bluff 'cause the tide was coming in, and then I got scared 'cause the waves was closer."

"Aye. And then?"

"I got to the rock the castle's on, and I knew there was this little cave in the rock. Eppie and Liza and I found it a long time ago. So I went in, and at the back behind some brambles is a little door. Ye can hardly see it. I pushed at it, and there was stairs what went up and up. So I went up 'cause I knew the tide couldn't get to me."

"And you found you were in Dunnottar Castle!"

Meg nodded. "And when the stairs stopped, there was a passage-way and a great door, and there was this room. And, Miss Annie, it had all sorts of strange things and boxes of brocade cloth—and jewelry—and then—Oh, Miss Annie!" Meg began to sob.

Annie stroked her hair lovingly. "It's all right, Meg. I'm here."

"All of a sudden some men came—and they grabbed me and brought me here and said I couldn't go home."

Annie pulled her close. "But you're alive, darling! We thought you'd been swept out to sea! Griselda found your apron and kerchief all torn, out by Bull's Head Rock."

Meg's eyes took on a knowing look. "The men took them and said they'd fix it so no one would come for me."

Annie's eyes searched Meg's earnestly. "Did they hurt you?"

"No. They left, and no one's come back. But sometimes I hear running and voices." Meg stopped and frowned. "Miss Annie, how did ye know to come here for me?"

There was a sound of footsteps and of the bolt being pulled back. Annie reached for Meg and froze.

The door opened, revealing a tall man with a lantern. His silhouette looked strangely familiar. He swung the lantern before him, peering into the darkness. It was Ian Fraser! Relief washed over Annie.

"Ian!" she cried, hardly daring to believe it was true.

"Master Ian!" shrieked Meg joyfully. "Take us home!"

Annie, grasping Meg's hand, almost ran toward him. "Ian, thank God you've come! How did you know?" There had been one miracle this astounding night. And here was another—

"Ye should never have come to Dunnottar," said Ian evenly.

"I know, I know! Please take us out of this awful place."

"But ye did come," he continued without moving. "And now there's no other way but that ye'll not be going home—*not ever!*"

Annie gaped at the sheepherder in astonishment. Then cold fear poured over her. "Ian, surely you—no!" she stammered. "You cannot be—be—part of the wreckers?" she ended almost in a whisper.

Ian's face broke into wicked merriment. He chuckled. "Not *part* of the wreckers, Miz Annie. I *run* the wreckers at Dunnottar Castle!"

Annie gazed at him, horrified. Ian a wrecker! Ian—genial, dependable, going about his sheepherding! Did Fiona know? Her stomach churned. How could such an appalling thing be? But it would explain the connection between Fiona's necklace and the ring that Malcolm held when he died. Treasure from wrecked ships! And Ian head of a wrecking operation! She felt momentarily dizzy.

Without warning, Davey Morrison stood in the doorway behind Ian. Annie gasped and clutched Meg in terror. If there was one person in all the world she could not bear to see, it was Davey—Davey who had betrayed her, who was a part of this whole ghastly business.

Davey strode toward them, a pistol in his hand. Ian whirled about. With a deft motion, Ian yanked Annie in front of him, pulled a pistol from his pocket, and pointed it at Annie. "Don't take another step, or Miz Annie here'll be dead!"

Davey stopped.

"And drop yer pistol! *Drop it!*"

Davey's pistol thudded on the floor.

"Davey Morrison!" snarled Ian sarcastically. "Sailor, are ye? Want to sign onto a fishing ship, do ye?" He laughed long and loud. "I know ye, Davey. I know who ye are! Agent sent by the coast guard to snoop about fer wreckers hereabouts, ain't ye? Well, much good it'll do you—or anyone else—because now ye'll *die!* Ye'll die with the rest of 'em!"

Annie's eyes blurred. Would the terror never end? Davey was *not* a wrecker! He had been sent to Stonehaven to *investigate* wreckers. But a pistol was pointed at her head. She felt a sudden terrible dizziness and nausea. The dungeon reeled, and she slumped into unconsciousness.

Annie crumpled, which distracted Ian momentarily. Davey sprang toward him.

"Hold it, Davey Morrison!" a new voice bellowed from the doorway. It was Hector, Ian's sheepherder. He moved toward Davey, his gun pointed, as Ian picked up Davey's pistol, which still lay on the floor. Ian watched in satisfaction as Hector seized Davey's shirt and roughly shoved him backward and to the ground. "Now stay there, will ye! We got enough to do out there without fussing with you in here!"

Davey, breathing hard, took the measure of the present situation. Several feet away, he could see Annie stir and try to sit. That was a relief. Meg ran to her, and the two sat huddled on the floor. If only there were not *two* men with guns! He could at least buy time by getting them to talk. He eyed Ian. "No doubt it was *you* who murdered Malcolm!"

Ian's lip curled in malicious satisfaction. "Malcolm Donnovan got too close to what he hadn't oughta. We took care of him and then carried him back down to where he began his walk—and where he oughta stayed!"

"How can you call yourselves men and do what you do?" Davey hissed.

Ian laughed derisively. "Men? What is a man but to get what he wants! Ye can sit about in here twiddling yer thumbs and thinking about yer inspector business. We got work to do."

"Work?" Davey said derisively. "Sheepherders are you?"

Ian smiled. "Oh, we get a little sheepherding in on the side. But listen to me, Davey. The end result of our *real* work is in the storeroom yonder. All kinds of stuff to sell when we move it little by little into the cities."

"Can't be just the two of you."

"Oh, I got me select group coming in from Huntley and Aberdeen." He turned toward the door. "Come on, Hector."

Davey cast about wildly in his mind for some way to stall Ian or tap into some kind of conscience. "Ian! How can you betray the people who've trusted you? What about Fiona! Isn't there some decency in you somewhere?"

Ian paused. "I should stand about diggin' into me inner soul for you?"

"You must have feelings," said Davey more gently.

Ian walked back and squatted in front of him—close but out of reach. "I'll tell you the truth, Davey. First time there was a wreck and I heard them pitiful cries and screams, me innards felt a mite bit squeamish. But I come to get used to it. And now it don't mean *nothing* to me but *treasure*."

"There's other kind of treasure, Ian. Things not gotten by pillage and killing."

Ian narrowed his eyes. "Oh, but there's something downright exhilarating about this!" His eyes glowed with excitement. "Listen— I'll tell you! Right now my men are walkin' a mule back and forth beside the castle, with lanterns tied to it. And out yonder—" he gestured grandly—"on the high seas, a ship's heading in. And there's *no light at Reef Point*."

"Your work, too, no doubt."

"Let's just say 'twas Rob Rafferty's sea demons a-helpin' us," he laughed.

"Fiend!" Davey's blood was boiling. It was no use to reason with a man this far bent on evil.

Ian strode back and forth in good humor. "Anyway, as I was saying, the ship's a-comin', and it's a boiling storm out there— black as the ace of spades! We don't need to do no moon cussing tonight. The ship thinks she's sailing toward another ship. But I tell you—she's gonna come apart on them reefs out there!" He moved to stand over Davey and spoke in measured tones. "And we'll take care of the rest of it." He motioned toward Hector, who kept his gun trained on Davey. "Ain't that right, Hector?"

"You're beasts!" yelled Davey.

Ian deliberately picked his teeth. "Cain't let nobody escape that could tell a tale somewheres else. Whether they're floating in on a ship's beam, screaming, or jest sittin' inside Dunnottar's dungeon."

Hector shifted on his feet. "Ian, time's goin'. We better go."

"Aye, ye're dead right. Why am I standin' around in here? Guess I never had such a captive audience before!" he sneered.

Terrible rage poured over Davey. He jumped to his feet and lunged toward Ian shouting, "Beast! You're a beast, Ian Fraser!"

Hector almost instantly grabbed him from behind, pinning his arms.

Ian grabbed his shirt until they were eyeball to eyeball. "Listen to me, Mister Inspector Davey Morrison! We're going to be done with you!"

Davey saw it coming. Ian swung at him with his gun, knocking Davey to the floor.

Thomas hung over his horse as sheets of rain pounded him mercilessly. Under him rippled the powerful muscles in the great animal's shoulders and withers as Blacky pounded over the dirt road. Scrubby pines bent in the wind. Ahead of him thick fog hung over moor and heath, outlined intermittently by the lightning.

Thunder occasionally blotted out the sound of the horse's hooves. Or was it the drumbeat in his head? He had unwittingly become part of a wrecking operation. But was he really so innocent? Hadn't he known something evil was afoot? And Ian Fraser. Ian Fraser was the masked figure who had met him in the forest. He had become sure of it at the fest when Ian had begun his story—even as he tried to push it from his thinking. The voice, physique, even the almost overly confident bravado had told him.

He tugged at the reins and dug his heel into the right flank, nudging the horse southeast over the brae toward Kilamon. His sodden clothes clung to his thin frame, and he shivered. The downpour lessened, but no star shone; and in the gray mist he thought he could see a strange blackness moving toward him in the thick fog. It seemed to float. Was a black cape streaming behind it? *Elvira Elphinstone!* "Nay!" he said aloud through his teeth. He could not think of her! Could not think of her threats. *Only Kilamon.* "Please, God," he breathed. "Ye be gettin' me there."

The rain had begun again full force as they reached the crest and began the descent to the road below. It stung his eyes, and he closed them and shook his head to free his nostrils.

With a sudden whinny, Blacky jolted to a stop while Thomas made out the sound of rushing water over the din of the rain. The road to Kilamon that lay before them had become a torrent of river. Somehow they had to cross it. The road wound about the heath. They would have to go up the moor and over to the other side.

The rushing river continued as far as he could see on either end before disappearing in fog and rain. There was no time to lose. The water before him looked murky and indistinct, but it could not be that deep.

He leaned forward, caressing the wet mane and patting the horse's throbbing neck. "Blacky, we got a job to do here. Ye got to get through to the other side. Come on now." He moved in the saddle and gave a light dig with both his heels.

Blacky put his head down and took a tentative step. Thomas dug his heels harder. "Come on, Blacky! Ye do it! Ye do it for me—and for Liza. Come on, boy."

The horse moved forward, seemingly with more determination. "That's it! That's it, boy! Go! Go!" Thomas urged.

The water rose to his boots. And to his knees. Then with a sudden jerking motion the horse lost its footing and fell. The reins were torn from Thomas's hand as he went under. The current yanked and pulled at him. He struggled up, gasping and sputtering. Fighting the rush of water, he dragged himself to the other side and up onto rocks and mud. A dozen yards to the south he saw the horse haul itself onto wet but surer footing.

"Blacky!" he yelled. But the wind tore the sound from his mouth.

An enormous crash of thunder rent the heavens. With a dreadful whinny the horse bolted and almost immediately disappeared in a gray wall of fog.

"*Blacky! Blacky!*" Thomas screamed. But there was only the mist and the moor and the rain. And the river that tore through the gully beside him.

Annie had screamed into clenched fists as Ian hit Davey. She felt as if her heart would stop as he slumped to the floor and lay silent and still. Thoughts tumbled wildly. Perhaps he was dead. She would not be able to bear that. She could never ask forgiveness for not trusting him. He had given her friendship, and she had thrown it away. How could she have been so horrible to him?

Annie held her breath as the door closed behind the two men and the bolt slid into place. She ran to Davey and knelt beside him. "Davey—"

"Is he dead, Miss Annie?"

"Davey—can you hear me?"

"He moved a little."

"Aye, he did! Davey? Please, please be all right!"

Davey stirred and gave a low groan. He opened his eyes. Relief poured over Annie. She stood up, clasping her hands tightly, feeling as if something in her heart were going to break loose. She turned away, and the tears began to come.

THE LONG NIGHT

Meg's voice behind her seemed far away. "Master Davey! We were so afraid for you. We thought they might kill you."

"Meg—what? Ian? Hector?" he mumbled.

"They're gone. They left the lantern, but the door's slammed and bolted."

"Curses!" There was a silence. "Annie?"

By this time Annie was shaking violently with silent sobs. The pent-up emotions of the day washed over her, and she felt as if she might shatter into pieces.

Davey staggered to his feet. "Annie, did they hurt you?"

"No."

"Thank God for that!"

She turned toward him slowly. How could she talk to Davey about *anything*? She had not trusted him. And here he was in this awful situation because of her! "I'm sorry. I couldn't cry before— about—anything! And now—I can't stop."

He came to her, unsteadily. He took her hands in his. "Don't try. You need to cry."

"Don't be nice to me," she said, pulling away.

"Why?"

"You must hate me."

"I could never do that."

"But—after all I said—what I called you?"

"It was a terrible time for you. I understood that."

"You asked me to trust you."

"You couldn't know."

"I'm sorry—"

"Annie—Annie, it's all right—it is." Suddenly Davey's strong arms were around her, pulling her close. She felt the strong beating of Davey's heart and clung to him. If only she might stay there in his arms and never have to deal with other miseries. Her sobbing began again, but more gently.

225

When she regained control, he released her. She wiped at her eyes. "What made you come?"

"Griselda found me. Your house was empty, and she was worried about you. I knew you would have gone to Dunnottar. By that time I also knew mischief was afoot up here. So I ran—and prayed all the way."

"What's going to happen to us?" asked Meg.

"There's nothing to do but wait," Davey returned thoughtfully.

Meg pulled the rags and old blankets closer to the window opening. She dropped down upon them.

Davey brought the lantern. "Come and sit, Annie. At least there's some fresh air to be had in this dank place." A faraway sound of fighting erupted.

Annie stared at them miserably, wearily. In the turbulence of her thoughts, one thing was clear. They were all going to die—she and Davey and Meg. What did it matter that Davey had forgiven her and Meg was alive? *We're still going to die!*

She dropped down beside them, trembling. "Davey, what are we going to do?"

He looked away and was silent for so long that she wondered if he'd heard. Finally he said, "*This*—what we face now, when we can't do *anything*—makes one look at things differently." He raked his hands through his hair. "Two months ago I was bitter, determined to cling to nothing! Now—I'm caught up short. And I'm hearing some of the things Duncan has been saying to me."

"Papa prays for you every night, Master Davey," said Meg.

Davey nodded thoughtfully. "I'm tired of being a rudderless ship going nowhere." He spoke slowly, "I feel like God's been calling to me. I feel like he's been saying, 'Davey, I know you! *Where* can you flee from my Presence?'"

Meg stirred. "I'm scared, too. But if—if something bad happens, Papa says Jesus'd pick me up in his arms and carry me because I'm his child and he loves me."

Annie, watching her, thought Meg's face beautiful in the lantern light. And it seemed to her the look was the same as that of Thomas and Liza at the funeral. The funeral yard—dark and foreboding. And now—here—the dungeon—ominous with violent portent.

Suddenly she heard the words of her mother—words of long ago. "Lassie," her mother had said, "when all is said and done, Jesus is all ye need. And it may be that ye'll not be findin' that out until *Jesus is all ye have!*"

Jesus was all that Liza and Thomas had. And Meg. She clasped her hands as tears rolled down her cheeks. "Jesus' voice has been calling out to me through my darkness—through my pain. I *know* he has—and mostly I've ignored it and—and looked for good and happy gifts—not Jesus *himself.*"

Abruptly, not caring what Davey or Meg did or thought, she found herself on her knees, murmuring softly to Jesus—the Presence she had so long neglected. When she was done, she looked up through tears. "I'm still frightened," she whispered, "but I know I'm not alone."

Meg threw her arms around her. "Maybe the wreckers are like the devil and superstitions and all the things that keep folks mixed up. And Jesus is the *light* in the lighthouse, calling to us out of the storm."

Davey clasped Annie's hand in his and reached out for Meg. "Listen to the words, Annie, Meg.

'Whither shall I go from thy spirit? or whither shall I flee from thy presence? . . . If I take the wings of the morning, and dwell in the uttermost parts of the sea; Even there shall thy hand lead me, and thy right hand shall hold me.'

When he had finished, the three sat quietly as the words echoed in their hearts—unaware of the sound of waves and storm and fighting—sensing that here or in the uttermost part of the sea, the Presence of Jesus was with them—that they would be *led*, would be *held* by him.

Ian Fraser, standing on Dunnottar's bluff outside the castle, held a loose hood over his head, shielding himself from the rain.

He glanced briefly to the side where Hector stood guard over the ragged figure who walked the mule back and forth, its odd lights swinging innocently against the animal's flanks in the darkness.

But his eyes sought the sea, restless in waves that rose in foaming ribbons to crash and swell again. Then he saw them— two tiny lights far out—lights that dipped and were lost to sight and then rose once more. His pulse quickened as a predator sighting his prey. *This! This* is what he was born for!

He threw back his hood, a great hulk of a man, unafraid of sea and tempest, unmoving even as rain and wind battered his body and pulled at his wet clothing. He clenched and unclenched his hands in anticipation, scarcely aware that he did so.

He searched for the lights on the horizon and then smiled. There was *no* horizon tonight. No moon nor hint of stars to show where sky met with sea. He again caught sight of the tiny lights far out, winking through the fog and rain, and he rejoiced.

He fancied he could see the faint outline of a hull, immediately obliterated by a wash of wave. A pity if it came apart too soon— on the high seas. He told himself fiercely that this would not happen, that the wild tempest that struck fear in the bravest of hearts would surely, inevitably, dump its treasure on his waiting shore.

Below, close to the seething sea, his men waited and watched as well. When the time was ripe, he would join them. But until then he would stand, a waiting sentinel as the ship floundered to her destiny on Dunnottar Rock.

Thomas had scarcely moved from the bank. The storm's river rushed by, inches from his feet. Exhaustion overwhelmed him, and time meant nothing. *Time* is what he had dealt frantically with. But now Blacky was gone, and Kilamon was too far for a man on foot in the storm.

He pulled his knees to his chest and bowed his head, tears flowing down his already wet cheeks. It seemed nothing was any use. Perhaps he ought to drown himself. "Oh, God!" he mumbled softly. "Why be I here when all has come to naught?" Only the rain and the rushing river thundered any reply. "I be needing a miracle!" he cried out. He lowered his head between his knees and sobbed, "And there be *none!*"

He twitched as something soft touched his back. Probably something blown by the wind. But when a more urgent nudge followed, he leaped to his feet. It was Blacky.

He stared dumbfounded at the animal, who seemed to stare back apologetically. Then Thomas threw his arms about its neck, laughing and crying. "Blacky! Blacky! Ye done come back! *Ye be my miracle!*"

Still laughing and crying and mumbling what was incoherent even to himself, he mounted. Grasping the reins firmly, he dug with his heels, and they galloped off over the moor.

Thomas had seldom been to Kilamon, but he knew the sheriff's house was next to the jail. Finally he stood before it. The shutters were securely closed, and no hint of light escaped from anywhere. He beat upon the door with both fists—long and hard.

He was about to repeat the action when the door opened a crack, just enough for one eye to survey him. "Please," he begged frantically. "I must be speaking with you!"

The crack widened enough to reveal a candle and part of a woman's face. "Sheriff ain't available," the voice said. "Ye be coming back tomorrow."

"Tomorrow be too late!" Thomas yelled. *"Please,"* he continued in lower tones, "open so I kin talk to you!"

The door swung back, and a woman with a puffy face and gray hair disappearing into a ruffled nightcap peered at him over her candle. After some silent consideration on her part, during which Thomas realized what a strange apparition he must seem— drenched to the skin and with his hair blown every which way— she motioned him in out of the rain.

He stood dripping in a small hall out of which were two doors, both closed. He nodded. He must make some kind of connection with this woman. "Thankee. Weather's right muckle bad out there."

"Aye, and a poor time of night to wake a body out of sleep!" she answered in obvious irritation.

"But I kinna help it. I must see the sheriff—"

"I tell you—he's not available."

Thomas felt anger and frustration engulf him. "But there be terrible trouble afoot. The sheriff needs to know!" *Please, God, help me,* he prayed. "It be *lives* in terrible danger!"

The woman stared back stoically. "Come with me."

He followed her to the first door. She opened it and preceded him inside.

In the low light of a dying peat fire a big man sprawled in a chair, eyes closed. He had a red nose, a thick beard flecked with gray, and a belly that hung out over his pants. At his feet was an almost empty whisky bottle.

The woman put the candle down and folded her arms. "I tell you, he ain't available." She pointed to the whisky bottle. "See that? It's the end of him for the night."

Thomas stared at the bottle and at the man, frantic fear grabbing at him. Had he come to Kilamon only for this?

"Go on," said the woman. "Try to wake him if ye want. I'm going back to sleep. When ye give up, let yerself out and shut the door." She took her candle and left.

Thomas gaped at the man, who suddenly let out a loud snort, making Thomas jump. The dying embers of the fire cast a feeble glimmering that left most of the room in shadow.

Whatever he did had to be done with the utmost speed. He bent over the man, grasped his shoulders, and shook him. One eye opened—then two—a brief grimace—and he sank back into his stupor.

"Sheriff! Sheriff—wake up! Ye must!" Now Thomas shook him as violently as he could.

The man's arms and legs flailed. He squinted at Thomas and then bellowed a string of curses.

Thomas glared back. "We be needing ye in Stonehaven! There be evil—"

"Stonehaven? Stonehaven? Nooo," he growled, his bleary eyes unfocused. "Not on a night like this. . . ." His voice drifted off, and he slept.

Thomas cast about wildly. On a small table by the door stood a bowl and a cup. He caught them up with one swoop and made for the out-of-doors. The rain was steady and caught in small pools here and there. Thomas scooped it up frantically with his cup, pouring it into the bowl until it was full. Blacky nosed him curiously and whinnied.

Back in the house he took aim and threw the cool, muddy water squarely in the sheriff's face.

The eyes flew open and the curses, sprinkled with sputtering, erupted again. "Ye be the devil himself!" he spat out finally.

Thomas leaned close. His eyes bored into the other man.

231

"Wreckers! There be *wreckers* by Dunnottar Castle! We need a posse! *Now!"*

The sheriff shook his head slowly. A hint of a smile crossed his lips. "Wreckers? No."

A new fear assailed Thomas. What if the sheriff was involved? Thomas had heard tales of outwardly respectable people—he pushed the thought away. With all the authority he could muster he glared at the man and shouted, "A posse! *Now!* There be wreckers at Dunnottar, and if ye be not helping, ye shall have blood, *blood* on yer hands, Mr. Sheriff!"

The sheriff gawked back. He roused enough to grasp the arms of the chair and try to rise, but he sank down. "Go next door." He jerked his head in the direction. "Ye ask for Jeb."

"A posse! We need a posse!" roared Thomas.

The sheriff blinked and nodded. "Jeb'll help you. He'll tell you what to do."

Duncan crept cautiously along the shore, keeping low behind outcroppings of bracken, dwarf oak, and clumps of tall grasses. Thunder seemed distant, but lightning continued to flash. The rain had let up, at least temporarily, but his footing was precarious.

He stopped and listened. There was only the sound of the relentless waves that rhythmically washed the shore a few feet away. Even the wind seemed to have lessened.

He looked behind him, where a slope of rock and grasses sent a long finger into the sea. It was not more than twenty yards away, and yet he could not see the men (at least a dozen) who hid in its shadows, waiting for his signal.

He moved on. His goal, a low but solid formation of heavy rock just before the shore rounded an inlet and led to Dunnottar itself.

He reached it and was ready to breathe a sigh of relief when a hand was clapped over his mouth, his arm was twisted behind, and he was thrown to the ground. A figure was on top of him, a knee pressed between his shoulder blades. Duncan grunted, and a voice hissed in his ear, "Now stay put, or I'll kill you!" A familiar voice!

Duncan lifted his face from the dirt enough to frantically whisper, "Jonathan?"

Instantly he was released and rolled over. The lighthouse keeper stared down at him, wide-eyed, in the semidarkness. "Duncan!"

Duncan rose from the ground and brushed himself off. "We got enough trouble without killing each other!" he said in low, irritated tones. "What are ye doing here?"

"Same as ye, I reckon," was the reply. Jonathan turned, and his voice sounded far away. "Exceptin' I come to purge my soul." He roused and tugged at Duncan's sleeve. "Sit ye here on that hillock. Now look where them two rocks join together—there's enough crack ye'll see 'em. Ye'll see wreckers waiting when the lightning flashes."

Duncan dropped down, peering ahead. Jonathan sat, too, but got up immediately. He paced, running his big hands through his hair. "I'm goin' to die tonight, Duncan."

Duncan glanced sideways at the lighthouse keeper. He knew Jonathan to be sometimes erratic—definitely eccentric. "No good can come of talking like that."

"Aye, but it can—for mayhaps it'll purge my soul."

"Now ye are blethering!"

Jonathan stopped his pacing. "I'm going to tell you because I'm going to die," he insisted.

Duncan stared at him in silent puzzlement. There was something different about Jonathan tonight.

"When I was young, I was first mate on a cargo ship."

233

"Aye," said Duncan, with one eye carefully on the crack.

"'Twas a night like this, and a terrible gale blew the ship upon the reefs. It was coming apart—coming apart, I tell you! And I couldn't—I didn't stay with the ship!" He clutched at Duncan's shoulders until their eyes were inches apart. "The captain did! He stayed!" He straightened and whirled away. "I let down a small lifeboat. 'Twas all I could find. I was going to pick up as many as I could—I was!"

Abruptly he sat cross-legged on the ground. "Then there was this terrible sucking sound as the ship was pulled under." He held his head in his hands. "I was afraid, Duncan. I was sinking in *fear!*" he sobbed. "So—I rowed away for all I was worth. And—and saved myself," he finished, barely above a whisper.

So that's it! thought Duncan. The weight the lighthouse keeper had carried on his soul for all these years. It explained many things. Duncan leaned forward. "But it was a terrible time—who knows what *I* would have done. And if ye ask the Lord to forgive—"

"Aye—aye. 'Tis true. But always I hear the cries—in the wind and the waves. I thought to atone if I kept a lighthouse, but still I hear the cries." He stared glassy-eyed at Duncan. "Do ye hear 'em now, Duncan—if ye listen?"

"Jonathan—please—"

The lighthouse keeper stood slowly. He thrust his hands into his pockets. "And do ye know—that taking the easy way out is a *lie!* It plays on a man's soul till there ain't nothin' left!"

Duncan gazed at him compassionately. Lightning lit the sky, followed by another flash. Duncan pulled his eyes back to the space between the rocks.

Another flash, and he saw them clearly. Men at the base of Dunnottar Rock. Some pacing, others looking out to sea. Suddenly they seemed not men but hideous creatures, monstrously inhuman in their ominous intent! His eyes were

THE LONG NIGHT

drawn to a great hulk of a man, larger than the rest, leaning against the rock. "Ian Fraser!" breathed Duncan, dumbfounded. There was no mistaking it.

"And look there." Jonathan pointed upward as they were plunged into darkness again. Swinging lights moved into view on the north edge of the bluff. "Tied to a mule. Someone's walking it back and forth."

Duncan tensed. "Our first job is to get rid of those," he murmured, "before they lure any vessel in to the reefs." He looked out to sea, and his stomach knotted. "Which they're about to do. See that ship—way out yonder. She's heading in!" He turned with sudden resolution. "We've got to get up there. We'll climb the path on the west side—through the tunnel and then the gate. It's been a long time, but I remember it."

"Ye can't," said Jonathan. "Wreckers are guarding it. Looked like about four of them." His eyes lit. "Wait! I know of a small cave in the rock, with a passage leading up to the castle. Liza told me of it in great detail."

"Where?" Duncan asked eagerly.

"To the sea—" Jonathan's face fell. "Right about where Ian and the others are."

"Then that passage and the west path are the only ways to the castle," Duncan mused. Jonathan paced restlessly. The wind picked up, and thunder rumbled in the east.

"The only way is to distract them," Duncan said finally. "This is what we'll do. I'll move along the inlet and heave a large enough rock to cause a commotion, and they'll all come running. If that doesn't do it, I'll howl like a banshee! I'll give my men the signal—three hootings of an owl, which means they come ready to fight! That leaves the cave entrance for you, Jonathan, and as soon as the wreckers leave the west path—which they will!—I'll go that way and meet you at the castle." He turned to go, muttering to himself, "I've got more than one reason to go up there." *I'd wager Annie's being held hostage at Dunnottar. And maybe I'll find Davey, too!*

Shortly, an enormous rock hit the side of Dunnottar's cliff with a startling, thudding crash. The night air was pierced with three long, lonely hootings of an owl, and two distinctly different groups of men moved swiftly toward their destinies.

Scrambling up the west path, Duncan was assailed with thoughts of Jonathan, the wreckers, Ian Fraser, Annie, and Donal. But through it all was the steady, aching drumbeat for Meg. Questions regarding her disappearance and probable drowning. Visions with which he could not deal. The happy beginning of a fest seemed long ago. The day had turned into a nightmare!

Reaching the top, he ran through the gate, wondering if Jonathan had preceded him. He stopped short as the sound of fighting erupted below. Obviously his men and the wreckers had found one another.

He moved warily through the darkness, eyes searching everywhere. Just past the stables a terrible braying rent the air. He ran toward the sound. Rounding a shadowy wall, he saw them!

Jonathan held a lantern in each hand as a man, stocky but short of stature, wrestled and grabbed at him in vain. A mule pawed the ground and brayed.

Duncan ran toward them, shouting. Jonathan twisted away from the wrecker. He swung the lanterns before him and let them fly, arcing into the sea. *"Ye be done with it!"* he shrieked.

The wrecker leaped at the lighthouse keeper, and at the same time Jonathan whirled about. They caught at one another, and with a hideous scream from the wrecker, they hurled from the cliff to certain death.

Silence had fallen in the dungeon as Annie, Davey, and Meg sat, busy with their own thoughts.

Suddenly Meg raised her head. "I hear something."

They froze, listening. Footsteps—far away but coming closer.

Davey leaped up. "Annie, Meg—take these rags and blankets. Get under them in the far corner—and then don't move!" He picked up the lantern. "This is the only weapon we've got."

He moved toward the door and positioned himself to its side, then blew the light out.

Annie and Meg huddled under the blankets. Annie tried in vain to breathe slowly. Was this about to be the end—a violent end to a day that had already held so much horror? But the Presence! The Presence of Jesus *was*—*would be* with them.

The footsteps stopped. Silence. The sound of a bolt—fumbling—then it clicked and slid. The door creaked open slowly. Annie hoped Davey was ready. She tightened her grip on Meg.

The dungeon was silent but for the sounds of storm and fighting at a distance.

"Annie? Davey? Are ye in here?" asked a familiar voice.

"Duncan!" boomed Davey in relief.

Annie's heart lurched. Could it be?

"Davey?" asked Duncan, "where in thunderation are ye?"

"Here. I was about to knock yer brains out with this lantern."

Annie threw off the blankets, and she and Meg ran toward them in the darkness.

"Papa!" screamed Meg.

"Meg?" They threw their arms around one another. "*Meg!* It can't be! Oh, darlin'! Darlin'!" Tears streamed down his face.

"Oh, Papa, Papa," sobbed Meg. "I was so scared! I wanted ye to come, but I didn't think—"

Duncan held her tightly. "Yer alive! Yer alive! I can scarcely believe it! How did ye get *here*?"

"The wreckers found her," said Annie. "Actually they found both of us. Duncan, how could you know to look for us?"

Still the tears came as Duncan held one arm about Meg and stroked her hair. "Griselda told me about Donal, Annie—I'm so sorry—and that she was sure ye'd come up to Dunnottar." Duncan took a deep breath. "I've been calling all over the bluff and the castle for you. Thank God, I was finally led to the right place—when I found a bolted door, I was pretty sure."

"What's happening out there?" asked Davey.

"The lights to lure any ships are gone, thank God!" Duncan buried his face in Meg's hair. "Jonathan is the one. He threw the lights into the sea. But he—he lost his life doing it."

Annie gasped in horror, and Meg began to weep against her father's shoulder.

"I'm going out there, Duncan. Give me your pistol. Stay here with Annie and Meg."

"I won't let either of them out of my sight!"

Davey moved toward the door.

"Davey," called Annie. He paused. She moved until she stood quite close. She could see his eyes only faintly in the starlight of a sky that was only now partially clearing. "Please be careful! If—if you should die, I don't think I could—Please, Davey," she whispered. "Please don't die!"

He looked into her eyes for a long moment. He leaned down and kissed her cheek. "I promise you—I don't plan on it!"

And he was gone.

The air smelled of dampness, fog, and seaweed as Thomas and the posse from Kilamon dismounted. The rain had ceased, but not the wind. A heavy bank of roiling clouds hung overhead as thunder rumbled and then left the sounds of a circling curlew and the smash of waves on rocks below as the men tethered their horses to mountain ash and larch.

Then with a sweep of wind came the sound of fighting from over the hills. They froze, listening. Lightning flashed. The man Jeb nodded, and they began their descent down a slope that would lead to the sea and along a jagged inlet and beyond a low bluff to Dunnottar.

Thomas, peering through the darkness, suddenly felt both his courage and determination leave him.

It had been exhilarating—pounding over the moor with the posse of ten men, Jeb leading them to higher ground where they had crossed what was still a river but with less difficulty. He had felt his blood coursing through him with something akin to joy as he bent low over his horse, racing against time and evil. He was doing what he could. His spirit felt almost free. Free of the guilt and consternation that his double life had laid upon him.

Now his joy, his exhilaration, vanished as he stumbled after the group. He had no gun, but someone had given him a club. He winced as a rough branch from a low, dying tree scraped across his face. Perhaps he was insane for having gotten himself into the present situation.

Still he set his teeth and followed. As he ran along the sea toward Dunnottar, he prayed a mixture of frantic half phrases, pleading with the Almighty for help, and cries for forgiveness for his lack of courage.

The clamor of battle grew louder. As they rounded the last outcropping of rock, lightning illumined the dreadful scene, and they found themselves abruptly in the thick of it.

Thomas instinctively raised his club, his eyes darting everywhere like a trapped animal's. Panic and terrible fear washed over him.

Suddenly a large hand grabbed his shoulder with such force

that he dropped the club with a cry of pain. He was yanked several paces to the side.

"Thomas Blacklock!" a voice hissed in his ear.

It was Ian Fraser. Thomas stared into eyes filled with more hate and loathing than he could have imagined in his wildest nightmares.

The big man clasped his arm in a viselike grip. With his other hand Ian pointed a gun at Thomas's head. "Went for help, did ye? Well, I'm going to kill you, but first I got to tell you what a vile piece of scum ye are, Thomas Blacklock!" A string of curses from Ian rent the air, along with a bullet from somewhere, which hit the ground inches from their feet.

Ian jumped, dropped Thomas's arm, and twisted, seeking the assailant.

It was Davey Morrison on a run toward them. Ian lifted his gun and took careful aim.

Thomas lunged in front of Ian, took the bullet, and slumped to the ground.

CHAPTER 34

Elvira

Elvira Elphinstone had not slept the night. After tossing restlessly for some hours, she rose, pulled on a velvet robe of deep emerald green, patted at her hair, and started toward the door.

Then she hesitated. No, she would not go downstairs. There would be no fire in the grate, and the autumn night was chilled. Besides, Nora had been stationed at the rear door to watch for the gardener, who had been sent to Dunnottar. He would bring word to them as soon as there was any to bring.

She moved to the window. The great oaks that ringed the grounds no longer bent in the storm, and to the west a patch of stars had appeared. Her mouth widened in a half smile. It must be over by now.

She settled herself into a soft cushioned chair in the corner of the room. She would be patient. The delicious details would come soon enough.

How long she sat thus before hearing voices downstairs, she didn't know, but she cleared her throat, arranged the folds of her dressing gown, and fixed her eyes expectantly upon the door.

Any moment Nora would come to announce the gardener, or perhaps he himself would appear.

However, the indistinct murmur of voices below continued— suddenly punctured by a shriek. Elvira sat up straight and frowned. Perhaps she should go down.

She had half risen when Fiona burst through the door. She was wearing her pink satin robe; her hair was disheveled, her eyes wild.

"Just *what* is the matter with *you?*" Elvira intoned, settling back into her chair with dignity.

For answer, Fiona ran her hands through her blonde hair in a frenzy and collapsed on the floor in a fit of hysterical weeping.

Elvira waited for the worst of it to subside. Then she leaned forward. "Fiona," she said loudly, "kindly *stop* this fit of hysteria, and tell me what is wrong with you!"

The sobbing lessened, and Fiona rose slowly. She stood facing her aunt, her hands folded in front of her almost grandly. "Just the worst tragedy of my *entire life* has occurred!"

"Indeed?"

"Ian—Ian—" she gave a great sniffle—"was shot! He's been *killed*, Auntie!"

Elvira flinched. "It was bound to happen to *someone*—in a fight. Ian was involved in dangerous business tonight, Fiona." Surely, Elvira told herself, even *this* did not mean the endeavor was not a success. Ian had always been one to throw caution to the winds. It was bound to catch up with him sometime. She fixed Fiona with her eyes. "You'll get over it."

The sobbing began again. "No, no—I never, never shall!"

Elvira gave a dismissive wave of the hand. "Oh, come now— don't be ridiculous!" She smiled. "Dear child, you will *love* playing the part of the poor 'almost widow' in your best blacks." She stopped, contemplating momentarily, and sighed. "Although Ian's death will be a great loss to—" she paused—"to the things he's been a part of—"

242

Her hands came down from her face, and Fiona glared at her aunt. "You *never* told me Ian was a—a *wrecker!*"

"Oh, pshaw! You're not stupid, Fiona. Of course you knew."

"Upon my word, Auntie, I didn't know! I—"

"Tell me the rest of it!" Elvira interrupted impatiently.

Fiona stood quite still. "The wreckers are all dead or in custody. Someone rode to Kilamon for a posse."

Elvira's face went white. *Thomas Blacklock!* Her hands shook. There was only the sound of a ticking clock. Then the blood slowly rose through her neck and upward until her face was flushed and livid. "Get out!" she screamed. "Get out of my presence!"

Fiona silently fled.

Elvira rose. She moved toward the nightstand and picked up a great brass candlestick. She hurled it against the ticking clock, where it shattered the clock's face and then fell to the floor with a loud thud.

Then she went to the window. With a mighty sweep she ripped the curtain down and threw the window open. Then she returned to her chair.

A chill swept into the room. The old woman (for her face was suddenly lined) stared out the window at the blackness beyond. Unfathomable—filled with evil portent.

She shivered, for she perceived the night air to be full of spirits—perhaps the haunting spirits of those who had been slain on Dunnottar and those who had drowned in the icy waters at its feet.

Did the spirits haunt for the rest of one's life? She trembled miserably. She would have to look it up in the little book.

CHAPTER 35

By the Peat Fire

Davey stared hard into the peat fire. It would soon be daylight, but none in the little group gathered at the Carmichael house was sleepy. Tired—yes! But at this point they needed to be with one another, to process the experiences they had been through, to both rejoice and sorrow together.

Davey tightened his hand on Annie's as she sat beside him. Perhaps Annie seemed the quietest and most weary of all.

"You all right, Annie?" he asked gently.

"I will be," she said slowly. "There's so much to be grateful for—although . . . ." Her voice trailed off.

"I know." He squeezed her hand. "We'll get through it. I promise."

Across from them Meg sat huddled in a blanket beside her father. Margaret had insisted, whether Meg needed it or not. After her initial shock, relief, and wild joy at Meg's survival, Margaret had collected herself enough to announce that everybody needed hot tea and biscuits, and had bustled off with Eppie and Griselda in tow.

Meg shivered. "I'm sorry, Papa! I know I shouldn't have wandered off."

Duncan pulled her close. "I still can't believe it. I was so sure ye were lost to us!"

"I won't never do it again."

"Never ye mind. Oh, darlin', I love you!"

Eppie danced into the room. "Mama says the biscuits and tea are almost ready." She plumped down on the floor in front of Meg. "Just think, Meg, tomorrow ye will be about the most famous girl in Stonehaven! What ye been into is just like some storybook!"

Meg shook her head. "Master Thomas is the one what was really a hero."

Eppie turned to Davey. "Warn't that the most bravest thing to do, Master Davey? Ridin' off to get that posse and then jumpin' in front of Ian Fraser so's ye wouldn't get shot?"

"Aye, Eppie, that it was! Thomas'll be all right, though. Letty Rafferty knows all the things to be doing for him. And there's no one to give more tender loving care than Liza. Even Rob Rafferty was impressed with Thomas's bravery."

Eppie's eyes were large with wonder. "Was ye much scared, Master Davey?"

"Aye, that I was, Eppie."

"Did ye shoot at many of 'em?"

"Eppie—Eppie," remonstrated Duncan.

Margaret hurried into the room with a tray of cups and a steaming kettle of tea, followed by Griselda. "Duncan, pour for yerself and Meg. Meg, are ye feeling feverish?"

"No, Mama."

"Griselda, hand around the biscuits to everybody. Duncan, ye sure ye don't need to change into somethin' dry?" She turned to Davey. "Ye have a mean gash on yer forehead. Gracious! I don't know when there's been as much to tend to all at once!"

Eppie munched excitedly on a biscuit. "Ain't it grand?"

Duncan, sipping his tea, looked grave. "It wasn't some kind of big adventure, Eppie. Actually, it was terrible, and it was sad."

"Wish I could've been there," she insisted.

Duncan put his cup down. "I still can't believe Ian Fraser was head of the wreckers."

Margaret poured tea into her own cup. She shook her head. "It beats everything I ever heard tell of."

"Could Fiona possibly have known?" murmured Griselda.

"There's no telling. Ian's dead, and Fiona probably wouldn't admit it if she did," said Davey.

Duncan rose to add more peat to the fire. "We're going to be missing Jonathan."

"Poor Master Jonathan!" sighed Meg. "We all loved him."

Griselda blinked at tears. She studied her hands thoughtfully. "I think he died the way he would have wished. And he seemed to know it was going to be tonight."

There was a stillness in the room but for a soft hissing of the fire.

Finally Davey broke the silence. "I reckon the end of it all is—the ship that was sailing toward her destruction tonight changed her course in time. And there'll be no more wreckers at Dunnottar Castle."

"And Jesus was our light in the darkness!" said Meg.

Epilogue

Annie and Davey climbed to Dunnottar Castle in a leisurely
fashion. The October sun was unusually warm, the breeze gentle,
and before them lay the sea, looking as if the sun had cast a million
diamonds over it.

They walked to the south side of the bluff and stood looking
down at the brief pebbly shore. A flock of curlews, with their
long slender beaks, was busy winkling crabs from among pools
formed by the rocks.

Davey pointed. "Look at that one, Annie. It's turning its head
upside down to get the best angle for his bill!"

Annie smiled. "So peaceful, calm. It's hard to believe that only
two weeks ago this whole scene was so dark and horrible."

"Aye, it was that. And some of its consequences seem to go on
and on."

"Like dear little Liza. She mourns so for Jonathan. And I wonder
about Fiona."

"Doory Wilson says her aunt took her to Aberdeen, and no one
knows when they'll return."

"Something good came out of it though—Thomas Blacklock.

He's considered quite a hero by the villagers. And Liza says he's been getting stronger every day."

They wandered past the old stables. Annie looked back at the castle. "I don't know if I'll ever go inside the castle again." She turned toward the sea. "But I'll always come up here—and think about Donal." She paused. "As for the Captain and my whole life with him, I'm just realizing I don't mourn for—for that anymore."

"I hope I might have something to do with it," Davey said jauntily.

Annie glanced at him sideways. His hands were in his pockets and his expression inscrutable. "Perhaps you have," she said softly. "But don't get too proud."

They came to the old stone bench with the stretch of stone hedge just beyond.

Davey leaned back reflectively against the wall. "For me, Dunnottar is a place of beginnings."

Annie sat down on the bench.

Davey chewed on a piece of grass thoughtfully. "It was right here that you and I first began to really understand one another—and to be friends."

Annie nodded, remembering.

"And then coming to Stonehaven has been the beginning of faith for me. Now I find I'm anxious to know more of what Jesus Christ wants of me."

Annie nodded, bright tears in her eyes. "And it was here—in the castle that I truly *found* the Presence—that I told Jesus what I should have said and done so long ago."

There was a silence with only the gentle sound of waves beneath them and the plaintive cries of the curlews above.

Finally Annie said, "Perhaps we could read the Bible together sometimes."

"Aye." He stared at her fixedly. "I don't know about spending a lot of time together, though."

Annie's heart skipped a beat.

"The thing is," he continued, "I told you once I was falling in love with you, and that's not true anymore."

She held her breath.

"It's only fair that you know—I've *already* fallen in love with you, Annie Mackinnon." He pulled her to her feet, holding her hands tightly in his. "Can you love me back, Annie?"

His eyes entreated her, and her heart beat faster even as she surveyed him solemnly. She looked down momentarily. "It seems you entered my life like a strange bolt out of the blue, sending the pieces of it flying every which way. But now—" she looked up—"you are my steady rock, and . . . and . . ." Annie took a deep breath. "I love you, Davey Morrison—I do!"

He dropped her hands and stared at her. Suddenly he reached behind her and with a deft motion removed her comb, releasing her hair to cascade down her back and about her shoulders. "I've always wanted to do that—to see you like this."

"Oh, Davey," she laughed, shaking her head, "still like the Scottish weather, y'are! Unpredictable!"

He held out his arms then, and she went into them. She felt the beat of his heart and reveled in his strength and the warmth of his body. And was content.

A curlew circled above them and then winged its way out over the North Sea.